Shirley Larson

SEE ONLY ME

Harlequin Books

TORONTO • NEW YORK • LONDON
AMSTERDAM • PARIS • SYDNEY • HAMBURG
STOCKHOLM • ATHENS • TOKYO • MILAN

Published October 1986

First printing August 1986

ISBN 0-373-70232-9

This book is dedicated with love
to Eileen Backstrom, a sister who is like a friend,
and Alice Coe, a friend who is like a sister,
both of whom live their lives
with intelligence, courage and love.

CHAPTER ONE

ONE AFTERNOON IN APRIL when he was twenty-one, Rourke Caldwell pushed open the glass door of the courthouse in the tiny town of Edgerton and stepped out into the pale sunshine. Winter in his eyes, he paused on the top step to brace himself against the bucolic charm of a western New York village surrounded by dairy country, its houses nestled complacently along the street. *The* street. There were four cars parked there. It was a big day for this backwater town.

His father's black Mercedes was not among those cars. Edgerton was only forty miles south of Rourke's home in Rochester, but Alcott couldn't be bothered to come to pick up his son. Rourke had been a fool to hope—again.

A rough wind tore his jacket away from his body. The violent gust pleased Rourke. It matched his mood.

In an effort to distract himself from internal pain with external sights, he lifted his head to examine the street and realized he'd missed two weeks out of his life. While he'd been locked in the Edgerton jail, spring had come to New York State. The snow was gone and the fuzzy pods of pussy willow were bursting into tiny yellow seeds, bright dots of sunshine matching the forsythia lining the sidewalk.

Across the road, the ice-cream parlor was still closed, the plate-glass window boarded up, mute testimony to his efforts to disprove the physical laws of matter. At three o'clock one morning two weeks ago, he'd gone too fast through a radar trap. He'd compounded his error by accelerating to a high speed in an attempt to elude the pursuing police car. When he'd come around a corner, he'd found another police car pulling in front of him to block him off, the driver still in it . . . and Rourke's car heading at him like a cannonball.

Rourke had twisted the wheel, not knowing where he was going, not caring about his own safety. He couldn't risk killing someone. Metal crashed into glass; a thousand shards had showered over the car. The parlor had been empty; he'd had his seat belt on. He'd hurt no one but himself, a slice lifted out of his cheek that had turned into a small, thin scar.

Rourke made no attempt now to zip his jacket or keep the wind from sending stinging nettles of cold over his ribs or ruffling his brown hair. He thrust his clenched fists into his jeans pockets, straightened his shoulders and welcomed the shivers that swam up his spine. The courthouse had been overheated. So had his jail cell.

Raising his head, he took a deep breath. The thirty-degree air smelled like wine. All around him, the small-town countryside was stretching and stirring with life. He exhaled...and as if on signal, the knot of humanity at the bottom of the steps broke formation and headed up toward him.

His nerves tightened from the pit of his stomach to the soles of his feet. He said a muffled word under his breath, squared his shoulders and galloped down the steps to wade into the maelstrom of reporters waiting for him, his face and eyes as cold as the air.

"Where's your father, Rourke?"

"Is it true he left you in jail two weeks to teach you a lesson?"

"Are you planning on going back to the university?"

Rourke met the rumor-hungry lions with his head up. It was his father the newsmen had come to see, not him, and now they were having to settle for second best. His father was rich and powerful, carrying in his veins aristocratic blood that went back to land barons who'd migrated from England to America before the revolutionary war. Addicted to the habit of acquisition, the transplanted Caldwell males had run true to form and now, two hundred and some odd years later, they owned real estate all over New York State . . . some of it on Manhattan Island. Rich enough to live off his investments, Rourke's father had spurned the life of leisure and had trained to be a surgeon who specialized in eye disorders. Yes, his father fascinated the press.

"Is it true your old man has disowned you?"

"And cut off your allowance?"

Reacting instinctively, Rourke made a fist and drew back his arm.

A hand like steel caught his elbow. "Away with you, boys. Go find some other lad to pester. This one belongs to me."

Scotty, he thought dazedly. *It's Scotty.* Then the relief vanished and he tensed under Scotty's grip, thinking of what he'd done, where he'd been. What would his scrupulously honest, police officer uncle think of him now?

Scotty MacDonald's eyes met Rourke's, and the half-teasing half-tolerant look Rourke knew so well was gone. In its place was an unspoken message of compassion and understanding one soldier gives another when they've walked off a battlefield together . . . and survived.

The older man inserted his lean body between Rourke and the reporters with the ease of an eel. "Okay, fellows, it's time to give the lad a break."

There was a slight hesitation before the circle around Rourke broke. But break it did. The reporters all knew MacDonald and they knew he was more dangerous than he looked. He was tall and lean, with a nose like a bird's beak, and his slimness was deceptive. He could pound his fist through a two-inch board, and under his soft burring speech he was a city cop, who had a mind like a computer and a will like granite.

The men knotted around Rourke bent to that will. Scotty commandeered his nephew as easily as if he were cutting a cow out of a herd, and had him bundled into the old black Saab before either the reporters or Rourke knew what was happening.

Inside the car, Rourke flexed his legs and ran a hand down his thigh. He didn't know where Scotty was taking him. He cared even less. What he did care about was his uncle's mood. What was Scotty thinking? After that one brief compassionate look of greeting, Rourke hadn't been able to read Scotty's state of mind. This was nothing new. If his canny uncle didn't want to be read, it was impossible to tell what thoughts went round inside his quick brain.

"Feeling a little cramped, are you? That doesn't surprise me. Edgerton county jail doesn't have the plushiest of accomodations. Now if you're in Monroe County the next time you feel the urge to seek lodging at the expense of the taxpayers—"

"There won't *be* any next time."

Scotty's face was smooth. "I'm glad to hear you say that. But just remember, getting apprehended is like having a baby. It's easier the second time."

Despite himself, the corner of Rourke's mouth lifted. "What would you know about having babies?" Instantly, he regretted his words. The remark was too close to the bone. Scotty had made the decision to put off having children. His wife Fran had died unexpectedly the year before Rourke's mother. Even as a child, Rourke had sensed the pain tearing his uncle apart.

"I listen to the ladies talk." Scotty's tone was casual, and he sounded faintly amused. The old wound had healed.

"You listen to everybody talk."

"And so, my friend, do you. I commend you for that. It's a useful gift to have, that gift of listening."

Rourke stifled the reaction he felt at hearing Scotty give him a compliment. He hadn't thought anybody had ever noticed his ability to listen. He wasn't even sure where he'd developed the trait... unless it was from the man sitting next to him. As casually as if he were asking about the weather, he said, "I'm surprised an upright, honest cop like you came to gather up the jailbird and take him home."

Scotty shook his head, a rueful lift to a corner of his mouth. "I thought you'd need someone."

"You knew my father wasn't coming?" Scotty's silence told Rourke he'd stumbled on the truth. "You never seemed very crazy to be around me when my mother was alive, and you were still coming to see your kid sister. Have you got a cigarette?"

"Alcott felt I was a bad influence on you."

Scotty handed the cigarette he'd pulled from his pocket to Rourke. Rourke took it and strove for a casual tone. "You? A bad influence?" Unerringly, without looking, Rourke punched in the dash lighter. "The straight-as-an-arrow gumshoe cop a bad influence on me? That's rich." In the silence that followed, Rourke fought to stay calm, to tamp down the anger filling him at the thought of those lost years. He lit the cigarette and exhaled a streamer of smoke in a long, satisfying breath. "He just can't stand to see me do anything I enjoy, can he?"

"Depends on what you mean by 'enjoy.' You're a bright boy, my friend...even though sometimes you don't act it. Twenty-one, and ready to graduate summa cum laude...until last Christmas. Like any father, Alcott wants what's best for you."

"He doesn't want what's best for me, he wants what's best for him, a son to be proud of, a clone who goes to his alma mater and graduates with the same honors he graduated with, and goes forth into the world to become what he became, a brilliant eye surgeon who can marry and produce another clone to go to his father's university and wear his father's clothes—"

His impassioned speech brought no response from Scotty, no expression of reproof or dismay. Equally important, it brought no denial. At last, in a soft burr, Scotty said, "You've a problem, lad, there's no getting around it. You could do what your instinct tells you and learn what it is you need to know, and because you've a bigger heart, you'd wind up being a better doctor than Alcott is. He'd never forgive you for that and well you know it. Your own quick brain has told you he'll hate you less if you rebel."

Rourke's throat constricted. Now he knew why he'd loved Scotty throughout the years with so little encouragement. The reciprocal love had been there, waiting for him, hidden under the surface, like the bulk of an iceberg. The browns and grays of the spring countryside disappeared and reappeared in Rourke's line of vision as he fought to control his emotions.

"What are your plans for the next few days?" Scotty asked.

Rourke relaxed slightly and let his mouth pull upward in a self-effacing half smile. "As if you didn't know."

"Well, tell me again," Scotty said softly in a tone that sounded far milder than it was.

"For three months, I'm to spend two days at the hospital, one day at the library and two days doing custodial work for the town."

"And you're going to do it?"

Rourke looked away, out the window. "What choice do I have? I need the money to pay for the window."

"And meanwhile?"

"What do you mean, meanwhile?"

"What are you going to do for the excitement you've become addicted to?"

"Excitement?"

"The thrill of the chase. What are you going to do about that?"

Rourke's lips twisted. "I'm not going to have any money to chase anything. Since I made the decision to quit going to the university, I've been kicked out, my Caldwell buttons stripped from my jacket, my Caldwell epaulets sliced from my shoulders by one strike of Alcott's sword. To say nothing of the damage to my credit rating. According to my father, I'm free to go to hell in my own way now." The attractive mouth curved in a self-mocking smile. "*Free* being the operative word. Where are we going?"

"Home. I'm doing what I should have done long ago...taking you into custody."

Rourke went rigid with a peculiar emotion, one he couldn't name. "You're going to let me stay with you?" Rourke turned in his seat, the cigarette dangling forgotten from his hand. "Why...now? Why after all these years did you change your mind now?"

"I've never changed my mind," Scotty said, looking straight ahead at the road. "It's your father who's had a change of heart."

"That time I went to you and asked you to let me live with you...you couldn't do it because he didn't want you to?"

"No man has a right to come between a father and his son, lad." Scotty hesitated in an uncharacteristic way. Then he said huskily, "I didn't have a boy of my own and I was...afraid my own motives were none too pure. I wanted you with me, lad. But I wasn't going to have you at the expense of another man's happiness. Now..."

"Yes," breathed Rourke, "now I'm expendable. An embarrassment to Alcott. He's only too glad to get rid of me. Meanwhile, like a dog in a manger, he's cheated me of the years I could have had with you. I won't soon forget that." He lunged forward and stabbed the end of his cigarette into the ashtray.

THE SUN WAS BRILLIANT on the green spring grass of the skeet field. Over the low house, the sky was an effervescent blue. The place was as deserted as a sea on the moon, and Rourke knew why. The sane people were inside their houses, keeping warm, while he was out there freezing to death.

Somewhere, on the ride from the courthouse to this combination target field and gun shop on a country road, he'd lost the urge to flagellate himself with the April wind. Being with Scotty was like being given a strong dose of common sense intravenously. In another minute, he was going to succumb to the humiliation of listening to his teeth clack.

Rourke had come here often as an observer; Scotty had never offered to teach him to shoot. But today he turned to his nephew and handed him the gun.

Rourke stared back at him, his hands at his sides. "Why?"

"Because it's time you learned some control. There's a cradle between your collarbone and your shoulder where the butt of the gun fits. Find it." Rourke did so. The barrel of the shotgun was still warm from Scotty's hand. "Now put your cheek against the comb...no, don't bend your head. Your nose should be an inch from your thumb. You ever see any old movies?" Here, Scotty's mouth twisted, as if reminding himself of the age gap between them. "About turret gunners? Well, that's what you're going to turn yourself into. A turret gunner. Now here's the way you stand...and believe me, my boy, in skeet shooting, as in life, position is everything."

With the correct head angle, the correct posture and the correct stance, Rourke missed the first four birds.

"You're stopping your sweep when you squeeze the trigger. Keep your sweep going."

By the end of the afternoon, Rourke was frozen and his shoulders and arms ached...but he'd learned how to sweep and lead, and he'd broken seven clay pigeons out of ten.

"You've more lessons ahead of you," Scotty said softly. "I've taught you the gentleman's sport. Now we must progress to something a little more businesslike."

Afterward, looking back on that time of his life, Rourke remembered it only as a blur. The odd incongruity of his days made him feel as if he were acting out a bizarre script of some science fiction story. He woke, his mind weary, his body aching from his midnight sessions with Scotty, to spend his daytime hours swabbing down hospital corridors, hauling enough buckets of water to qualify him for a job as a sorcerer's apprentice.

When six o'clock rolled around, he climbed into Scotty's car and was transported into the city, where he descended into Scotty's inner sanctum of a basement. There he spent another four hours learning how to handle the full recoil of a .357 Magnum handgun, to ride out the impact and let his elbow flex to protect his shoulder from injury.

When the lesson was over, Scotty looked at him through eyes that told Rourke that whatever it was Scotty had on his mind, it was serious.

"I don't like listening to lectures or giving them. But I'm not too old that I can't remember what it was like to be your age. A boy takes what he wants, a man doesn't. A boy tells himself sex is all right as long as a woman's willing. A man knows better. A man knows there are right times and wrong times and he knows how to tell one from another. He learns to say no to a woman when he aches to say yes. He learns to think before he acts. He learns control." The words echoed through the empty basement eerily, and in that moment Rourke knew Scotty understood him better than any living being. He was filled with a rush of love that nearly overwhelmed him.

"Do you understand what I'm saying?"

Rourke nodded.

"In this rough-and-tumble world of ours, it isn't easy, being a man. We've thrown the rule book away. Maybe we shouldn't have. Maybe we should have kept a few of those pages. What do you plan to do with your life, son?"

"I ... don't know."

"I've got a friend who's opening an agency in New York ..."

"Scotty, I don't want to be involved with any law agency."

Scotty shook his head. "I know you don't, lad. That way is not for you. I'm talking about working in industry as an investigator of white-collar crime. You could learn something about the business world...yet you wouldn't be stuck in a nine-to-five job. No, don't shake your head. You've a brain that works like lightning, and the ability to listen when others talk. Those skills are rarer than you think. At this time in your life, you'd be a natural. You're young enough to go into a company as a new employee but you're tough enough and smart enough to discover whoever is committing a crime. I think you should give it a try. Don't say yea or nay tonight, lad. Think about it. It wouldn't be a life for a gregarious man but it would suit you. You've the temperament to survive the loneliness...and you have the creativity to enjoy the change. And you'd be filling a desperate need."

If there was more Scotty wanted to say, he didn't say it. When Rourke went upstairs that night to the roll-away bed Scotty had installed for him in a small room, despite his weary mind and body, he had trouble sleeping.

Even though he hadn't decided to act on Scotty's suggestion, Rourke began to take the hours he spent with his uncle more seriously. He graduated from his course on firearms into another form of torture. Scotty transformed a corner of the basement into a gambling casino. While Rourke faced his own image in a mirror, Scotty taught him to play blackjack and poker. The stakes were real. Rourke learned that the slightest gesture indicating emotion could cost him money. He fell into debt. One hundred dollars. Two hundred. Three hundred dollars. Until the night he learned to use the knowledge that

Scotty had gained about him to his own advantage... and began to win.

Spring melted into summer. The days were long stretches of boredom, the nights torture. Scotty pitted Rourke against all of his own forty-nine years of expertise. He heckled him while they played cards, he needled him while he practiced shooting targets to improve his performance and made quiet, disparaging comments when he missed. Rourke knew it was a game, but it was a game that was becoming very real. He gritted his teeth and developed the ability to wipe every trace of feeling from his face.

But when Rourke reported to the town constable for his work duty on one particular Friday, and was told his task for the day was to clean out the horse stable that belonged to the owner of the ice-cream parlor, he nearly forgot every lesson he'd learned.

The constable, a man small enough to qualify as a jockey, obviously took great pleasure in informing the rich kid about his undesirable chore for the day. Rourke's fists clenched. He longed to knock the man flat on his back. But pride and control, the control Scotty had worked to instill in him night after night, won out. Without a word, Rourke climbed on his bike and headed for the stable.

By the end of the day, he stood under the shower in Scotty's bachelor establishment, scrubbing at the grime. Despite three soapings and clean hot water, he remembered every pungent odor. He wondered if he would ever feel clean again. To make things worse, Scotty sensed his irritation and twisted a knife in the wound.

During Rourke's target practice with the handgun, Scotty said in his soft burr, "You shouldn't have missed that target, lad. Maybe I was wrong about you. Maybe you just don't have what it takes."

Furious, Rourke swung the gun in a ninety-degree arc, pointing it at Scotty's chest.

There was a long echoing silence like that of the crypts of Egypt. "I'm not armed," Scotty said softly, his eyes never leaving Rourke.

He stared at Scotty. Then, carefully, he clicked the safety on and tossed the gun down on a table.

Scotty smiled. "Now, you're beginning to see what these lessons are all about. Pointing the gun at me was a boy's stunt. Tossing it away was the act of a man."

Rourke clenched his teeth and dismissed the thought that standing in front of him was the only person in the world he had ever loved. The fury accumulating over the long days and weeks and months rose in his throat and exploded in front of his eyes like a thousand firecrackers. "I'm going to hit you, Scotty."

Scotty's face didn't change expression. He looked almost relieved, as if he'd been waiting for the volcano to explode and was glad the suspense was over. "Hit away, son. You might find I can do more damage to your handsome puss than that plate-glass window did."

In the next moment, he blocked the angry punch Rourke threw, and gave the younger man a sharp uppercut to the jaw. The boy sagged in his arms, and Scotty laid him back against the pool table.

When Rourke opened his eyes, Scotty said, "There now. Feel better?"

The next morning at the hospital, when Rourke got out his scrub bucket and the detested mop, the nurse in the emergency room looked at him and made a muffled sound of dismay.

Not wanting her pity, Rourke met her gaze head-on, defying her to say anything. His uncle had examined him with the same expert hands that had knocked him senseless, and the results had assured them both that his jawbone hadn't been broken. Still, it hurt to move any part of his head.

The nurse, whose name was Janet, was not intimidated by Rourke's fierce stare. "You shouldn't be working here, you should be checking in for treatment. What happened to you?"

"I ran into a door," he replied.

He could see she didn't know whether to laugh or to chide him for telling such a blatant lie. "Some door. Although I must say you look good even in shades of lavender and blue." Rourke stiffened. It was the first personal comment any woman in the hospital had made to him. Had she noticed his immediate withdrawal? He thought she had. She stood for a moment, and then, as if she'd come to a decision she wasn't going to rescind, she took the mop from Rourke's hands. "Look, kid, we're paying people to come in at night and do that. Why don't you try doing something we can't hire people to do for love or money?"

Janet smelled of starch and looked like a woman who'd eaten a few too many chocolate sundaes, but he'd seen her soothing hand move over the back of a child in pain. It made his throat ache to think if he'd been luckier someone like her might have been his mother. Now, she was challenging him on purpose, he knew that, yet he still couldn't resist asking, "What job?"

"There's a kid down the hall not much older than you. He's been through eye surgery and he's come out with less vision than he had before." Brown eyes sought his. "How would you like the job of cheering him up?"

Rourke's insides clenched. "I can't talk to a blind person—"

"Oh, he's not completely blind," she assured him. "He can see your rainbow makeup."

"What would I talk to him about?"

For the first time since he'd come into the hospital, the nurse's face softened. "How do I know what you should say to him? You're a bright boy, you think of something. Unless," she said gently, watching him, "you're scared to try."

He pursed his lips . . . and steeled himself not to wince from the pain of moving his jaw. "Where's his room?"

"Just follow the yellow line to 118. He'll be there."

When Rourke walked into the room, the first thing he noticed was the bruising under the bandaged eye. This young man's face looked as bad as his own felt. An urge to back away seized him, but as he stood in the doorway, the young man in the bed turned his head and said, "Mom? Jessica? Is that you?"

"No, it's not Mom or . . . Jessica." Who was Jessica, Rourke wondered, his girlfriend? Did the poor devil have a girlfriend? Why had he let Janet needle him into walking in here?

"If you've come about the money for the television rental, it's there on the stand."

This guy watched television? Wishing he'd never let go of that mop, he said, "I'm not here to collect your money. My name is Rourke Caldwell. The nurse sent me to . . ." He hesitated, his honesty at war with an urge to dissemble. Honesty won. "To talk to you because she thought we were the same age, but . . ."

"Rourke Caldwell? I've heard about you." The young man extended his hand. Rourke caught it and was surprised at the eager strength. When he withdrew his hand, the young man chuckled and the unbandaged eye ranged freely over Rourke, able, it seemed, to see him more clearly. "You look like the one who needs cheering up. My name's Gavin Moore. I'd ask you to sit down, but the only chair in this place is hard as a board and I don't recommend it. Try the windowsill."

"I'll do that," Rourke said, telling himself that now that he was in, he wasn't going to be able to leave without spending a few minutes, but knowing he was really being drawn in by his curiosity about this fellow's apparent good humor in a bad situation.

"You're the guy who drove your car through old Pepper Brown's ice-cream parlor window, aren't you? You sure provided everybody with a few days' entertainment. They were all talking about you. They said if you had been drinking, they would have locked you in jail and thrown away the key. Why did you put your 'Vette through the window?"

"It seemed like a good idea at the time." Rourke's tone was dry.

"I'll bet it was a girl. With us guys it's always a girl causing trouble, isn't it?"

With a twisted smile that Gavin couldn't see, he said, "Yeah, I guess so."

"If that one didn't work out, you'll find another. Rich guy like you probably has lots of girls. I'd introduce you to my sister, but she's a little young for you. She's almost seventeen. The only trouble is . . . she has the same problem with her eyes that I do. It's hereditary from our father, developing cataracts. We could both see when we were kids, but as we get older the problem gets worse."

Lord, Rourke thought, that was all he needed, to have a blind, teenage female pushed at him. She probably had a face like a horse. He slid off the windowsill.

"Hey, don't leave. Look, I'm sorry. If talking about girls makes you uncomfortable, we'll find something else to talk about. Cars. Do you like cars? The one you were driving was a Corvette, wasn't it? How fast will it go?"

Eager and willing to discuss anything that would keep his visitor from leaving, Gavin launched into a learned discussion about compression and engine size and gasoline octane that challenged Rourke to follow. From there they went to college football teams, and after they'd discussed the strengths and weaknesses of the coaches and players, they discovered they both had a love of music. Gavin played piano, a feat that, by this time, surprised Rourke less than it would have before he walked into the room forty-five minutes ago. He heard himself telling the other young man that he, too, played the piano, and that the blues was his specialty.

He visited Gavin again the next day, and when it was time for him to go, he wasn't sure who had gained the most from their session. It was then Gavin asked, "Are you going to be around tomorrow? They're coming to take me home. Come in before ten. I want you to meet my parents...and Jessica."

Feeling a twinge of guilt, Rourke shook his head. "I can't. I have to work at the library."

"Ask for some time off. Please, Rourke."

He didn't promise. All that night and the next morning at the library, he watched the clock move, filled with guilt. He stayed very busy but he was tense as a high wire, until at last ten o'clock came and went and he breathed more easily.

The next Saturday afternoon the phone rang. It was Gavin. He wanted Rourke to come to dinner at his parents' home that night.

Desperately, he tried to think of a reason to decline. He heard himself saying, "Yes, I'll come. What time?" Almost the minute he put the phone down, he regretted his impulse to accept.

He found no help from Scotty in wriggling out of the invitation. "It will be good for you to talk to a lad your own age," Scotty said, and handed him the car keys. Rourke's license had been restored a week ago.

He'd been given directions by Gavin. He followed them, driving forty miles to Edgerton on the expressway and then past the town into the countryside of dairy farms, finally turning into a lane beside a mailbox that read Moore. The house was neat, traditionally white, and there was a barn on the place but no other buildings.

Rourke got out of the car and, facing up to the task head-on, he ran up the steps.

The door opened under his ready-to-knock fist.

"Hello," she said, "I heard you coming. I'm Jessica," and she held out her hand.

CHAPTER TWO

ROURKE DIDN'T WANT to take Jessica's hand. It seemed wrong to touch a girl like this, a girl with tawny hair that reached to her waist, and slim graceful hands, and skin that looked as if it had been dipped in a moon stream. Her face was smooth, untouched by any reaction to his physical appearance, yet when his hand captured hers, he felt her tremble. Under the petal-soft skin, a rosy color seeped upward.

"I'm Rourke Caldwell."

Her attractive color deepened fractionally. "Yes, I know. Nobody else around here runs up those steps like that. Won't you come in? My brother's still upstairs." She hesitated and then said shyly, "He wanted to look good for you so he's spending extra time getting ready."

"What about you? Didn't you want to look good for me, too?" Was he actually flirting with her? He needed his head examined.

"Of course," she said with a guileless charm that was both enchanting and enslaving. "I started two hours earlier than he did. Can I get you something to drink? Iced tea, coffee?"

"Iced tea sounds good."

Jessica turned to escape to the kitchen and nearly tripped over her own feet. She felt as if a thousand fire-crackers were going off inside her. All the long hours of waiting were over. He was here.

He was here…and she'd already blown the first of her friend's edicts read to her from Anita Raskin's *Manual for Attracting Men*. She'd let him see how eager she was to meet him. She hadn't been able to help herself. His voice was velvety steel, and so warm, so honest. He hadn't sounded as if he felt at all awkward about being with her. He'd sounded easy, relaxed. And he'd teased her. She recognized that tone of voice because she'd heard boys talk to other girls that way, but no boy had ever talked like that to her. And he had the most delicious smell, some terribly expensive cologne that he'd splashed on while he stood in his beautiful bedroom and got ready, she supposed. Gavin had told her that Rourke came from a rich family but he wasn't conceited and didn't talk about his money.

All last week, she'd sat in her room and opened the dormer window to feel the May breeze caress her face and had fantasized about how wonderful Rourke Caldwell would be. As the evening progressed, she realized her fantasy was a pale nothing compared to the real person. He talked easily with her father about farming, he sparred with Gavin about their favorite baseball teams, and he complimented her mother on the supper with the same, straightforward honesty he said everything.

With a little urging from Gavin, he even consented to play the upright piano in the living room. Jessica sat on the sofa and listened to the earthy blues tune he'd told them was called, "Goin' Nowhere, Doin' Nothin'" and wove dream after romantic dream about the young man whose mind seemed to be opening to her, note by note. He was lonely, his music told her that. He needed her as much as she needed him.

It was only as he said good-night that the bubble of her dream burst. He shook hands with every member of the family but her. She could hear him doing it, the satin swish of his arm moving up and down against his jacket. To her, he only said, "Good-night, Jessica. It was nice meeting you." *So polite. So correct. So remote.* He put a distance of a thousand light-years between them and walked out the door.

She went upstairs and sat at the dormer window and whispered violently under her breath, "I want to be someone else. I want to be someone else. Dear God, please. Please make me into someone else."

But He couldn't do that, of course, and there were some things in her life she wouldn't change. There were Gavin and her dear mother and father. She rose from the dormer, knowing that she would never see Rourke Caldwell again because of who she was...and what she was. She didn't cry...but she lay awake long into the night, wondering if she would ever forget him.

THE NIGHT ROURKE SPENT at Gavin's house stood out in his mind like a beacon. The family had so little...yet they made it seem like so much. Gavin and Jessica's parents were visually impaired, too, making Gavin the one who had the best vision. Even though he'd lost the sight of one eye during his operation he could see fairly well with the other. As for the rest of the family, nobody seemed to realize he or she couldn't see...especially Jessica. She moved around the house like a young gazelle, mainly, he supposed, because the rooms were kept so neat and orderly.

The Moores seemed to do everything well. The meal was delicious, the conversation easy. Theirs was a real home, a real family. And the warmth they shared was something he hadn't known since those very first years, before his mother had gotten ill.

He told himself he had to stay away...but the next week Gavin called to extend another invitation. Tantalized by the glimpse into a family life he'd never had, Rourke accepted and found himself looking forward eagerly to the next Saturday.

When he went the second time, Jessica didn't greet him at the door. Not only that, she seemed more subdued and not nearly as open and friendly. He told himself he was lucky she hadn't developed a schoolgirl crush on him...and then wondered why he felt a twinge of disappointment.

At the end of the meal, Mrs. Moore insisted he come again the next week. He agreed, telling himself he was being kind. But as the weeks went by, and he became a fixture at the Moores' Saturday night supper table, he faced the truth. This family, with their severely limited vision, saw through him, straight into his lonely heart.

"JESSICA. YOU'D BETTER come inside and get ready. Rourke will be here soon."

"In a minute, Mom." She gritted her teeth in frustration. One, two, three, four, five, six, seven. There were seven steps on their porch, she'd known that for years, but she'd never tried to run up and down them before. She'd taken them cautiously, counting. Now, she threw herself at them in angry frustration, trying to run up and down them as quickly as Rourke did. "One, two, three—ouch!" There was a rough spot on the banister and she'd gotten a sliver. Now she'd have something else to do before Rourke came besides get ready. She'd have to go to Gavin and ask him to use the magnifying glass to get her sliver out. But she'd do that later. Right now, she was going to run up and down these stairs if it killed her.

Actually, it was the bottom two steps that killed her. She always slowed down on them, never quite sure if she had counted right, never quite sure that the ground wasn't going to come up and hit her.

"What on earth are you doing?"

She was at the top of the stairs, and Rourke was there at the bottom, just a few feet away from her. In the bright sunlight she could see his outline, but even better, she could smell that wonderful distinctive cologne of his.

"You're early," was all she could think to say.

"That's better than being crazy like you are. What are you doing?"

She lifted her head, feeling her long, unfettered hair blow around her arms. She'd washed it but she hadn't taken the time to braid it because she'd wanted to imitate the way he ran up the stairs. Did he guess she was so besotted with him that she was trying to do everything he could do? "Exercising."

"Exercising?" He was close, standing at the bottom of the stairs looking up at her, she knew that. She could see his tall figure hazily outlined against the sky. She didn't back away but it took all the courage she had not to.

"Yes. Exercising. You've heard of it, surely? Jogging and pumping iron are out so I thought I'd—"

"Jessica." He said just that, her name. "Try it again. I'll stand at the bottom and catch you if you start to fall."

She shook her head, knowing that tumbling into his arms would be far more dangerous than falling down. "No, I've got to do it by myself. No!" His shadow and marvelous scent came closer. "Just...stay where you are. I'll get it right this time."

Blanking out all the years of cautious warnings and scraped knees, knowing that Rourke's eyes were on her, she flew down the stairs in a quick run that brought her triumphantly to the bottom, her shaky hand clutching the rail. "There. I did it." She fought to hide her nerves from him and looked at his hazy gray shadow, wishing with all her heart she could see his face. He seemed so very close, closer than he'd ever been to her.

"So you did." The admiration in his voice warmed her skin more than the exertion. "The victory run."

He wasn't mocking her, she knew that. He was rejoicing with her. Joy exploded inside her. "I'll tell Gavin you're here," she said, and turning, she dashed up the stairs and into the house, leaving him standing there, staring after her, wondering if he'd ever known a girl with more courage.

An hour later, when she finally admitted she'd collected a sliver, it was Rourke who offered to take it out.

They went upstairs to the bathroom where the bandages were kept, and for the first time, she was alone with him in close quarters. All the while he worked over her, probing her hand gently with the needle, she fought to hide from him the powerful effect his nearness had on her. She could feel his warm breath on her face, feel the strength in his hand holding hers.

"You do that very well," she said, when she felt the sliver leave her flesh. "You must have your father's skill."

He was silent, the tempo of his breathing changing as if she had shocked or insulted him.

"Rourke." She reached out and connected with his arm, her fingers closing around his wrist. "You never talk about your father or your family."

They were shut away from the rest of the house and everyone in it. It was so quiet that she could hear him breathing, feel the tenseness of his body under her fingers. "There's nothing to say."

"There must be something—"

In a brusque, cool tone, he cut her off. "You'd better let me look at it next week when I come back." She didn't have to see to know that he was different than he'd been a moment ago. Cool as snow, he daubed disinfectant on the wound and covered it with an adhesive bandage. The warmth, the strength vanished. He became as impersonal as he'd been that first night. What was there about his family that bothered him so?

Afterward, she thought of that night often, and gradually she began to realize that Rourke wasn't a fantasy figure to fit into her dreams. He was a flesh-and-blood young man with depths she could only guess at, secrets that tantalized her. He was a private person, as self-contained as she was, and he lived with a complexity that she could only guess at. She wasn't naive enough to think that the life they lived on the farm was similar to his. Yet he fit in like a glove. He was relaxed, and he seemed to enjoy being a part of their family... almost as if... as if he were one of them. But some instinct told her it was Rourke's chameleon ability to suit his surroundings that made him seem so compatible. She was sure that if he were invited to a party at the most expensive house in the city, he would look equally at home. Yet with all his abilities, all his money, all his intelligence, Jessica sensed that Rourke needed a friend. So she set about to become what he needed.

There was a thawing in Jessica's attitude toward him that he discovered he liked. She seemed easier with him than she had after that second night, and he found himself spending as much time with her as he did with Gavin. Both the young man and the girl became his friends... at a time in his life when he desperately needed friendship.

After he'd known the Moores for a few weeks, they insisted he come early one hot July day, to help with the haying and to stay for Jessica's birthday supper. He found himself out under a broiling sun, stripped to the waist, riding on the wagon behind a tractor driven by a farmhand. They were headed for the field, Jessica holding a hay hook, a sinister-looking piece of metal that reminded him of the sickle on the Soviet flag.

When the tractor swung into the rows of cut hay and the baler began to spew the bales onto the wagon, Jessica lifted the hook. Rourke's stomach rose to the same height. Unerringly, Jessica drove the lethal weapon into the bale in front of her.

Rocked by a force stronger and deeper than he'd dreamed possible, he cried out, "Good God, Jess!"

Genuinely startled, she let go of the handle and turned too quickly. She overbalanced and teetered on the edge of the wagon.

All his ability to think gone, Rourke reached out and yanked her into his arms.

The shock of contact with her almost-woman's body nearly made him drop her. Young firm breasts, unfettered by a bra, nudged his chest. The slim cradle of her hips seemed to fit against his to perfection. In the next instant, he thrust her away, pushing her against the bale with such force that she plopped down on her rear on the tightly packed hay, the breath exploding from her lungs.

"Get up," he said to her, in a tone that shouldn't have carried above the noise of the tractor. Evidently it did. She got slowly to her feet. He grabbed the hay hook and shoved the bale to the back of the wagon. "As long as I'm here, I'll handle this thing. Go stand in the back where you can hang on to the guard."

She stood where she was. "What gives you the right to order me around like... like some second-class citizen?" Her face was flushed. If she had had the ability to express her emotions in her face, she would have looked furious, he was sure. "I've been stacking bales since I was ten." She groped wildly for the hay hook. Discovering it wasn't there, she turned on him. "Give it to me."

"No," he said, knowing she couldn't find it as long as he didn't want her to. "I'll use it."

"Stop treating me as if I'm blind," she said furiously. "I'm not blind. I just can't see!" With a cry of frustration, she groped for the hay hook. He snatched it out of the bale and held it to one side of her. When she reached in the general direction of his arm, he shifted the hook to his other hand. Realizing that he was moving it from side to side, and that it was hopeless for her to try to wrest it away from him, she whirled around to jump off the wagon and fell over the second bale that was being extruded onto the platform. She pushed it angrily to one side and leaped off the slowly moving wagon, falling to her knees in the hay stubble with a bone-jarring thump that Rourke felt to the pit of his stomach.

"Jessica!"

She scrambled to her feet and faced him, her sightless eyes bright with unshed tears, her long tawny braid swinging. "You're so sighted and competent, you do it alone!" She whirled around and began walking toward the house.

His heart in his throat, he jumped off the wagon. "Jessica, listen to me—" She wouldn't stop so he did what he'd swore he'd never do again and grabbed her. "Jessica, dammit—"

"No," she said, the tears streaming down her face, "damn you, Rourke Caldwell, for reminding me I'm as blind as *you think* I am. Now let go of me."

Every instinct screamed to him he was a prize fool, but he let her go. She stomped over the hay stubble away from him, in a direction that he could see would lead her to the house.

He stayed for the birthday supper but it was a subdued affair. Jessica was there, but only in body. Her usual good spirits were gone. And he had been the one to banish them. He drove home with a heavy heart, his mind working furiously.

The next Saturday, it rained. He left Scotty's early because he wanted to talk to Jessica. When he got to the farm and asked where she was, he was told she'd gone riding. Wondering why they'd let her out in a cloudburst, he left the house and went into the barn to saddle a horse and look for her.

Before he could lift the saddle down off the wall, she rode into the barn. Both she and her horse were soaked to the skin, her hair hanging in long strands, the tawny color dark with moisture.

She dismounted, and her head came up, like a doe smelling the air. "Rourke?"

He didn't stop to ask himself how she'd known he was there. "What the hell were you doing, riding in the rain?"

"I know the roads—"

"I don't mean that. Damn it, even a sighted person wouldn't go pleasure riding in a downpour like this."

"Well, I'm not sighted," she said in a bitter tone he'd never heard her use before. "I thought you'd noticed that." With the easy grace that typified everything she did, Jessica unsaddled the horse, hung the saddle over a hook on the wall and began to rub down the satiny moist back of the bay with a towel. Rourke ached to rip the cloth from her hands and order her into the house to get dried off herself, but he knew he didn't dare. She would dislike him more than she already did. And he'd come to talk to her because he had something important on his mind.

"You told me once that you see a little. What do you see when you look at me, Jess?"

The cloth faltered for a moment, then went on. "You're a dark form, an outline. I have to fill in the outline with my imagination."

"You can distinguish light and dark?"

"If the room is well-lit, yes. Not here."

"Then there is probably a chance, if you had an operation to remove the cataracts, you could see."

"My folks were told when I was a baby that they'd have to wait until I was older to try. Now, after what happened to Gavin, I'm not sure they ever will agree to an operation.

"But you're different from Gavin. You have no sight to lose."

She stiffened with pride and he cursed his quick tongue.

"Why . . . why did you want to know?"

He was silent for a moment. He hated to raise her hopes. "I'd like, with your permission, to talk to my father about you. Have you heard of him?"

"Yes, I've heard of him."

"Didn't you ever think of asking me to talk to him about you?"

"Yes, I thought of it."

"Then why didn't you?"

"Because you were my friend...not...someone to use. If I did that—used you—I wouldn't be able to live with myself."

At seventeen, he thought, *she knows more about life and herself than I did four months ago.* "So it's all right if I talk to him, then?"

"If you want to, as a favor for a friend."

To cover his reaction to her words, Rourke picked up another rag and began to rub down the horse's flank opposite Jessica. Unused to so much attention, the animal moved nervously in the stall. "Whoa, boy," he said in a low, assuring tone and the horse quieted.

Jessica raised her head and stared at him across the expanse of horseflesh, and for one eerie moment, he thought she saw him. Then she threw the rag down and ran for the stable door. Unable to get it open, she turned around and flattened herself against it. "Don't touch me."

"Jess, for God's sake, what is it?"

Pressed against the wall to avoid his touch in a way that made him ache all over, she said, "You shake hands with my father every time you come and you shake hands with Gavin. You put your arm around my mother and tell her her apple pie is wonderful. Then you come in here and you start rubbing down my horse." She stopped, swallowed, lifted her chin. "You touch everybody and everything on this farm...except me. You can't stand to touch me. I know it's because I can't see and I understand why you feel that way, but sometimes, I can't stop...hating you for it. So don't touch me now because you feel sorry for me."

There in the darkened barn, with the smell of horse and hay all around, and the patter of rain on the roof, and the dim shadows revealing the lovely face of the wretchedly unhappy girl looking up at him, he saw what he hadn't seen before. She was struggling against the same relentless force pulling them together that he'd been fighting.

Cupping her jaw, consciously controlling the racketing of blood through his brain caused by the slightest contact with her flesh, he tilted her head up to him. "You want more than touching, Jess. And so do I..."

Her mouth was cool, velvety, her clothes wet, the nipples of her young breasts taut from the cold rain and from her first encounter with a male.

He slid his fingers down her rain-slick hair to the curve of her hips where it stopped, gathered up a fistful and wrapped the silken strands around his wrist like a tether. He brought the hand wrapped in her hair up to the nape of her neck. Capturing her in the fragrant, wet tangle, he bent his head to the lips he'd been waiting all his life to taste. "Ah, Jess, you're open, and sweet...oh, God, so sweet..."

At seventeen, Jessica wasn't too young to have been kissed before, but he suspected she hadn't been, because of her blindness. It was painfully obvious that she hadn't expected his tongue, didn't know what to do with it and was about to withdraw into shyness. He flicked the tip of her tongue with his, enticing her into a playful game of come-hither-and-run. With an eager shyness that rocked him more than any experienced seduction could have done, she joined in the game. Cautiously, he became bolder, kissing her more deeply. When she didn't draw away, he thrust deeper still, drinking from her with a thirsty eagerness that threatened to take over his soul. Her willingness to let him guide her through this foreign territory of passion made him want her more than ever. But even while he took her mouth and then taught her how to take his with the same greediness, a dark under-current in his mind cried out to him to stop.

"Jess—" He pulled away, and like a bee seeking the honey, she followed him, pressing against him and slipping her slim, clever hands around his waist. "Don't push me away," she whispered. "Not again. I couldn't bear it if you pushed me away from you again."

"Jess, you don't know what you're doing—"

"I want to touch you all over," she whispered. "Please, let me. I've been dying inside, wanting to touch you, wanting to... know you."

His unwillingness to hurt her and the slight trembling of her cool fingertips on his face stopped him from moving away.

How incredibly sensitive her fingers were. The slow, exploring path she traced over his forehead and down his temples couldn't possibly be setting off that heated charge of dynamite in his blood. But it was. Oh, it was.

He stood still, stoically accepting the punishment of those fingers on his face, knowing he wanted to feel them on his chest, his abdomen, his thighs, his feet... and in all the other places of his body that cried out for her touch.

"You have high cheekbones."

"There's a Viking lurking in the ancestral closet somewhere, so they tell me."

"You have a scar...there." She drew her fingers along the line of his injury.

"It's from the accident. I was... lucky."

"You could have been killed."

"I could have... but I wasn't."

"I'm glad you weren't. I would have been missing you all my life if you had been." She said the words with a sincerity that brought a lump to his throat. As if she realized she'd said too much, Jessica slid her fingers on to new territory. "Your nose is nice. Long and straight."

"No Caldwell baby would dare show up with a crooked nose."

She smiled, and the sight of her response to his self-deprecatory words made his mouth lift.

Unerringly, her fingertips found his lips. She traced their shape with a careful reverence that sent depth charges through him. "I like your mouth...it's you, Rourke. So very much you. Firm on the outside, but warm and tender underneath. I've always wondered what your mouth was like, what it would feel like to kiss you. Now I know."

"Jess—"

She went up on tiptoe and brushed her lips over his, a brief butterfly kiss that had his heart hammering like a drum. Before he could move, she relaxed back away from him.

"That's my thank-you kiss for staying alive."

He was alive. Too alive. Her hands wandered lower, and he gritted his teeth. She traced his shoulders and then followed his arms down to the bones of his wrists. She felt the tendons in the backs of his hands, the valleys between his knuckles, the blunt shortness of his fingernails. Turning one hand over, she found the blisters the hospital mop had made on the soft fleshy part under his thumb. Before he realized what she was doing she brought his palm to her mouth and pressed her lips against flesh gone so sensitive he wanted to cry out. "Jess...Jess, that's an—" he stumbled over how to tell her what he thought she needed to know "—an intimacy you shouldn't...shouldn't share with a man unless you—" His words ended in a groan.

Her hands had returned to his chest, and in his clothes that were damp from the wetness of hers, she discovered the sweep of his stomach. "Unless I . . . what?"

"Unless you're . . . going to make love with him."

For a moment she faltered, her fingertips lingering at his belt. Then, as if it were her right, her hand glided over the swelling under the zipper of his jeans. He said her name, a hissing sound between his teeth. "Jess—"

"No, don't back away. I've already felt that...part of your body touching me before, when you were kissing me—"

By the time he'd sucked in his breath and tried to brush away her hand, she'd ducked down, kneeling to stroke the muscles of his inner thighs and his calves.

It was gradually growing darker in the barn. She was a slim form kneeling, her hands lingering at his knees. No longer able to watch her there at his feet like a suppliant, he stooped to lift her up but she stopped him and brought him down to his knees in front of her. The straw crackled under his weight, and his heart thumped like the thunder rumbling outside the barn. He was being ravaged by a primitive need to absorb her into himself.

"I want to kiss you again," she whispered. "With my tongue, like we did before."

Kneeling in the sweet-smelling hay, she took him in her arms and her mouth found his with unerring accuracy.

With the scent of her rain-damp hair and skin all around him, and her slim body pressed against his at knee and hip and chest, he ached to succumb to her sweet temptation. It would take so little to undress her and nestle her into the hay and bury himself in her sweet body. He'd already pulled her wet shirt from her jeans and smoothed his hands up her bare back. She'd accepted his touch on her naked flesh with an eagerness that told him she was ready to do anything he asked of her. Even now, she was kissing him with all her newly learned skill, instinctively tasting him in delicious little sips. She seemed to have been born knowing how to please him.

Cold reason hammered inside his brain... and won. Breathing hard, he exerted a supreme effort of will and grabbed her arms to push her away to arm's length. "No, Jess. No. No more. You're cold and wet and you need a hot bath and a change of clothes."

"I don't want a hot bath and a change of clothes. I want you. I want you to kiss me and make love to me. Why won't you, Rourke? Because you don't want to make love with a girl who can't see?"

In the quiet barn, his feelings of desire fed his guilt and fired an explosion. "No, dammit, because I don't want to make love with a seventeen-year-old girl who isn't dry behind the ears—"

"I was out in the rain. It's hard to stay dry behind the ears when you've been out in the rain."

Her irrepressible humor was back, but it didn't help him. He loved her sense of humor... and everything else about her. He grasped her under her arms and pulled her upright with him. "Go into the house, Jess."

"Rourke—" She moved toward him. Hating himself for taking advantage of her blindness, he sidestepped her. But how he wanted to go into the circle of those slim arms and never leave them. "No, Jess. No." His tone told her there was no arguing with him. She dropped her hands with a sudden dejected acceptance that tore at his heart. Pride made her chin rise. "You'll come up to the house with me?"

"I can't. Not just now."

"Rourke..." She moved toward him, a soft feminine yielding in her voice. The pain he was in sharpened.

"Dammit, Jessica, use your head. I need...some time...alone."

She froze and he felt as if he'd kicked a puppy. "Go on up to the house. I...have something to do. I'll be back as soon as I can." Steeling himself, he reached forward and brushed his lips on her forehead. "I'll come back," he said huskily. "Trust me, Jess."

The face she lifted to him was a pale shadow. "I do trust you. I love you, Rourke."

Her words were so simple. Such a simple declaration of love, given without strings. She loved him, she wanted him to know. He wanted to tell her he loved her, too, but he couldn't. The words stuck in his throat. "Go on up to the house, Jess."

She turned and went out, and after he waited a few minutes to make sure she would be inside the house, he left the barn, climbed into Scotty's car and drove back to the city as if the demons of hell were after him. He was going to see his father.

The big house on East Avenue, when he entered it, seemed cold and strange. He felt as if he had never lived there. Alcott was seated behind the desk when the butler escorted Rourke into the study like the guest he was.

In the soft light of the desk lamp, his father looked tanned, fit, and much younger than Scotty. What was Alcott? Forty? Did he resent having a maturing son because it reminded him that he too, was getting older?

"Good evening, sir," said Rourke, walking into the book-lined room filled with priceless walnut antiques, Tiffany lampshades and first-edition books. His father's objets d'art did nothing to soften the austere atmosphere. The heavy, stifling odors of satin, velvet and furniture polish stirred the memory of the scent of Jessica's rain-dewed hair.

Alcott relaxed back in his expensive leather chair and didn't invite his son to sit down. "You obviously want something. Why don't you save yourself and me time and simply tell me what you need?"

Rourke had guessed this interview wasn't going to be easy, but he hadn't understood the depth of his father's vindictiveness. The old familiar resentment arose. Why should he have to explain himself to his father like a defendant on trial? Why couldn't his father, just once, unbend a little and try to understand him? Angry and hot and knowing he'd been wrong to try the impossible, he said stiffly, "I'm sorry to have bothered you. Perhaps another time would be more convenient."

He turned to go, thinking he was only postponing the inevitable. Jessica's need was more important than his pride. Alcott's voice stopped him. "You've aroused my curiosity. Come, come sit down. We'll have a drink. What would you like?"

Reluctant to toss away the advantage of approaching his father at his request, Rourke turned, his cautious blue eyes playing over his father's bland face. "I'll have some of your excellent brandy, if you're offering it."

Alcott pressed a button, and half of the bookshelves behind him swung out to reveal a bar.

When his father had handed Rourke the snifter and poured his own drink, he pressed the button and the bar disappeared. Rourke watched, thinking his father would never have installed the bar at all if Clark, the chief surgeon at Ontario General, hadn't remodeled his house and added a bar in *his* library. His father hated to be bested...in anything. After Rourke's mother's death, Alcott had married an eminently suitable woman with social connections and money of her own. Rourke's stepmother was caught up in her own interests, overseeing one worthy project after another. Rourke wondered if they ever went to bed together. He doubted it. He also doubted that his father was doing without female company. Fidelity was not one of Alcott's virtues.

Alcott sniffed the brandy appreciatively but didn't drink. "Now, what was it you wanted to see me about?"

Rourke knew his father would treat any evasion with scorn. "I'd like you to perform an operation on a friend of mine."

"I wasn't aware you had any friends among the visually impaired. What is his name?"

"Her name is Jessica. Jessica Moore. She lives on a small farm outside of Edgerton."

His father held out the brandy snifter and stared at the ruby liquor in the curved glass. "And where did you meet Jessica? In an adjacent jail cell?"

Rourke forced his hand to lie quietly on his thigh and the other to remain on the brandy glass, while he called on all the lessons he'd learned from Scotty in the past four months to leash his temper. It was for Jessica he'd come here, and for Jessica he'd swallow his pride and deal with Alcott the way Alcott loved best, from a position of submissiveness.

In an even tone, he said, "Jessica's brother was in the hospital. I got acquainted with him while I was working there and then, later, with the whole family."

Alcott turned the brandy glass and stared at it, his face smooth. "Are you having sex with her?" He lifted his head and looked at Rourke across the top of the glass.

Rourke met the calculating blue eyes that were the same color as his and kept his face carefully expressionless. "She's only seventeen."

"The question," his father said softly, "still stands."

There in the soft lighting, surrounded by the expensive antiques, the leaded Tiffany lamp in a delicate shade of pink, the huge walnut desk, the framed diplomas on the wall, all the accepted accoutrements of wealth and power, Rourke wished desperately that this man was not his father.

But he was. And if it hadn't been for Scotty, Rourke might have thought every adult male in the world was like his father, obsessed with the competitive need to play the game and be "best" at all times. Alcott's obsession made any man anathema who had the potential to be stronger, smarter... including his own son. In a low voice that scarcely trembled at all, he said, "No."

His father sat back in his chair, a new expression on his face. "Do you love her?"

Years of learning to protect himself by denying that he loved anything—since whatever he loved would promptly be snatched away from him—made Rourke say, "No."

"So. You aren't having sex with her and you don't love her. What is your interest in this girl?"

"I want her to be able to see again."

Alcott twisted his chair a little to angle his face away from Rourke. "I see. I find your concern rather... curious. But never mind that. I'm more curious about her problem. What is it, exactly?"

Rourke told him.

"Your friend's problem is not an uncommon one, and though we didn't have the technique to handle young eyes with cataracts fifteen years ago, we certainly do now. I've had several successes with young people like your Jessica." Alcott was playing his best role, the competent surgeon any man could trust. This was the motive for his personality, the base of his power. He had money and prime real estate, but that hadn't been enough for Alcott. He'd studied for years, turning himself into the cool surgeon who gave blind people sight. He enjoyed playing God. "I can't promise anything, though, until I examine her to see what can be done and when."

All professional caution now, Alcott sat up and put his brandy glass down on the desk. Facing Rourke, he folded his hands on top of the green suede blotter. "How will Jessica pay my fee?"

Rourke leaned forward and set his glass on the desk, knowing that his father was at least serious enough to begin bargaining with him. This was what he had both hoped for and dreaded. He had nothing to bargain with except his inheritance, which wouldn't be his for another four years.

"They don't have any money or insurance, and they're too fiercely proud to accept assistance. They do own a dairy farm. I thought perhaps you could take back a mortgage on the land, just to soothe their pride. I would sign an agreement with you to pay it off in a few years—"

Alcott's snort of derision stopped him. "You surely can't expect me to do that. Farmland is the least valuable commodity anywhere in the nation right now. Prices have been dropping for the past three years."

"Then I'll get a job and pay your fee," Rourke said through gritted teeth.

"At the age of twenty-one, with your education interrupted and no skills except those involved in driving an expensive car through a plate-glass window, how do you expect to pay me two thousand dollars? Not to mention an equal amount in hospital bills."

"I don't know how I'll do it . . . but I'll do it. I'll pay back every penny for everything she owes."

Alcott relaxed back in the chair. "My boy, my boy. There's no need to do anything so drastic as look for a job. You have the means to give your little Jessica her operation with one quick, clean transaction."

Rourke's eyes narrowed. Effusive, Alcott was a man to be watched. "What kind of 'quick, clean transaction'?"

Alcott hesitated, his eyes flickering away. His son steeled himself. This was Alcott at his most dangerous. When the older man's gaze returned to Rourke, the blue eyes held the calculating look of a predator. "I'm talking about the trust fund you'll inherit in four years when you're twenty-five . . . along with the right to sit on the board. If you want this operation for Jessica, I'll take a mortgage on the farm, and we'll strike a bargain. You sign off your inheritance and agree to relinquish any rights you have to vote in the Caldwell conglomerate, and I'll promise to do everything in my power to restore Jessica's sight to her, if at all possible. If I am successful, the mortgage will revert to you . . . and you can do whatever you like with it."

Here it was. The battle joined . . . with Alcott clearly favored to be the winner. He would best his son and stay at the top, spared the threat of having Rourke beside him on the board.

His father misinterpreted his silence. In a voice as smooth as silk, Alcott said, "Perhaps you've decided you don't want the operation for Jessica as badly as you thought you did. Are you just now realizing you'd be completely without funds?"

Feeling as if a great load had been lifted from his shoulders, Rourke got to his feet. It could have been a long bitter battle. This way, it was over quickly, with very little bloodshed. "Have your lawyer draw up the papers and send them over to Scotty's by courier. I'll sign them as soon as I receive them."

For a moment, Rourke considered that the soft light must be playing tricks on him. He didn't see the triumph he expected to see. Instead, those eyes that had looked at him a moment ago with such dispassionate blandness held a flicker of uncertainty. Had Alcott thought his son wouldn't accept such a lopsided bargain? "You're sure this is what you want to do?"

"I'm sure," Rourke said. Standing up, he looked down at his father, thought of what he was signing away...and felt nothing at all. "I'll wait for your call." He turned away, wanting very badly to leave this house and never return.

He was at the doorway when his father called out to him.

"Rourke! What will you do now?"

Rourke pivoted around slowly, his feet dragging on the waxed, silken floor, knowing that this was the last time he would ever look willingly on the face of the man who was his father. "That's really none of your concern, is it?"

His father's face showed no reaction to the cutting words. Alcott merely tilted his head and studied Rourke as if he were a curious toy whose inner workings Alcott didn't understand. "It seems rather...odd. You...caring so much for a little blind girl that you've given up everything for her."

"Love does seem...out of place here in this house, doesn't it?"

His father reddened with anger. "I loved your mother."

"But not enough. You didn't love her enough to stay faithful to her when she was dying."

Deathly silence filled the room. "You were nine when she first became ill, twelve when she died. You saw things through a boy's eyes."

"I'm not a boy now. Explain it to me, father," he mocked, his voice rich with irony as he addressed Alcott by his parental title.

Alcott's eyes blazed with remembered anguish. "You want me to bare my soul to you? All right, then, listen and try to understand, if you think you're man enough. I took her to four specialists, the top men in the country. None of them could help her. I was a rich man. I had everything...but I couldn't do a damn thing but come home every day and watch her die. I was helpless." He stared at Rourke. "I felt...emasculated. I began to look for ways to ease that...feeling." Alcott's eyes raked over his son. "Your mother never knew."

"She knew."

Rourke's blue eyes were ice. Alcott's were nearly black. Aware of a rather strange, stark look on his father's face, he turned on his heel to leave. "Come back here," his father called, but Rourke kept walking down that shining, pristine hallway. His father had no hold on him now.

When Rourke told Scotty about the inheritance, that gentle, controlled man said in a mortiferous tone, "If he were not your father, I would kill him. Please, think of what you're doing. It's your right as his legitimate son, to have that money and be part of the governing board of the Caldwell conglomerate. I know you're fond of Jessica and her family but surely—"

"It's the one time in my life I'm getting something I want from my father."

"But at what expense?"

Rourke's rueful smile was self-deprecatory. "Easy come, easy go."

Scotty said nothing more. His hours of teaching had come to fruition. Rourke had become a better man than Scotty had dreamed he could be.

A few days later, after Rourke had signed the papers and sent them back to Alcott, Scotty took his arm and said soberly, "You've cut yourself off from your father's money and friends. Have you thought any more about my suggestion?"

"Yes."

"And you'll let me help you finish school?"

"Yes. But I'm going to pay you back as soon as I can."

For a moment, Scotty seemed to lose the ability to breathe. "It will be the best investment I ever made." Another pause. Scotty said carefully, "You haven't been out to the farm."

"No," Rourke said.

"Why not?"

For a moment, anguish shone from Rourke's face, dark, tortured anguish. Then it was gone. His shoulders lifted. "I have nothing of my own to offer her." Defiance and a cold, hard new pride gave his features a look of maturity beyond his years.

The hardened policeman who had seen everything was moved. Rourke recognized the emotion in his uncle's eyes. "So you've given up everything... for her."

"She deserves a chance to live a normal life."

Scotty murmured something he didn't catch. Words didn't matter. In those wise eyes was a look of love and admiration that, for Rourke, made the pain easier to bear.

CHAPTER THREE

JESSICA STOOD at the open dormer window waiting, her tawny hair swirling around her waist. It was raining, a hard, pelting rain that beat against the earth with a rhythm she could feel through her skin.

She had bathed her body and changed her clothes and now, in the swish of air between the outdoors and her room, a tendril of hair brushed her elbow and the cool breeze kissed her face. As Rourke had.

Rourke. Not a knight in shining white armor. A man. A man who had kissed her and touched her and made her feel...loved. She was loved.

This was what being loved felt like, this glider ride into heaven. She soared with elation one minute, and swooped down into a deep, quiet pool of joy the next. This was the elusive beacon in the darkness that had beckoned to her all her life, humming to her through space like a star nebula, bright, beautiful...and light-years away.

The rain eased, the rhythm of the soft plops changed, slowed, decayed. In breathless suspense, she waited for the next...and the next.

Let time go by, she prayed. *Let the hours, the minutes, the seconds fly by quickly, oh so quickly. Let it be time for Rourke to walk through the door...*

She strained, listening to the soft, warm-wet summer sounds of the air for his car. The crisp smell outdoors was a delicious counterpoint to the tantalizing odors wafting up the stairwell, the baking ham Jessica had stuffed with cloves, the scalloped potatoes rich with cheese, the bubbling pineapple sauce scenting the air with tart fruit and brown sugar and mustard.

Two hours later, the sticky-sweet smell of the food clawed at Jessica's throat.

Rourke had not come.

Her hands clutched the cold, damp cloth and circled around the kitchen countertop she'd already wiped six times. To Gavin she said, "Please go look again. Maybe we didn't hear him drive in."

"I've looked till I'm blue in the face. He's not coming." The sound of her brother's footsteps striding out of the kitchen told Jessica he'd finally become so impatient with her repetitious plea that he'd left the room.

She wasn't fooled by his show of temper. He was as upset about Rourke's unusual tardiness as she was.

Jessica's mother said in a resigned tone, "If he were coming, he'd be here by now. I don't like eating burned food. Take his plate away from the table, Jessica."

Why did it suddenly hurt to breathe? "Please, can't we wait just a few minutes more?"

"Rourke's not coming, child, and you must accept it. Now do as I say, remove his plate and call your father and brother to the table."

With unwilling hands, Jessica reached for the plate she'd laid out with such anticipation two hours before. The china felt slick and lifeless in her hands. Cold. Dead. As dead as she felt inside.

She lifted the plate into the cupboard and let it slide into place on top of the others. When she shut the cupboard door, her hands were as empty as her heart.

What a fool she'd been to think he cared for her. It didn't take caring for a boy to kiss a girl, Anita had told her that. Boys kissed girls all the time when they wanted...something. But she'd offered her body to Rourke and he hadn't taken it. He hadn't wanted her...because she couldn't see.

"You want more than touching, Jess. And so do I..."

If only she hadn't shown him how much she loved him. If only she had gone on treating him as a friend. If only he were here now, she would show him—

Show him what? That she didn't want his kisses, that all she wanted was to be his friend again?

Be his friend again. Could she do that? Could she turn back the clock and forget the feel of his body under her fingertips, the mobility and strength of his mouth, the gentleness of his hands, the steely comfort of his body? She didn't think she could.

She'd driven him away. She'd driven him away because she'd kissed him and touched him intimately and now he was afraid to come back. The question was...how long would he stay away? One week? Two weeks? Forever? She had to know.

"Please, mother, let Gavin call Rourke's uncle. Suppose he's had an accident and he's lying on the road somewhere?"

Her mother was silent for a moment. Then she said, "He is rather reckless with that car of his."

"It won't cost that much to call long distance and talk for just a few minutes."

"All right, then, child," her mother said, reaching out and touching Jessica's hair, "he can call. But tell him not to stay on the line long."

She followed her ears to find her brother. He was playing the piano, a tinkling, aimless progression of notes that sounded as if a cat was running over the keys. "Mother says you can call."

"About time." She heard Gavin slide off the piano bench and head for the phone in the kitchen. She trailed after him.

Her keen ears couldn't hear what was being said at the other end of the line, and all Gavin was saying over and over was "yes" and "I see." But something was wrong. Gavin took a long time replacing the receiver.

The rustle of his clothes told her Gavin was turning toward her. By the sound of it, her mother had stopped dishing up the food in order to hear what Gavin had to say.

"He's gone. He left town two days ago. He went back to California to finish his education."

"Gone?" It wasn't true, it couldn't be true. Jessica's hand went out to the countertop, groping for support. Her legs felt numb. So did her heart. "He left without . . . without saying anything to us?"

"So it seems." Gavin sounded grim. "I guess he didn't like us as much as we thought he did."

Jessica lifted her head. "Don't say that."

"Well, he couldn't have liked us much, could he, to just go without saying goodbye or telling us where he was going or dropping us a card? He probably didn't have time to bother with his low-class friends. He probably had to get on his father's jet and fly back to see his rich girlfriends."

"Don't talk about him like that," Jessica cried and flew at her brother, her fists clenched and ready to pound on his chest. "Don't. I won't let you—"

Gavin cried out and knocked her hands away. "Jessica, for God's sake—"

A dish clicked, a piece of silverware fell to the floor. "Children! Gavin, I dropped a spoon. Will you get it for me? Jessica, go upstairs and rinse your face in cool water to calm yourself. Then I think we'd better eat our supper."

Jessica fled from the kitchen and ran up the stairs, stumbling when she reached the top. Standing at the bathroom sink, she splashed handfuls of cold water over her face, knowing that nothing would take away the pain of this day. Rourke was gone. Rourke, who had tangled his hand in her wet hair and kissed her rain-damp mouth, was gone, and he wasn't coming back.

She buried her face in a towel and sank to the floor on her knees, a small, crumpled figure. Had he hated her so much? Had he been laughing at her even while he talked to her in that dark, husky voice and taught her to do things with her mouth she'd never read about in any braille book?

She wanted to hate him, needed to hate him. But she couldn't. She could only hate herself.

How stupid she'd been. Stupid and foolish. She doubled up, her head nearly touching her knees, her hand pressing against her stomach. It hurt terribly there. How could it hurt like this to lose someone? It was a physical pain that touched every part of her.

She would never be able to go back down to the supper table. But if she didn't, they would guess how much she missed him, how much she cared, and they would pity her.

Never again. She would never love anyone like this again.

Jessica clenched her fists and beat them against her knees. *Never, never, never.*

She lifted her head, stood up, rinsed her face once more and dried it on the towel. No one but Gavin would be able to see her distress, and he had already guessed how much Rourke meant to her.

There was silence at the table when Jessica finally slid into her place. They had been waiting for her. Her mother began to urge food on her and Jessica put things on her plate, knowing she wouldn't eat any of it. Her father said, "Gavin, your mother tells me Rourke is gone."

"Yes, he's gone," Gavin said in a bitter tone that matched Jessica's mood.

"'Tis not a good thing to go without saying goodbye...unless the goodbye is too painful to say. Have you thought of that, my son?"

"He could have called."

"Perhaps he couldn't. Perhaps his errand was too urgent. Or perhaps...he was afraid."

"Rourke isn't the type to be afraid."

"No. Nor was he the type to willingly hurt anyone. Would you sweep away the memory of all the happiness and good times he brought us just because you don't like the way it came to an end?"

Sweep it away. That was what Jessica wanted to do. And yet, as she sat at the table with nothing to sustain her but the bitter thoughts in her heart, she knew she couldn't. She would carry the memory of Rourke with her as indelibly as he carried the scar he wore on his cheek.

DURING THE NEXT FEW DAYS, Jessica's goal was survival. It wasn't easy to survive. She moved stiffly and carefully through the days, walking as if she'd been in an accident and bruised every muscle in her body. It hurt to lay out the plates for an evening meal. It hurt to listen to the patter of the rain on the window. It hurt to go into the barn and saddle up the horse, to smell the fragrant hay and remember those moments she'd felt Rourke's mouth on hers.

It hurt to feel the swish of her hair around her waist and hips and remember how Rourke had tangled his hand in it and brought it up to wrap it around her neck while his mouth pressed down on hers with such devastating accuracy.

By Friday, she knew she couldn't face Saturday, Rourke's day, without doing something to ease her burden. But she would need help. And Anita Raskin, her longtime school friend, the girl with fiery red hair and fierce loyalty who had defended Jessica and been her champion since the two of them had walked into the first grade room together, was the only one she could trust to do what she wanted done. Jessica went to the phone and began to dial.

An hour later, Anita arrived. Shutting away the turmoil in her mind, Jessica led her friend upstairs, away from the rest of the world, closed the bedroom door and picked up a pair of long-bladed shears to hand to Anita. "Cut my hair."

The blades lay on her palm, cool, steely, unyielding. Anita did not lift them away. Jessica felt her hair shift and fall. Anita was touching it. "Jess, no. I know you're upset about Rourke, but this won't help." Anita sounded worried and faintly maternal.

"Please, Anita. This is something I want you to do."

"Jessica. You know I'd do anything for you, but...not this."

"I want it cut."

"You don't know what you're asking. You don't know how beautiful your hair is, how it swings when you walk—"

"I don't care how it looks." Then, Jessica added bitterly, "I can't see it."

"Jess, you're not thinking rationally—"

Aching with the pain of memories that wouldn't go away, she said shortly, "Forget it. I'll do it myself." She grabbed a handful of hair, pulled it away from her body, and jabbed the scissors at the heavy mass. One quick clip and the long strands fell over the back of her hand.

"Oh, Jess, look what you've done...oh, Lord. I don't believe I just said that. Jess, listen, please..."

Once set on the track, Jessica knew she didn't dare stop or she would burst into tears. She reached, found another long trailing lock and clipped it. Anita cried out in distress. "Stop. Please stop." There was a long silence. Then, from behind her, Anita lifted the tattered remnants. "Oh, Jess. It looks...awful."

Jessica's stomach tightened. "Then let go of it and let me finish."

"You've already butchered it. I couldn't do any worse than you've done. Here, give me those scissors."

The next morning, Gavin told their mother, in less than flattering terms, what Jessica had done to her hair.

"She looks like a ragpicker."

Her mother came close and touched her head, exploring the hair that came just to her shoulders. In that soft voice that told Jessica so much, her mother said, "Why? Why did you do this?"

"I...was tired of taking care of it."

Jessica's head came up and there was pride in her tone, pride and a defensiveness that she'd never used with her mother before.

Don't come close. Don't ask questions I don't want to answer.

Her mother touched her arm. "This Saturday will be a difficult day for all of us," she said, and turned to walk away.

Her mother's understanding brought a flood of tears to her eyes. It was difficult to suppress them. But she did. Over the past week, she'd had hours of practice.

During the next few weeks, in alternate bouts of depression and courage, she bitterly regretted cutting her hair and then told herself she was glad it was gone. Wearing hair that long was childish...and she was no longer a child.

Anita agreed, telling Jessica her shorter hair made her look older. Jessica didn't care how she looked. She only knew how she felt. She felt older, deep inside, in her heart.

Summer days melted into autumn with hot afternoons and crisp, cool nights. This would be Jessica's last year in public high school. When she first started school, she had been able to see well enough to keep up with her schoolwork. But as she grew older and her sight failed, there had been murmurings in the community about her inclusion in a sighted classroom. Jessica's mother refused to listen. Year after year she fought the battle for Jessica, until at last the new policy of mainstreaming the handicapped into regular classrooms made the struggle unnecessary.

In other years, starting back to school had made Jessica's nerves pound in anticipation. She would lie awake the night before, dreaming wild dreams. There would be a boy, she'd think, a special boy who would like her so much he wouldn't care that she couldn't see as well as other girls. He would be tall and handsome and the other girls would die with envy. He would give her his arm instead of grabbing hers and dragging her along the way sighted people sometimes did, and he would understand if she held on to his a little too tightly.

This autumn, she did not dream or plan her clothes carefully or have Anita help her with makeup. This year she dressed and combed her hair with a heart heavy with memories she didn't want to remember and dreams that were cold and dead.

One day after she'd been in school for about two weeks, she was called to the office. She went, her heart pounding with trepidation. Had she broken some rule she was not aware of?

She'd been in the principal's office a few times, and thought she remembered where the desk was, but sighted people had this fondness for changing things around and forgetting to tell her.

"Jessica, come straight forward. There's a chair there by the corner of the desk, and the phone is off the hook in front of you. You have a telephone call from a Dr. Caldwell." Mrs. Whitney, the principal's secretary, had a low, friendly voice, and her immediate and no-nonsense description of the room stole Jessica's heart away forever.

"A doctor?" The familiar name didn't register. "Is there something wrong with my parents?" There was a minute's hesitation during which Jessica's heart seemed to stop.

"No, dear, nothing like that. If the call were an emergency, I'm sure the doctor would have said so. The best thing to do would be to talk to him and find out what he wants." A warm, smooth hand guided hers to the receiver lying on the desk. With shaking fingers, Jessica picked it up. "Hello?"

"Jessica, this is Dr. Caldwell. I believe you know my son."

Rourke. The man on the other end of the line was Rourke's father. The numbness she'd been living with since Rourke left cracked like an eggshell. He hadn't forgotten. He'd kept his promise. Every cell in her body vibrated with joy. Rourke had remembered. "He...he told you about me?"

"Of course, my dear." There was a pause and then the crisp voice so totally unlike Rourke's asked, "Did you think he'd forgotten about you?"

How could she admit to Rourke's father that there were other things she was sure Rourke had forgotten, his mouth on hers, his hands sliding up her back? For if Rourke had remembered, he would never have gone away. "People sometimes say things they don't mean and he left in such a hurry that I...I thought..." Suddenly aware from the rustling of papers that Mrs. Whitney had not left her desk but was sitting just inches away from the phone, Jessica halted.

"I would have contacted you sooner but I had a heavy schedule, and then I was out of town for two weeks, speaking at a seminar. I want to examine your eyes, Jessica, and see what can be done for you. When can you come into my office?"

Feeling more than a little wretched, wishing heartily that Rourke's father had called her at home, she said with a quiet dignity, "I'm sorry that you've gone to the expense of this call, Dr. Caldwell. There's really no way my parents could afford your fees right now."

"My dear girl, I'm sure that if an operation is called for, something can be arranged. There will be no charge for the examination. Now, when can you come for an appointment?"

He'd swept away the barrier of money as if it had never existed. She should have felt ecstatic. She didn't. Jessica knew her parents would not want her to go through an operation. "I'm not sure that I can. Neither one of my parents is sighted enough to have a driver's license, and my brother has a limited one that only allows him to drive to Edgerton and back."

There was a silence on the other end of the line, as if Rourke's father was absorbing the fact of their limited world. "I'll send a car for you. Would you be able to come on the twenty-seventh of this month, a Tuesday? I'll schedule you for my last appointment, at four-thirty in the afternoon. That way, you won't miss any school."

"There may still be a problem. My parents may not approve. May I have your number and call you back?"

"Of course. Do you have something with you to take down the number?"

"No. It doesn't matter. Once I hear it, I'll remember it."

"Are you sure?" He sounded skeptical.

"Quite sure." She was annoyed. Did he, like the rest of the world, think she was a dunce simply because she couldn't see as well as other people? She had expected more from him.

He must have detected her irritation. A faint chuckle sounded in her ear. "I didn't mean to question you, Jessica, but in my world, the ability to remember a telephone number after hearing it once is extremely rare."

"I would trade it in a minute for the ability to see."

There was another little pause as if he wasn't sure how to respond to her heartfelt words. Then he said in a sober tone, "It's possible I may be able to do something about your inability to see. If your parents give their permission for you to have an exam, I shall look forward to seeing you on the twenty-seventh. I'll have my driver call your brother for directions.''

She rode home on the bus, aware that her chest was rising and falling more quickly than usual with her excitement. What would her father say? And her mother? Would they give their permission for her to see Rourke's father? They had become more disenchanted than ever with doctors and operations since Gavin's surgery had not been a success. What would they do about this extraordinary offer by Dr. Caldwell?

''It's useless,'' her mother said flatly. They had finished eating supper and Jessica, too anxious to sit still, was on her feet, clearing the table of dishes. ''A waste of time. Nothing will come of it...except that Jessica's heart will be broken again.''

''But suppose you're wrong?'' Jessica's father spoke softly. ''Suppose there is a chance he can do something for her? Can you deny her the opportunity to let him examine her and see?''

''He'll break her heart,'' her mother said as Jessica turned around to the sink, ''just like his son did.''

Jessica froze, thinking she hadn't heard her mother correctly. But the words echoed in her head with a stark clarity that told her she had. She turned around, holding her head high. ''Then your answer is no?''

''You'd go back to them for more—let them hurt you more?'' Her mother's voice was full of pride and indignation.

Jessica had her own pride. ''If you'll excuse me, I'd like to go up to my room.''

Her mother cried out, ''You can't run away and hide from this any longer. You have to stop moping and face the facts. He's gone and he won't come back.''

"For heaven's sake, Elaine," her father cried, "let her go. Hasn't she been hurt enough?"

Jessica gave a muffled cry and ran up the stairs to her room.

She threw herself down on the bed and buried her face in the pillow. How stupid she had been to think she'd hidden her pain from her parents. She was suddenly furious with Rourke for leaving behind a legacy of hurt that seemed to go on and on, angry with herself for being so transparent.

Much later, how much she didn't know or care, her father came up to her room and knocked on the door. When she didn't answer, the sound of his footsteps told her he had come into the room and across to her bed.

"Jess, darling Jess." The bed gave as he sat down beside her and a work-worn palm cupped the back of her head. "Your mother didn't mean to hurt your feelings. It's just that she knows how unhappy you've been since Rourke went away, and she feels responsible because she encouraged the boy to come here in the first place. Do you understand that?"

Jessica gave a muffled affirmative. She felt weighed down by her inability to respond to her father's attempt to console her. She lay unmoving under his hand, listening, waiting.

"We both love you so much, you know that, don't you? We've always wanted you to live a normal life, to go out in the world and meet people and eventually find a man you could love and marry." The gentle hand caressed her hair. "When Rourke came here, we thought he was good for you. He accepted you as a friend, and for the first time in your life you came out of your shell. You learned how to talk to a young man and be around him and laugh with him and work with him. We saw him as a stepping stone, Jessica, the first man in your life to break through your shyness, but certainly not the last. You must learn to think of him in the same way.

"He gave you the confidence to reach out to him as a friend. He wasn't afraid to let you see how much he needed you. And you took the example of his courage and reached out to him. You'll have the memory of that courage for the rest of your life. You can use that memory as a drawbridge to reach out to other people, Jessica, if you'll try. Or you can pull up the drawbridge, close the castle door and shut yourself away from the rest of the human race forever. If you do that, you'll be far unhappier than you are right now."

"That's not possible." Her words were muffled by the pillow.

Her father sighed and the fingers on her head squeezed with a gentle pressure. "Oh, Jess. You're so young. Don't let this experience send you back into your shell. You were ready to fall in love. If you want to condemn, condemn us, your parents."

"It's not your fault" came the muffled protest.

Jessica's father smiled. "We should have known better. We knew he was an honest, caring lad, and that we could trust him with you. We should have known that you, with all the love you have stored up inside your heart, would want to give every scrap of it away.

"You'll forget the pain and remember only the good times, believe me, Jess. But it will take time. We don't want to see you suffer another blow before you've had a chance to heal. Could you stand going to see this doctor without being too disappointed if he says nothing can be done for you?"

"I . . . think so."

"Good." The hand on her head stroked her soothingly. "We've tried to strike the right balance for you and Gavin, giving you the support you need and yet not stifling you with our love." Her father's voice sounded full, thick. "It hasn't been easy."

"I know," Jessica said into the pillow.

"Someday you'll have children of your own and then you'll understand—"

Raising her head, she rolled over and sat up, brushing her hair away from her face. "I'll never have children."

There was a smile in her father's voice as he said, "You say that now, but later, when you're older and meet another man, you'll change your mind and you'll want children very much."

"No. Never."

"Well, we shall see." Her father seemed amused by her adamant declaration. "You're young yet. There's time to talk about this another day, when you're feeling more yourself. Let's see if we can weather this current crisis first before you start your mother and me worrying about our lack of grandchildren."

"Then you're going to let me see the doctor?"

She could hear herself breathing in counterpoint to her father's more quiet respiration. "Your mother and I have discussed it and we feel that you're old enough... now... to make your own decision. No, don't say any more tonight. You're upset. Calm down, sleep on it and we'll talk in the morning. If you still want to go, you shall go." Her father gave her an awkward pat on the shoulder and left the room.

In the quiet warmth, Jessica reached out for the bed, needing to touch something tangible. She felt alien, lost. There was no one to push against anymore. She was to make the decision herself.

She touched her closed eyes with her fingertips and let herself consider the possibility of having that ancient, longed-for dream come true. Suppose she could open her eyes...and see? Suppose she could see the room drowned in white ruffled dimity with its border of tiny purple flowers, the material that Anita had described and Jessica had chosen because it smelled heavenly and felt soft? Suppose she could walk outside and see the sky and trees and bushes and flowers and horses and...Rourke. Suppose she could see Rourke...

Just once. She wanted to see him just once.

But he was gone. And even if the operation were successful, she wouldn't see him again.

But if she were able to see, there would be other things she could do with her life. She could work, have a career, be independent. A fierce and desperate longing for that ancient dream to come true swept over her. If there was the slightest chance for her to see again, she had to risk it. She would go.

She got up and walked to the dormer window, opening it, letting the breeze play over her face...where Rourke had touched her.

Her father was wrong. If her sight was restored and she lived to be a hundred and met a thousand men, she wasn't going to have children. She couldn't bear to think of allowing another man to touch her body and make love to her the way Rourke had. There would be no other man for her. Ever.

On Tuesday, the twenty-seventh of September, she dressed for school and tucked a comb and lipstick in her purse, numb with anticipation.

Her mother had planned to go with her, but that morning Elaine woke with the flu. Jessica's father insisted that his wife stay in bed and Jessica make the trip alone.

She walked through her day at school with only the haziest sense of what was happening in her classes. By the time the driver arrived at the principal's office to pick her up at three-thirty, she was in a high state of nerves.

The chauffeur escorted her out of the building. To Jessica, he sounded young, somewhere around Gavin's age, and he wore shoes that squeaked, but he must be quite perceptive to sense her nervousness. He took such pains to put her at ease.

She hadn't imagined Dr. Caldwell would send his own car for her, but it was, it had to be. There was a lingering aroma of pipe tobacco in the air and the seats were velvety and luxurious. The speed with which the car accelerated once they were out on the thruway told her that the car was as well-made and costly mechanically as its upholstery was. Had Rourke ever sat where she was sitting?

She tried to put thoughts of Rourke out of her head, but an hour later, when they arrived at what her companion cheerfully described as a huge brick building across the street from the university, she wondered if Rourke had walked through this door, ridden this elevator up to his father's office, stepped onto the same soft carpeting in the hall and walked into this office.

The driver's hand on her arm, her nose assailed by that familiar medicinal smell that sent waves of apprehension to the pit of her stomach, she was taken to the receptionist's window. A typewriter stopped rattling and she was announced as if she were royalty.

"Come back in an hour, Chuck," the receptionist said pleasantly. "She should be ready to go home by then."

"I can wait for her here."

"That won't be necessary. Dr. Caldwell will page you when he's ready to have you take Jessica home."

The woman escorted Jessica into Dr. Caldwell's office. "Here she is, Doctor." In an undertone the receptionist wrongly assumed that Jessica couldn't hear, she murmured, "Perhaps you'd better find another driver for her the next time she comes. Chuck is quite smitten... and I can see why. She's a lovely girl."

Jessica didn't know whether Dr. Caldwell disagreed with the receptionist or was more aware of the possibility that Jessica was listening. He made a low noncommittal sound and said, "Thank you, Angela."

A door closed, then she heard a faint creak of wood and leather as if the doctor had sat down and leaned back in a chair made of the same kind of soft leather as the one she was sitting in. This room smelled different than the outer office had. It was filled with a stronger scent of the same tobacco she'd smelled in the car, and the aroma of leather, and books, and well-polished furniture. The sounds of the city were shut out but there was a strange sound, a rhythmic tapping. Dr. Caldwell was bouncing a pencil off his desk blotter, making her wonder whether perhaps he was thinking troublesome thoughts.

"You're in my consulting office, Jessica, and the light is on. Can you see anything?" His voice was low, crisply accented with that well-educated placing of vowels and consonants that reminded her of an English teacher.

"I can see that it's light."

"Tell me what you see."

Jessica hesitated and felt the same frustration she always felt when people asked her what she saw. How did she know what she saw? She had nothing to compare it with. She hadn't seen the days and nights, the clouds, the sky, the sun, the trees in so long she'd forgotten what they looked like. Was her world like the fog they talked about that felt like damp velvet on her cheeks? Or was it like the mist Anita had told her rose in thick tendrils from the river in the autumn?

"I see what I think might be you. You're a slightly darker form in front of me."

He went on asking her questions about her father, about her mother, about her general health. Then he said, "Do you know where we get the word cataract from, Jessica?"

"The word means waterfall. It's what the ancient men of medicine thought they saw when they looked into a person's eyes."

"You've been doing your homework."

"I . . . wrote a report on diseases of the eye once for a school project."

"Why did you do that?"

"Why?" She was nonplussed. To her, it seemed that the reason was obvious. "Because my teacher suggested it. She thought it would help if I understood what was wrong with me."

"And did it . . . help?"

"No," said Jessica, her voice husky, realizing this was the first time she'd ever dared to voice this thought, "not really. It made me angry to be singled out that way."

The pencil slapped against the blotter sharply. "I would imagine it did." The chair creaked again and the pencil stopped tapping. She suspected that he was leaning forward. "Since you've studied about your condition, you must also know that the retina is the main sense organ in the eye.

"The problem in your case is . . . a retina needs light to develop. You began to form cataracts almost from the day you were born. It's very possible that you could go through the operation, have the cataracts removed and still not be able to see anything because of your undeveloped retina.''

''I've . . . been told that before.''

''Which was the reason your parents never consented to your having the operation.''

''Well, not exactly. My parents have . . . a basic distrust in operations . . . and doctors.''

''You said that as a child, you learned to read and were able to distinguish color. This indicates to me normal retinal development. Even now, you can distinguish light from dark, which means that some light has been filtering through those cataracts. I'll know more after I examine you. Let's do that now, shall we?''

When the examination was over, Dr. Caldwell helped her out of the examining chair and back down the hall to his consultation room. She was seated again, and felt the slight movement of the air on her cheek as he sat down at his desk across from her. While she sat with nerves stretched like wires, a match scratched, and the same woodsy odor of tobacco she'd smelled in the car mingled with the pungent odor of sulfur from the match head. The soft puffing sounds told her he was lighting his pipe.

In the silence, Jessica's nerves pulsed. He was preparing himself to tell her the bad news.

She wanted to cry out in angry frustration. She'd wanted desperately to have that old, ancient dream come true, to have this man, Rourke's father, wave the magic wand that would enable her to see. And now this dream, this elusive dream she'd had all her life, was going to be put to rest. Irrevocably. The tears began to gather. To stop them, Jessica closed her eyes.

''Did the drops bother you that much?''

She kept her eyes closed and moved nervously in her chair. "No. No, not really." How very closely he must be watching her with his educated, trained mind. What an advantage it was to be able to see. A fierce hatred for what she was, for the trap she lived in, filled her. She would not subject herself to this again. She would go home and resign herself to being what she was. Blind.

He was quiet for a long moment until at last he said, "The cataract removal will be simple. What vision you'll have after that . . . I have no way of knowing."

She waited, braced, breath held, anticipating the same words that other doctors had spoken before. *"It's not worth the risk . . ."*

"Are you a gambler, Jessica?"

The words, so unlike those she had expected, were difficult for her to comprehend. "I don't know. I've never done it."

"It's easy for some, hard for others. Some people close their minds, shut their eyes and toss everything away. Others think ahead, know what they are risking, calculate the odds and limit the amount they will lose. I think, at this point, you have very little to lose and a great deal to gain. Are you willing to risk your chance to see on the throw of the dice?"

"What . . . is my chance?"

"About fifty-fifty. I must tell you, I don't like those odds. I prefer better ones."

"If I did take the risk and you were success-ful . . . what kind of vision would I have?"

"I don't know. It could be perfectly normal . . . but there's no way of knowing until the shields come off. I doubt if we can schedule the operating room until after

Christmas. We'll shoot for the first or second week in January, how does that sound?''

Too far away, thought Jessica. Much too far away.

CHAPTER FOUR

THE HOSPITAL SHEET was a light weight on her, crisp and cool and smelling of bleach. Her supper lay on the tray beside her, untouched. Surrounded by the strange sounds, the rattling of trays, the whisper of rubber-tired carts trundling up and down the hall, the relentless hum and chatter of television in the next room, Jessica was too nervous to eat or sleep. She tossed and turned and finally settled on her side, facing the open door of the room.

A woman came in, said something bright and cheerful, made concerned noises about the food she'd left on her plate and took her tray away. The sounds of the hospital were gradually changing from day sounds to evening sounds. The rattle of the dinner trolleys had ceased and the voice over the intercom spoke in a softer tone.

She was listening to the radio when she heard the soft step on the floor and smelled the scent of roses.

"Who is it? Who's there?"

"There's no need to panic, lass. It's Scotty Mac-Donald, Rourke's uncle, come to see how you're holding up."

He smelled of good wool and cigarette smoke and the crisp cold of the out-of-doors, and he wore shoes that didn't make a sound as he moved from the doorway to her side of the bed. He had taken hold of her hand almost before she realized he was inside the room.

"These are for you. A belated Christmas present." Fragrant, rustling flowers were laid into her arms, the source of the rose scent she'd smelled when this man walked in.

"What color are they? I'll have to ask the nurse for a vase—"

"They're red, and you don't need a vase. They've been specially prepared, dethorned and fitted with their own little individual plastic vials to keep them fresh. You're to keep them on the bed around you where you can touch them and smell them, sleep with them like you did with your teddy bear when you were a wee lass."

"But I'll ruin them."

"Ruin away. You'll find another batch waiting for you tomorrow."

How could he have understood so well what she needed? Her eyes stinging with tears, she gripped his hand tighter. His fingers were warm and strong, like his voice. Like him. "Thank you so much."

He was quiet for a moment as if he were weighing something in his mind. "The flowers aren't from me, lass."

Rourke. Rourke had sent flowers. But he hadn't come. "Where . . . is he?"

"I can't tell you that, lass. I can only tell you that he's thinking of you and sending you all his good thoughts for tomorrow."

"I think I'd like a vase for these."

There was a silence, as if her request had surprised Scotty. "Perhaps we could just lay them on the night-stand here next to your bed."

"Put them on the window. They'll be cooler there."

She was rejecting the lad's peace offering, Scotty thought, shaking his head, thinking how sad it was when the young felt a need to throw a cloak of pride around themselves.

To Jessica, the flowers seemed to rustle in protest as Scotty took them from her. Her hands felt empty. She steeled herself to keep from asking for them back. She couldn't resurrect the old dream about Rourke. Not now, not tonight, when she needed her concentration for tomorrow. Tomorrow, she'd be wheeled into the operating room, and when she came out she'd know whether or not the other dream she'd had all her life had come true. "I've been very rude. Won't you sit down?"

"I think not. You look as if you've had enough excitement for one day. I'll come back again when you've traveled a little bit farther along this road."

"I . . . Thank you for bringing the flowers."

"It was my pleasure, lass. Next time I won't need an excuse. I'll come under my own steam." And he would, he thought. He liked the cut of this one's jib. She was proud, lovely and honest. A rare combination. One to be treasured.

"SHE'S NOT forgiven you, lad."

Rourke tilted back in the chair in Scotty's kitchen. He'd gone back to school for the second semester, and doubled up on courses in an attempt to graduate in the spring when he should have. It had seemed like a good idea at the time. It didn't now. Since the second week in January, his life had been a blur of classes and homework. He'd wanted it that way. Flying back to Rochester from California, he felt as if he'd emerged from a tunnel. He'd taken off two previous days from classes that would set him back a week, but he'd had to come.

"I was afraid she wouldn't. Did the nurse tell you anything about her chances?"

"They're fifty-fifty."

"That's not too good, is it?"

"When you think it could go as easily one way as the other, no."

Rourke's fist clenched against his jeaned thigh. "Whichever way it goes...when it's over, I'm going in to see her."

JESSICA'S ONE MEMORY of the operation was of lying on the gurney, waiting to be taken in and hearing a soft whisper, "So this is Caldwell's pet project...." The rest was lost in the haze of her sedated mind.

Jessica woke in the afternoon, knowing she had another long wait ahead of her. Thirty-six hours. Dr. Caldwell had been specific, ordering a slightly longer hospital stay than usual because the condition of her retina was so crucial that a bump could be disastrous.

How could she possibly wait that long, all the while lying like a stone on this bed?

Just when she thought she would scream or go mad, the flowers came. Gardenias, wonderful, delicate blossoms, filled the room with their fragrance and took away the aching loneliness and the feeling that she couldn't stand waiting another minute to know the truth. She wanted, tried to resist their lure, knowing they were from Rourke. She couldn't. Eventually, she dozed with them spilling over her hands.

That night, Anita came into the gardenia-scented room to see her.

"How did you get here?" Jessica asked, listening to Anita bustle around the room and pull up a chair, feeling her friend's vitality reach out to her.

"Clinton Adams brought me."

Jessica's heart did a flop. "Are you . . . going out with him?"

"He was coming into the city and I wanted to see you." Anita sounded casual. Too casual. "How are you feeling?"

"They've given me medication for the pain. I just wish they could give me something to make time speed up."

"What you need is a fast forward, like we have on the videocassette recorder we got for Christmas. If..." Anita stopped, swallowed, tried again. "Maybe..." She breathed in sharply, "*When* you get out of the hospital, you'll have to come over and see it."

"That sounds . . . impossible."

"Well, it's about time the impossible came true for you. I'll be thinking of you. Listen, I can't stay. Clinton's waiting, and you look tired." A cool mouth brushed Jessica's forehead and Anita's heady, expensive scent surrounded her. "I'll see you tomorrow."

Anita's heels clipped out of the room. Drowsy from her evening dose of medication, Jessica drifted into a field where gardenias and roses mingled together in a sweetly scented garden that stretched to the horizon.

The next morning, there was more waiting, more taking liquids through a straw, more asking what time it was. Then time ran out and Dr. Caldwell was there. Slowly, carefully, she was raised to a sitting position and pillows were tucked under her back. Then, before she was ready, the shields were removed.

Light. Blinding, stunning, brilliant light. White. She was seeing white. Too much white.

"Jessica." Dr. Caldwell's voice sounded crisp, commanding. "Can you see anything?"

"No. No, I can't." She was sick with disappointment. "All I can see is white, white and too much light. I still can't see. *I can't see*."

"Jessica, you're looking at the window. The curtains are white and the sun is very bright on the snow. It's too bright for you, more light than you've ever been able to take into your eyes before in your life. Look at something else." A hand clasped her chin and turned her head at a different angle. "Look at me."

"No. No, I still can't see anything—"

"You've closed your eyes. Don't be afraid." The fingers on her chin tightened. "Open your eyes, Jessica. The light will hurt but we'll put the shields back on in a minute. Just tell me what you can see."

Distorted, somehow very different from what she had imagined, a man's face came into view. She saw deep-set eyes, a chin as sharp as a blade and a nose. A straight, wonderful nose that looked several inches too long.

No Caldwell baby would dare show up with a crooked nose.

"You look . . . odd. Your nose is too big." Fascinated, she watched his lips turn up slightly at the corners. He was smiling. Slowly, carefully, the fingers on her chin turned her head. "Look at your mother, Jessica."

"I can't see her. All I can see is a big blob of . . . red. I told you I couldn't see—"

The first cautious bit of optimism came into Caldwell's voice. "You can see, Jessica, you are seeing. Your mother has a maroon-colored coat on. Your colors are a bit rusty, but they'll come back. Anything else?"

"Yes," she said, letting the excitement seep through, letting the truth wash over her in waves, remembering when she was a child and she'd had a picture book that talked about birthdays and getting presents. "I see boxes, lots of boxes, big boxes on the walls and a little box on the ceiling—''

"The windows and the television," the doctor murmured. "You can see, Jessica. Your brain isn't accustomed to receiving images so you don't know what it is you are seeing. But I think we can safely say that the operation is a success. Once we can take the shields off and leave them off, you'll soon get used to being able to see."

A snatch of conversation drifting in from the hallway that afternoon convinced her that it was all true. "I hear Caldwell did it again. The miracle worker. Stripped out the cataracts, implanted lenses and gave a blind girl normal vision. There's a rumor he's being considered for the top spot on the staff. Any truth to that?"

You'll soon get used to being able to see.

That evening Jessica lay in bed listening to her old world, the world of sound, the voices of the nurses, the soft pinging of the doctor's call bell, the wail of a siren. A whole new world would open to her when the shields were finally removed forever, the glorious world of light and color. The world of the sighted.

Rourke leaned against the doorway. Silent, unmoving, he stood there and devoured her with his eyes. Her face looked thinner and paler to him, but maybe it was because she'd lost her summer tan. She looked older. What had happened to her hair? That gloriously beautiful long hair he'd loved was gone. She was wearing it short, like a cap.

Something wrenched deep inside him. He hadn't wanted her to change. He'd wanted her to look exactly the way she had when he'd left her.

God help him, he'd tried to erase her from his mind for the past five months. He hadn't succeeded. He carried the image of her with him no matter where he went, how frantic his schedule was or how late he studied. Now he would have a different picture to carry around in his head, a picture of an older girl with shorter hair.

He looked down at the violets he held in his hands. Scotty said she'd rejected his roses. Would she reject these...and him?

Jessica had been served vegetable soup for supper and the smell lingered in the room. Suddenly, there was another smell, subtle, intriguing, fresh and green.

Spring violets...mingling with a drift of cigarette smoke and the faint creak of a leather jacket. "Rourke?" The whispered name sounded strange, unfamiliar to her tongue. "Rourke, is that you?"

Silence greeted her words. She'd gone mad. Her whispered incantation had brought no response. Excitement vanished and panic flooded in. "If you don't tell me who you are in the next second, I'm going to scream."

"Don't you think it would be much simpler if you punched the nurse's call button?"

His voice flowed over her, an achingly familiar rough velvet sound, and her nerves pulsed with urgent sensation replacing the fear. Before she could fold her hands together to stop them from trembling, they were filled with the cool moistness of flowers.

Shaken, she tried to rally. "You've got a nerve, coming in here silent as a ghost and scaring the heart out of me."

"You've got a nerve, lying there threatening to scream and scaring the heart out of me." That low voice held the faint trace of teasing amusement that she remembered so well.

She opened her mouth to answer him, but shock stole the breath from her lungs. He was touching her, folding his hands over hers, wrapping both their fingers around the violet stems, lifting the flowers to her nose. "Smell, Jess."

They were like a miracle, those violets in January, a sweet-smelling miracle of love and caring that only Rourke could have designed. She breathed in deeply. Mingled with the sweet fragrance of the flowers was the scent of Rourke's skin, clean and faintly aromatic with the soap he used. "What are you doing here?"

"Looking at you."

"I can't imagine why you'd want to do that."

His soft breath stirred the violets, making them release even more of their lovely greening smell. "You have a better imagination than that."

If only he could tell what she was thinking. He couldn't. Jessica's smooth, expressionless face was turned down toward the violets. He felt her brace herself. Then she said, "Yes, I must have a very good imagination. I even imagined you cared for me. But I was wrong, wasn't I?"

For Jessica, the need to know the truth, to kill the dream once and for all and root it out of her heart gave her the courage to say the things to him she had never been able to say before.

The warmth of his hands left her as his fingers slid away. "Were you?"

His voice sounded strange, husky, barely audible above the beat of her heart. "Yes, I was... very wrong. Wrong and stupid. I must have embarrassed you."

"I wasn't embarrassed."

"You needn't worry. I realize you were just being kind because you...felt sorry for me." She waited, praying he would deny it. Silence filled the room. He wasn't going to deny a thing. The only emotion he had for her was pity. She rushed on, rolling over words like a car on a roller coaster. She didn't need his pity now and she wanted him to know it. "Have you heard the news? I'm going to be able to see now."

"Yes, I heard. I'm very glad for you, Jess."

"I haven't forgotten that you made it possible."

His leather jacket creaked. He had moved as if her attempt to thank him was disturbing. "You don't owe me a thing, not a damn thing."

She gave a half laugh. "You don't even want my gratitude, do you?"

"Listen to me, Jess..."

Overreacting, Caldwell, you're overreacting. After months of maintaining control, you're losing it with her.

Rourke knew why. She was the only person besides Scotty he had ever trusted. He wanted, even needed the closeness they'd had. He was starved for it. And if he stayed... if he stayed one second longer, he wouldn't be able to stop himself from folding her in his arms... and staying with her the rest of his life.

He couldn't do that. He had to finish his schooling, find a job. He couldn't claim her now, when he had nothing to offer her. She'd regained her sight and she deserved to see the world. And, it occurred to him with a shock that jolted him, she deserved to see other men. He couldn't tie her to him now, just when she'd regained her sight. She was too young. She needed time to grow, time to expand her horizons. He couldn't close them off for her again. Not when she'd just had the world opened to her.

"What was it you wanted to say?" Jessica asked.

"I wanted to say good luck, Jess. And...goodbye."

If he'd been thinking, he'd have known her still face and her silence were sure signs she was hurting. But he wasn't thinking. He was clenching and unclenching his hands, knowing that if he didn't walk out of that room soon he wouldn't be able to walk away from her at all.

"Goodbye, Rourke."

Lying very still in the bed, Jessica heard him go, quickly, as if he couldn't wait to leave her. The violets lay heavily in her hand. She gathered them up and laid them on her nightstand. Opening her fingers, she let them fall away. She no longer wanted to feel their velvet petals touching her skin.

THE NEXT MORNING, the ceremony heralding the arrival of Dr. Caldwell began. There were voices, his crisp accent mixed in with others, the curt announcement by a nurse that Dr. Caldwell was on his way to see her, and then his quick footsteps coming through the door.

"Ah, Jessica. Nurse, remove the shield over her left eye, please. How are you this morning, my dear? Did you sleep well?"

She treated his words as a rhetorical question and didn't answer. Tensely, she waited for the flood of light. It came again, like a tidal wave inside her head.

"Beautiful. It's a beautiful eye, Jessica, with a nice, healthy retina. Let me see the other one."

The tidal wave came again, then vanished. "Equally as beautiful. You'll be reading in no time."

A week later, sitting in her farmhouse bedroom with Anita, a restlessness seized Jessica. She had come home from the hospital, but just as she was steeling herself to return to school, they'd had a horrendous blizzard for three days that had closed schools and brought everything in western New York to a standstill.

Now it was Saturday, and Anita had braved the snow and walked over to Jessica's house to keep her company. Jessica was grateful for her friend's chatter. It was better than listening to the incessant thoughts inside her own head.

Anita dumped the schedule of television programs she'd been studying on the floor and went to the dormer window seat where Jessica sat. "You've got to forget him and go out with somebody else. Lots of guys will want to take you out now that you have your vision."

Jessica turned away from Anita to look out the window at the falling snow. People had always told her snow was white, but it wasn't really. On a day like today, it was a pale shade of blue.

"Why should I want to go out with a boy who wouldn't look at me when I couldn't see?"

This was a running argument between them.

"Jessica, that's foolish and you know it. I think Roger likes you and if he asks you out, you should go...."

"He already has. I told him no."

"Roger asked you to go out with him, and you refused?" Anita cried. "You've got rocks in your head."

"Too bad I can't have those surgically removed, too, isn't it?"

Anita laughed, as she always did, and tranquillity was restored, temporarily, at least.

Winter wore into spring, and outside Jessica's dormer window, a million shades of green beat against her eyes. Trees. She'd known there were trees, but she hadn't known they were everywhere with tiny little buds that miraculously unfurled into leaves. Signs of spring...and hope. Silly to hope. Silly to think of Rourke. But she did.

On her eighteenth birthday in July, Jessica waited all day, foolishly hoping he would remember her. But the phone was silent, and no sleek car pulled into the driveway. She went to bed that night feeling...empty.

Which was why, when the invitation came to join Anita, Clinton and Roger at a pop concert the following Friday night, Jessica agreed to go.

The concert was held in an outdoor shell in a hilly, grassy area. Listeners could either sit on wooden seats or on blankets on the lawn beyond. Anita spread blankets; Clinton opened the trunk of the car and produced soft drinks and snacks.

Jessica's depth perception was exceptionally acute, and she had never been more aware of it than at this moment. The sweep of grass curved downward to the bleacher seats built into the hill and farther down to the theater shell that served as a backdrop to the stage. Technicians were testing the spotlights, and the glow flashed from one point on the stage to another.

Roger treated Jessica with a sober deference, his manner a sharp contrast to Clinton's familiarity with Anita. When Jessica's friend bent to flip the blanket out on the grass, Clinton's hand rested casually on her derriere, as if it was his right to touch her intimately.

Jessica turned her head away, but the heat rose in her cheeks. For most of her life, she'd had no expressions to hide. Now, since she'd regained her sight, her features were becoming mobile, which was natural, but she found it difficult to hide her responses to what she saw. Her face was far more transparent than those who had learned from childhood to disguise their thoughts.

A gentle hand caught her elbow. Roger turned her toward him, away from Clinton and Anita. "Would you like something to drink?"

In the half light, he looked down at her, his face serious, radiating kindness, as if he understood what she was feeling.

"Yes," she whispered.

He hesitated for a moment, as if he wanted to say something more. He didn't. He released her arm and walked to the ice chest. He was tall, lean to the point of thinness, a basketball star, a gentle boy. Why didn't his hand on her arm make her pulses pound in her veins the way Rourke's did? Why didn't his eyes on her make her skin burn? Why didn't his voice send shivers swimming up her spine?

She knew why. There was no restrained violence in Roger, no void she ached to fill, no loneliness lurking behind the prosaic words he said. And it wasn't only that. There was that . . . what was it? Response to her? When she was angry, Rourke answered her anger. When she was lonely, he reached out to her. He'd come to her in the hospital, as if he'd known how desperately she needed him. Her presence changed Rourke, made him feel differently, think differently. When she felt an emotion, there was an answering resonance in him. Her presence affected him, she knew it did. Unable to see, but supremely sensitive to nuances of voice and movement, she had known he responded to her as she had to him.

But it hadn't made any difference. He was gone, and he hadn't come back.

"Jessica? Is a cola all right?" His brown eyes moved over her quizzically. "Are *you* all right?"

"I'm fine," she said, taking the can of soda from him.

The sun slipped behind the hill, and the combo began to play the soft rock music they were noted for. The black male vocalist whose name the group bore spun a caramel-sweet rhythm into the night air. Jessica leaned back on her palms and closed her eyes, letting the ache of Rourke's absence ease away a little. The darkness enclosed her in moist sweetness, Roger's arm a foreign warmth against hers.

The earth whirled on, the night grew blacker, the stars shone. As the air chilled, Roger drew her closer to protect her from the dampness. She found herself sitting inside his open thighs and raised knees, her back against his chest, her head on his shoulder. And sometime, it seemed much later, when the music had grown soft and unashamedly romantic, her head turned and Roger bent toward her. She could have moved away...but she didn't. She was filled with a strange curiosity. What would it feel like to be kissed by someone who wasn't Rourke?

Roger began to taste her mouth with soft, undemanding kisses. His breath was sweet, not smoky dark like Rourke's, and his lips were tentative, not demanding.

Farther up the hill, Rourke stood watching, his shoulders hunched in the leather jacket to ward off the pain, his mouth lifted in self-mockery. And he'd thought Gavin had done him a favor, telling him exactly where to find her.

He'd gone back to school and studied till he felt as if he was going blind, but in the back of his mind she'd been there with him...and he'd known he was going to come back to her.

But while he'd been waiting, she'd been going out with another guy. Obviously, she'd worked fast. They didn't act as if it was their first date...and it obviously wasn't going to be their last.

Well, what did you expect? his mind mocked him. *Did you expect her to sit at home and wait for you? You knew she wouldn't. She's only eighteen, for God's sake. She deserves a chance to find out what life is all about.*

But had she had to start with that skinny giant? He wasn't much older than she was. Probably he wouldn't have enough sense to come in out of the rain....

Rain. Rourke remembered Jessica's hair, shiny wet, her face, cool and moist with raindrops....

Admit it, you fool. You thought what you shared with her was so special she would never look at another guy. You thought she loved you, belonged to you. Well, take a good look at what your woman is doing, Caldwell.

Something hard and painful and searing twisted inside Rourke. He pulled the cigarette out of his mouth and tossed it to the ground, grinding it into the plush grass with his heel. He'd thought she loved him. Yet there she was, nestling into another man's body as if she belonged there. She'd been experimenting, learning with him, like a kid with a bicycle. It looked as if she'd certainly learned how to keep her balance. What an idiot he was. She didn't love him...and never had.

"Hey, buddy," a voice behind him said. "Sit down. You're blocking the view."

"Sorry. I was just on my way out." Turning his back, he tightened his face to hide his pain and began to climb the hill toward the exit.

Jessica broke away from Roger. She felt unclean, as if she had broken a sacred vow. There was only one mouth she wanted on hers. Rourke's. But he wasn't here. He'd been a part of her world for a brief moment...and then he'd gone, leaving her to discover that in another male's arms, she felt more lonely than ever.

IN THE SPRING OF THE YEAR that Jessica turned twenty, Anita became engaged to Clinton. In August, on the day of her wedding, Anita wore a long sleek glide of satin and a big floppy hat, the brim shielding her eyes like a forties movie queen. As the bride's only attendant, Jessica wore a dress designed for sweet femininity, yellow chiffon with a fitted bodice, a ruffle around the peasant neckline and a long sweep of skirt ending in a ruffle. In the room off the sanctuary, an hour before her wedding, Anita leaned over Jessica helping her with her makeup. Anita was bigger than life, vital, feminine, sensual.

Jessica, looking up at her friend, saw a shade of reserve in those green eyes she had never seen there before, as if Anita was hiding something. Jessica's heart ached. At twenty-one, Anita was surely old enough to know what she was doing.

"Close your eyes," Anita ordered her, "or you'll have black stripes on your upper lid from the mascara." She picked up a dryer and Jessica felt the warm stream of air directed at her newly mascared lashes.

"You look adorable, as virginal and untouched as I should be."

To Jessica, with her eyes closed, the wry tone of Anita's voice brought back the years when that self-deprecating tone was familiar . . . and dear. "Anita, are you sure you—"

"Close your mouth and suck in your cheeks. I want to shade your face with blusher. And keep those eyes closed." Jessica felt the light tickle of the sable brush on her skin. "Although heaven knows, you hardly need it. What I wouldn't give for your cheekbones. There. Perfect. Now your lips. I'm not sure how to put lipstick on another person. Let's try it with your mouth open. Yes, that works. Now some blusher on your forehead and on your nose to give you color. You haven't been out in the sun much this summer, have you?"

The sable brush feathered over her forehead, down the slope of her nose, swished across the base of her chin. "Summer school doesn't leave much time for sunbathing. I'll make up for it in a couple of weeks."

"I just hope that double degree is worth it." Jessica opened her eyes to gaze at Anita, watching as the other young woman gave a delicate shudder. "Why you want to have an electrical engineering degree is beyond me. Computer programming sounds complicated enough."

"I like the challenge." Jessica hesitated. "Scotty wanted me to thank you for inviting him to your wedding."

"No problem. I like Scotty. He and I have something in common." Anita stood back to look at her handiwork. "We both need you in our lives to keep things in perspective."

Jessica's heart gave a silent, offbeat skip. "Anita, if you don't want to marry Clinton, don't."

Anita looked at her in mock horror. "What ever gave you the idea I don't want to marry him?"

"You're not in love with him—"

"No," Anita drawled, "but he's the only man I've ever found who isn't bowled over by my beauty and my money."

"There's more than that, isn't there?" Jessica looked up into Anita's eyes. "There has to be more."

Anita stood very still, her eyes locked with Jessica's, the sable brush motionless in her hand. "He's safe, Jess. He'll be kind to me, kind to my children. That's worth something, isn't it?" As if she regretted her excursion into the truth, Anita tossed the brush on the counter, looked into the mirror over Jessica's head and adjusted her hat. It was heart-wrenching, watching her put on that facade. Jessica ached to say more, to comfort her.

Anita wasn't looking for sympathy. Whirling around, she picked up her bouquet, looking as if she were girding herself for battle. But when Jessica rose from the seat in front of the mirror, Anita's hand grasped hers. It was icy cold. "Don't let my getting married come between us. I still need you as my friend. No, don't kiss me, you'll smudge your makeup. Just . . . don't change, Jess. For God's sake, don't change."

CHAPTER FIVE

THE OCTOBER SUN shone brightly through the window at Jessica's back, the window her co-worker, Todd Wainwright had rhapsodized about. "Nominated for most valuable employee in Consolidated Photographic Products, Distribution, and then awarded a window. What greater glory is there for you to attain?"

An office of my own, Jessica thought ruefully, as the sound of the ringing phones and voices filtered around and over the angled six-foot-high partitions sheltering her from the rest of the floor.

It was four-thirty on Friday, and it seemed to Jessica that the noise level was the highest just before everyone left for a weekend. Her hearing, still more acute than most people's, registered every noise. It had been a constant battle since she'd taken this job with Consolidated two years ago to teach herself to block out extraneous sounds and concentrate on her work.

But she had learned. Jessica returned her gaze to the seductive glow of her computer screen, groped for the pencil behind her ear and tossed it down on the desk. The computer program she'd written had passed the last test. On Monday, it would be operative.

"Jessica?"

Her nerves jumped. Despite her acute hearing, Brewster Hilton, her boss, managed to enter her cubicle and come and stand behind her without her knowing it. His shoes were rubber soled. Todd swore he went to twenty stores looking for the quietest pair.

"Yes?"

"The security guard tells me your friend, Ms. Adams, is outside in the portico waiting for you."

Anita had fallen into the habit of stopping by the office building on Friday afternoons to wait for Jessica, but it seemed too early for her to be there now. "I'm sure she won't mind waiting...."

"You're finished here, aren't you? I'll give you my permission to leave early." Brewster attempted to smile. Only on him it looked like a grimace.

The largess was so unexpected that Jessica didn't know how to react.

"Go on, Jessica," Hilton said again, and this time it was an order. "I'll see you on Monday."

"I have some things to secure...."

"I'll do it."

There was no doubt about it. He was telling her to leave. And he meant it.

She was still puzzling over his uncharacteristic behavior when she walked into the bright sunshine of the autumn afternoon. She was even more puzzled to discover the portico was empty. There was no sign of Anita.

Jessica stepped back through the double glass doors and went to the security guard. "I was told that a friend of mine, a Ms. Adams, was here. She has red hair. Were you the one who called Mr. Hilton?"

The guard's eyes flickered away from her for a moment, then returned, as if he suspected she wasn't quite sane. "No, ma'am. I'm afraid I don't know anything about a Ms. Adams."

Feeling vaguely disturbed, Jessica walked out of the building again. For ten minutes, she stood waiting, afraid to leave for fear Anita had gone somewhere and would return any minute.

It was five minutes to five when a cab pulled up and Anita appeared.

A whirlwind of restless energy swathed in a white fox wrap coat hanging open, Anita looked like raw energy drawn in vivid shades of red tresses and ivory skin. Her face was bright with carefully applied makeup and the added stimulation of the cold air. Her hair, cut by the best hairdresser in town, was a bright cap of red curls. Her eyelashes were long and darkened, her lips bright with coral sheen and her dress understated designer elegant. Jessica had a sudden vision of what a contrast they must make, facing each other, her own gray suit worn with a tailored white blouse, her shoulder-length chestnut hair pulled back into a chignon.

Anita grasped her arm. "You're here. What a great surprise."

"Weren't you waiting for me?"

"No, why?"

"I received a message that you were out here waiting for me."

Anita frowned and then shrugged her shoulders. "Must have been some kind of crazy mix-up with some other woman's friend."

"The message came from my boss."

Anita's mouth curved. "Count Dracula?"

Jessica, her eyes alive with laughter, shook her head in warning. "Careful. Those walls might have ears."

Contrite as always after an attack of impulsiveness, Anita said, "Oh, Jess, I'm sorry. If he fires you, you can come and live with me." That problem dispensed with, she grabbed Jessica's arm as they headed for the parking lot. "Are you busy tonight?"

For just a moment, Jessica had the urge to be less than truthful and say yes. Anita's divorce had become final a few days ago and Jessica had spent many hours with her friend over the past few months, helping her survive the trauma of her breakup with Clinton. Anita's relationship with her husband had always been volatile and subject to arguments, almost from the first day they married, but when the break came, it had been abrupt, cruel and a complete surprise to Anita. Clinton had simply packed up and left one night while Anita was out, and a few days later, a letter arrived saying he'd found another woman he truly loved and wanted his freedom. The blow had been to Anita's pride and her femininity more than to her heart, but the divorce had been no less devastating. Now, with the marriage behind her, Anita was plunging into the singles scene with a vengeance, making the rounds of all the hot spots in town. Though Jessica enjoyed going out occasionally, there was something about Anita's regular and relentless search for another man that made her uncomfortable. "I thought I'd go home and soak in a pink bubble bath and then curl up with a good book."

"Oh, Jess." There was a wealth of expression in that single uttering of her name. "I'm almost ready to give up on you."

"Why don't you? Think of the energy we'd both save."

"What do you need to save your energy for? All you do all day is sit around in front of a computer. A machine isn't going to keep you warm on a cold winter night—"

"No, but it will certainly pay for the bedclothes to do the job."

"I know being independent and successful is important to you but . . ." As if she realized what she was saying, Anita faltered.

"Ah, the all-encompassing but," Jessica said coolly. "Don't stop just when it's getting interesting."

"I read a book the other day about creative visualization," Anita said in a rush, as if she was extemporizing. "The idea is you have to visualize what you want to happen and experience it as if it were already true. And then—" Anita's eyes met Jessica's and at the look on her friend's face, her bright bravado collapsed a bit "—it happens."

"That's no problem for me. I can see that bubble bath right now." Jessica linked her arm in Anita's and guided her out of the portico toward the parking lot.

"But you can't see a man in there with you."

"I don't know any males with a penchant for pink bubbles."

"Nor are you ever likely to, the way you go about it. When I think about Steven... There you were, going out with the hunk of the century, and after a few months you tell me you like him as a friend. I thought you were kidding, but I found out you weren't. He's such a good friend, he asks you to preside over the guest book at his wedding."

"Steve is a thoroughly nice man. Why shouldn't I be his friend?"

"And then there was Rich, and Marc—"

A tawny eyebrow raised. "You *have* been keeping track, haven't you?"

"Married to Clinton, what else did I have to do that was interesting? I'm not paying him alimony, by the way. The judge didn't think he'd done anything to earn it. I couldn't agree more." Before Jessica had time to laugh, Anita plunged on. "All right, so tonight's out. What do you have planned for tomorrow? More fun trips to the Seneca Park Zoo with those blind kids so they can listen to the lecture about the animal of the month, a knobby-kneed dromedary who has nostrils he can shut like doors, interlocking eyelashes to keep the sand out and snowshoe feet that stop him from sinking into a sand dune?'' Anita tilted her head thoughtfully. ''Now that I think of it, he sounds a lot like Clinton.''

Relaxing, Jessica laughed. ''Yes, he does, doesn't he? But I'm not taking anybody to pet the zoo animals. Actually, I have to work.''

''*Have* to work? Or *want* to work?''

''No one's holding a stick over my head. The choice is mine. I just like to keep ahead of things.'' She kept her tone light. It was an ongoing battle between them, carried on in a constant state of impasse.

''Jessica, don't you ever want to...to be with a man?''

''I'm with men every day.''

Anita's eyebrows shot up. ''Every day? Lady, either you've been holding out on me, or I'm blinder than you ever were.''

''Every day,'' Jessica repeated, smiling. ''Right here.''

The disgust in Anita's face made Jessica's smile broaden. ''Here,'' she said one hand gesturing backward at the building they were walking away from, ''does not count. What about after work? Like right now?''

''Hey, Jessica.'' A man, blond, friendly, came around from behind them. Todd Wainwright was on his way to his car just as Jessica was. He caught Jessica's elbow and halted both her and Anita in the aisle between the rows of cars. ''Why don't you come along to Eddie's with us? A bunch of us are going for a drink, and dinner afterward...'' His eyes drifted to Anita, following the neat legs in nylons, up past the trim body clothed in the green sheath dress to the classically beautiful face. As men often did in Anita's presence, he lost the sense of what he was going to say.

Jessica's lips curved. "Todd Wainwright, Anita Adams."

Todd found the coordinating link between his tongue and his brain. "Are you—do you work here?" He sounded as if he already knew it was too good to be true.

"No, I'm a friend of Jessica's."

Wainwright straightened himself, his hand going to the knot of his tie in an instinctive grooming gesture. "Any friend of Jessica's, etcetera. You're welcome to join our party."

Dark lashes swept down over those sultry green eyes. "I'm sure I'd like to...if Jessica's going."

Anita should go into undercover work, Jessica thought later, as she sat at the bar and raised the glass of wine to her lips gingerly to avoid jostling the man who stood squeezed in beside her. Except that it would be impossible to miss her in any crowd. Jessica could see that glossy red head in the bar mirror. At the opposite end of the bar, Anita was keeping three men enthralled. One of them was Todd Wainwright.

Jessica drew her eyes away from Anita's fiery-haired image. She knew it was her own fault she had been dragged along on an evening she had neither wanted nor enjoyed. She'd done it because of...old debts. She owed Anita a million of them, from the time Anita had shoved a classmate up against the washroom wall because the girl's idea of a joke was to push a book in front of Jessica's feet and watch her stumble over it, to that year Rourke had left. In those gray days, Anita had been her only bulwark against the pain.

Why? Why had Rourke walked away without any explanation?

She'd told herself he hadn't wanted to get involved with her because she was blind.

But it was when she could see again that he'd disappeared from her life entirely. Which meant he'd never really cared for her at all. He'd felt pity for her...nothing else.

Even now, the thought of Rourke's rejection had the power to bring a pain that never seemed to go away. It was that pain that drove her to pour all her energies into her work. She was going to be successful. She needed neither sympathy nor adoring men to give her life meaning.

An ironic smile curved her lips. Why, buried in eligible men three deep dressed in their finest yuppie array, was she thinking of Rourke? She should have forgotten how it felt to run her fingers down over his lean, hard body, how his touch expressed his tenderness and yearning.

She should have forgotten...but she hadn't. Whatever else had been a lie, that rainy afternoon in the barn had been real. He'd wanted her then. And yet...he'd walked away.

She didn't even know what he looked like. She knew his scent, the feel of his silky hair, the warmth of his skin; on a summer night when the moon rode high and the breeze touched her face, she could call up his presence so vividly every nerve under her skin trembled. But it was all an illusion. Like their time together. He'd been as elusive as the breeze, as far away as the moon.

She felt warm suddenly. She sipped her wine again, and wished she'd followed Anita's advice and taken off her suit jacket. The room was warm with the crush of bodies.

Someone jostled her elbow and it was only her quick reflexes that saved her from getting her drink dumped in her lap.

"Jessica. I'm sorry. Can I help you?" A large hand closed solicitously over her shoulder and half turned her stool till her knees bumped the new arrival who'd crowded in next to her. Flushing, she set her glass on the bar and turned to face her boss, Brewster Hilton.

She brushed self-consciously at her skirt, her fingers moving over the fine wool that was perfectly dry, sliding her shoulder away from his hand. "No, I'm fine. Nothing's damaged."

"I'm certainly glad to hear that." He gave her that look, the one he thought was sexy and she thought was obnoxious. He had a personable, attractive wife and two teenage children, and she liked all three of them far better than she did him. He was six feet four and towered over everybody in sight. He had the added advantage of being blond. He was forty-five, but with his trim, tall physique and his lack of gray hair he looked ten years younger. During those first few weeks when she was new with the company, he'd had the unnerving habit of touching Jessica whenever he came anywhere near her. It was all very proper, a hand on her elbow to help her into the elevator, or accidental, a brush of the fingers when they looked at printout sheets. But no matter what the context, she hated having him close to her. The touches weren't sexual, they were more an attempt to show mastery. *I have the right to touch you because you work for me and you are female.* They were chauvinistic, those touches. She became very adept at avoiding them.

She wasn't the first woman her supervisor had tried to intimidate in this way, and she was afraid she wouldn't be the last. The two women who'd held her job before had quit in record time.

Jessica had been lucky. After the first two weeks, she'd been ready to confront him about his efforts to intimidate her physically, when she'd discovered a glitch in the distribution system that was needlessly expensive. She'd stayed late and worked weekends, devising a new program that solved the problem. Her efforts had paid off handsomely. She'd been nominated immediately for an employee award. The day after the announcement of both her name as the winner and the date of the luncheon at which she would be honored, Brewster had come into her office to offer his congratulations. Best of all, he'd walked around her warily, and Jessica had gradually begun to work in a more relaxed frame of mind. This year, when she'd been nominated as a candidate for outstanding employee, he'd treated her with a polite deference she found amusing. She wondered if the number of drinks he'd had was the reason he'd reverted to his old habits.

"I'm glad you decided to join our party tonight."

Jessica waited, wishing she'd left five minutes ago.

"It saves me having to call you tomorrow. I don't want you to come in to work, Jessica. We're having a bit of remodeling done that involves turning off the electricity and we'll be having intermittent power all morning."

"That's all right. I won't need to use the computer. I have other things I can catch up on."

He shook his head. "Not at the office. Safety regulations. No employees permitted in the building while this work is being done."

"I see." It seemed strange. In the year Jessica had worked at Consolidated, she'd never been prevented from working by changes being done by maintenance. If she had, she would never have gotten anything done. The partitions, the phones, the desks were constantly changing, and most of the work was done during office hours while the employees were there. "Well, I'm sure I can find something to do at home."

"I'm sure you can." He lifted the squat glass to his mouth, drank half the amber liquid it contained and put it on the bar. "Let me buy you another drink."

"No, thank you. I was just thinking about going home."

"Not before dinner surely?" He looked amused. "You should take more time to play, Jessica. Working all the time makes Jill a dull girl, you know."

"Actually, I was thinking about spending some time in bed."

Stupid, stupid, *stupid* to give him such an opening. A glance up at his face told Jessica he meant to take advantage of the opportunity. His eyes were bright with alcohol-glazed laughter.

"To each his own playground," he said in a carefully light, teasing tone, his fingers clasping her shoulder again.

She eased away from his hand.

He lifted his palm in a gesture of defense. "Far be it from me to discourage an employee from leading a . . . well-rounded life."

Soon, but not soon enough for Jessica, he left, sliding out from the crush of people on an exit line she pretended she didn't hear but that was the standard "have a good night," said in a low, ironic tone.

She made a conscious effort to slow her breathing and unlock her teeth. In the past few months, she hadn't let anything Brewster said bother her. Why had she let him get under her skin tonight?

Because I'm thinking about Rourke... and whenever I do that, I feel vulnerable... and alone.

She dropped a bill on the bar and made a valiant attempt to detach her wool skirt from the wicker seat. When she succeeded, she shouldered through the crowd and got as close as she could to Anita.

The other woman's face was flushed, her eyes bright. She was enjoying herself...and forgetting. Forgetting to feel like a failure.

After several frustrating minutes of trying to attract Anita's attention, Jessica caught Todd's eye. She'd never make him hear. She mouthed, *Are you,* she pointed at his chest, *taking her,* she pointed to Anita, *home?* and she turned her hands in a half circle as if they were wrapped around the steering wheel of a car.

Her answer was a long slow wink and a silent mouthing of the words, *Absolutely, my pleasure.*

Relieved, knowing Todd could be trusted to see Anita safely to her door, Jessica collected her coat and walked into the dark, cool night.

As she drove home, she pondered the problem of Anita's life...and her own. Was it worse to marry a man you'd known all your life and then discover he wasn't the man for you as Anita had, or to live your life in limbo, waiting, hoping a man would come along to erase the memory of someone you couldn't have... and couldn't forget?

A year or so ago, she'd swallowed her pride and asked Scotty if Rourke had ever married. They'd been in the pocket-sized yard of Scotty's pocket-sized house, raking leaves. Scotty was silent a long time, considering his answer. Jessica had laughed then, suddenly self-conscious. "Oh, come on, Scotty. It's just a matter of a simple yes or no. I couldn't care less if he is. I'm just ... curious."

His lined face was dappled with shadows from the bare-branched trees. Golden leaves were piled around his feet. "Curiosity is a troublesome trait to have."

Her face had become flushed and she'd said brusquely, "Forget it. It isn't important." She'd turned away from him and raked desperately at the unfortunate leaves closest to her.

"He's not married, lass. Or at least if he is, he didn't ask me to the wedding."

She had stopped to lean on the rake and catch her breath because her heart was thumping so hard. "Which, if he's smart, he never will. You'd strut like a peacock."

Scotty had grinned. "Think you know me pretty well, eh? Best look out when it comes to your own wedding."

The words had made her laugh . . . and want to cry at the same time. She'd always secretly hoped her wedding and Rourke's would be the same. Now she knew it would never happen that way.

TWENTY PEOPLE SAT around the luncheon table in the posh restaurant, their faces turned up toward the head of the department, Jack Savage. He was talking about Jessica, how skilled she was, how much the company valued her as an employee. Next to Jessica, Todd prodded an elbow into her side. She'd confessed to him in the car on the way over to the gathering how nervous she was, and he'd laughed and said she couldn't be as uptight as old Brewster would be. Now Todd didn't say anything, merely flicked his eyes across the table toward Hilton, who sat next to Savage. In slow pantomine, Todd rubbed his hands down his trousered thighs under the table where no one but Jessica could see him. *Sweaty palms,* his gesture said.

Jessica wanted badly to smile and knew she didn't dare. As usual, Todd had assessed the situation accurately. Hilton's face looked determinedly affable. Having this much attention showered on Jessica by his immediate superiors did not please him.

Savage's speech had ended. He was asking her to come forward and accept her check and the small wooden plaque. Todd gave her another nudge, and under the cover of the applause, said out of the corner of his mouth, "Go get 'em, tiger."

Jessica kept her remarks short and honest. She thanked the people in her department for their support and patience with her during the first days of her employment and said she looked forward to making each year as productive as this one.

"You should have seen Hilton's face when you mentioned productivity," Todd told her later in the car as Jessica rode back to the office beside him. "Savage looked so pleased that I thought ole Mountain Brew was going to have a heart attack on the spot."

"He doesn't need to worry. Any success I have can only make him look better."

"Well ... yes ... and no. Just remember, you're young and a woman. That gives you a definite advantage over him. This company looks for women to groom for executive positions."

At the mental picture of going to Brewster Hilton's cubicle and putting her hand on his shoulder, Jessica laughed. "I don't think he has anything to worry about."

"Maybe not. And then again, maybe he does."

Jessica dismissed Todd's ideas as ludicrous. There was no denying, however, that as October drifted toward Halloween, Hilton's attitude toward Jessica had changed. Other than the night they'd gone out for cocktails, he'd refrained from touching her. His manner was cordial but businesslike. Jessica breathed a sigh of relief. Things were going to be all right.

Throughout the last weeks of October, Jessica worked steadily, trying to keep up with the pre-Christmas madness that normally reached its peak then. Another few days and there would be a wonderful, blissful lull, Jessica expected, but until that time, it was her responsibility to see that the transfer of information from the main computer to the terminals went smoothly. Refrigerated trucks were being loaded with film in anticipation of the Christmas demand. Twenty semitrailers, dispatched by the computer program that Jessica had written, would leave the plant in western New York and head for major cities in the United States: Cleveland, Atlanta, Baltimore, Chicago, Dallas, Sacramento, San Francisco, Seattle.

The day the last truck left, Jessica heaved a sigh of relief. For a few days, she could relax...at least until the next crisis.

Disaster came quietly, insidiously, with one single ring of the telephone.

"Somebody screwed up royally," Todd said tersely into her ear. "The driver in Cleveland's got the wrong order. With our luck, the truck with the right order is somewhere in upper Sandusky." He cursed softly. "Can't anybody make little mistakes? Why do they have to be gigantic blunders?"

"That's not possible. All the orders and destinations were fed into the computer and I double-checked everything myself before the information was dispatched to the terminals at the warehouses."

"Well, you're right about that. The computer directions were followed to a T. I checked the order with the info in the computer. The driver has the load the computer told him to take to Cleveland, but it isn't the *right* load. The information in the computer is wrong. We're going to have to go back to the original orders."

Jessica was silent for a moment, trying to tell herself that there had to be some rational explanation for this mess. Computers didn't make mistakes. People did. She would have bet her life on that system. How could a mistake of this magnitude possibly have been made? "What are they going to do with the film?"

"The truck's been ordered to come back to the warehouse, what else? Nobody has a clue as to whose order he actually is carrying. Listen, Jess, we were lucky it wasn't worse. Cleveland is only a day's drive from here. He can be back in twelve hours, load with the right order and only lose a day or so."

"I suppose you're right. I still don't understand how it happened...."

"Ours is not to reason why. Ours is to deliver film, undeterred by snow, sleet or computer error."

The second jolt came when Jessica asked for a printout of the order files. Julie, the young woman whose job it was to retrieve order information came in an hour later, her face puzzled. "Here's Cleveland's order. It tallies exactly with the one on the main computer."

"Then where is the mistake?"

The look in Julie's eyes told Jessica where she thought the mistake had been made. Her nerves tightening with tension, Jessica made her voice sound calm and confident. "Thank you, Julie."

But when she walked out of the building that night and headed for the parking lot, the drizzling rain and the gray skies matched her mood exactly. If the load for Cleveland was the one listed in the computer, what about the other nineteen trucks? If they were all wrong, the software program, the one she wrote, would have put millions of dollars worth of film at risk ... not to mention what the company would lose in customer faith.

Unable to eat or distract herself with television, she sat on the couch, thinking. How was it possible the order files matched, that everything tallied so beautifully and looked so good when it was all so wrong?

She dressed for work the next morning without her usual enthusiasm, her body numb. Surely she was imagining things. Every order couldn't be wrong. Somehow, in some mysterious way she didn't understand, an error had been made in the Cleveland orders. Surely the others were correct. But that afternoon, Todd came into her office cubicle and flopped down on the chair, his face gray. "We just had a phone call from Cleveland. He's canceling our order. Get this: he said he had another company standing by, ready to deliver exactly what he needed."

"*Exactly* what he needed?" Jessica felt her skin grow cold. "How is that possible?"

"Evidently our competition keeps a better record of our orders than we do," Todd said dryly. "Maybe we should investigate and see how they do it. We might be able to adopt their technique."

Todd was keeping his temper and his head and refusing to blame her, and as yet others in the department knew nothing about their trouble. She tried to pin a smile on her face when she went down to the cafeteria to buy a sandwich to eat at her desk. She wasn't sure why she was bothering with the food. She had no appetite. She was waiting, anxious to hear confirmation that other trucks had reached their destinations and delivered their orders.

In the afternoon, Todd returned and the look on his face told her her worst nightmare had come true. "We got a call from Chicago. And Atlanta. And Baltimore."

Jessica's stomach dropped. "They all have the wrong orders?"

"Every one of them. And at every place, the rival company was standing by, ready to supply what we couldn't."

"It's not possible—"

"I did the same thing I did with our Cleveland order. I checked the program that was dispatched to the terminals. In every instance the computer did exactly what you...what it was programmed to do."

"The mistake is in the program?" She felt cold in the warm room, very, very cold.

"So it appears."

"That's not possible. I checked and double-checked...."

"Well, so have I. And the computer matched the trucks and destinations exactly the way the program told it to. You must have one hell of a bug, sweetheart. I have a feeling Brewster is going to be delighted with this." He shoved a hand back through his hair and frowned.

"He couldn't be that...vindictive, could he? After all, the problem is in his department...."

"But the computer program was your baby, and Brewster won't hesitate to lay the whole mess right on your well-shaped shoulders. Not only has he lost the business of the five major distribution centers in the East during the holiday season, he's due to lose the entire country. He's still got fifteen trucks rolling over the western plains, all of them carrying the wrong orders. The amount of money this company is losing, they're going to want an explanation and fast. Have you got your defense ready?''

''I don't have any defense.''

Todd shook his dishevelled head. ''And I don't have any to give you. According to the computer, the trucks were loaded correctly and sent to the right destinations.''

''Which turned out to be the wrong destinations.''

''Well, there's your answer. You can tell Brewster the trucks took a wrong turn on Interstate 90.''

''And have him think me more of a fool than ever.''

Todd gave her a quizzical look. ''I don't want this to come as a shock to you, lady, but in this business, honesty is not the best policy. I'd hunt for a way to lay the blame on somebody else and I'd find it fast.''

Jessica stared back at him. ''No.''

Todd shook his head. ''Well,'' he said as he clapped his hands on his knees, ''if you aren't going to look for a good excuse, you'd better look for your resumé. You'll be needing it. I'm going to go and see if I can find mine. I have a feeling I'll be out in the street right along with you. When are you going to tell Mountain Brew what's happened?''

Jessica straightened slightly, meeting his eyes. ''Now, I guess.''

He rose to go. ''We who are about to die salute you.'' He gave her a mocking grin and disappeared around the divider, leaving Jessica alone . . . very much alone.

Half an hour later, in Brewster's office, she told him what had happened, her voice catching only when she told him about the orders being filled by their competitor. When she finished, he didn't bluster or explode as she had expected. He sat back in the chair, his face as smooth as stone and as undecipherable. ''I warned Jack something like this might happen. I told him you were young and inexperienced, and that he was giving you too much responsibility when you didn't have a track record behind you. But he wouldn't listen. He was impressed with you, especially your past history."

Jessica flushed with anger. "My past history has nothing to do with our present crisis."

Brewster looked as relaxed as a cat. "It has everything to do with it. Being blind during your school years, there has to be gaps in your education."

"There are no gaps in my education. My school record is excellent—"

"Because your teachers felt sorry for you."

Jessica clenched her hands in her lap and stared at this man. He was prejudiced. Prejudiced because she had once been handicapped. His was a small mind, unable to conceive of anyone with such a handicap, whether in the past or present, being a capable, productive member of society.

"There is a mistake in the program," she said, struggling to keep her voice low and calm. "I'm sure I'll find it. I'll come in tomorrow and work on it—"

"No. I don't want you in the building on Saturdays, Jessica. I'm taking your name off the security guard's list." Jessica's nails went deeper into her palms. She was to be treated as a pariah, a person no longer worthy of trust. "I'll be taking this up with my superiors immediately. When I've talked with them, I'll get back to you on Monday morning." He said the words easily, but Jessica knew the implication was clear.

Later, leaving the building, she felt angry and unsettled. Brewster was being unjust…and idiotic. She hadn't expected any concessions from him but she had expected him to demand that she go back through the system and discover what went wrong. Wasn't he even curious to find out what had happened so that it didn't happen again? No matter who sat at her computer and punched those keys on the keyboard, the software was in place. The same system would stay in use, unless someone else instituted a major overhaul. And he had said nothing about either finding the bug, or having someone else go over the system.

Why hadn't he? There was something wrong with the system . . . something major. Why hadn't his first priority been finding that bug?

CHAPTER SIX

IT WAS A GRAY SATURDAY that matched Jessica's gray mood. She did laundry and cleaned her apartment, but nothing eased her mind. Thoughts raced around inside her head with no sense or logic. Pictures flashed in her brain: the expression on Brewster Hilton's face when she received her award, the look in his eyes when she'd told him about the mix-up. A voice inside her head changed, *The right load, the wrong destination, the wrong load, the right destination. Everything checks. There are no mistakes.*

But there had been a mistake somewhere, a mistake that could not be undone. And worse, a rival film supplier had somehow known that a mistake was going to be made far enough in advance to have their trucks loaded and ready.

She stood stock-still in the gray light of the afternoon. Someone had given the competition the correct orders. Someone from inside Consolidated. But that was impossible! Only Todd, Brewster and she had the level of security necessary to access that information. No matter how vindictive Brewster might be toward her, he would never commit a theft of such magnitude just to make her look incompetent. And Todd simply wasn't capable of such a crime, morally or emotionally.

She would be the company's prime suspect: it was only logical.

About four o'clock in the afternoon, Jessica's head ached from trying to come up with a solution to the mix-up. When the gloom in her mind threatened to surpass the gloom outside, she considered calling her parents. After a moment, she discarded the idea. She couldn't worry them. They'd been so proud of her when she got the job, and again when she received the award. So proud . . . and now, there was nothing to be proud of at all.

An hour or so later, she was unenthusiastically staring down into a bowl of chicken soup she'd poured out of a can and heated in her microwave when her apartment door began to rattle and bang under the assault of an enthusiastic fist.

"Open up. We've come to rescue the princess from her dungeon."

Jessica opened the door to a red-cheeked Todd, who looked and sounded as if he'd had too much to drink. He hadn't. His eyes were bright, but he smelled of nothing more potent than a rainy, fall day and Anita's perfume. Anita stood beside him swathed in her fox fur, looking happier than she had since her breakup with Clinton, her arm linked in Todd's.

"We're going to the Fall Festival and we want you to come with us," Anita said, smiling up at Jessica. "We'll go off our diets and eat sauerkraut and drink beer."

"Not *want* you to go with us." Todd patted Anita's arm and, gazing down at her fondly, corrected her with mock severity. "Insist." He turned back to Jessica. "We insist."

"I'm not going out in this rain to—"

"We'll give you an umbrella," Anita said soothingly. "Now go do marvelous things with your hair, and jump into something casual but chic. We'll give you exactly—'' Anita paused to consult her expensive gold digital watch ''—twenty minutes.''

''I'm hardly in the mood to—''

''All the more reason you should come with us.'' Todd was adamant.

''Would you mind—''

''No, we don't mind waiting.''

''—if I finish a sentence?''

''No finished sentences. We decided that on the way over, didn't we?'' Anita smiled up into Todd's face.

His ruddy complexion reddened a shade and he nodded solemnly. ''Yes, we did. We knew if we let you finish a sentence, you'd say no.''

Jessica knew that was what she should say. But Todd and Anita's sudden appearance in her too neat apartment made her realize how much more alone she would be if she sent them away.

''Come on, Jess,'' Anita cajoled. ''Don't sit here and think gloomy thoughts about your job when you could eat, drink and be merry with us.''

''Todd told you what happened?''

He said quickly, ''I told her you'd had a spot of trouble, but that it was nothing serious.''

Silently, she thanked him with her eyes. ''Sauerkraut does sound better than chicken soup.''

''Well, what are you waiting for?'' Anita gave her a little push. ''Do as I say and go get beautiful.''

She thought about refusing and knew what would happen if she did. Relentless thoughts about work would begin again, and this time, as the night closed in, they would be unbearable.

''All right. I won't be long.''

The downtown festival tent was awash with activity. Lanterns dangled from the tent poles, colors flashed as the people polkaed around the center pole to the stolid rhythm pumped out by an accordion. A *fräulein* dressed in a khaki green skirt and a shirred top that lifted her plump breasts and exposed the rosy rounded cleavage had subsided after singing a song, not a word of which Jessica understood. Jessica stood on the sidelines, holding a stein of beer, her eyes on Todd and Anita. They were making a passable attempt to dance the polka, Anita the more adept of the pair.

Jessica leaned her head back against the pole behind her. She'd worn a soft peach silky blouse and her cream wool pantsuit, and sometime within the past two hours she'd grown oblivious to the cold, too, and shed her jacket. Where she stood, the tent was surprisingly warm.

Humming the lilting song under her breath, she tapped to the beat with the tip of her toe, conscious that the combination of the beer she was sipping and the music and the crowd was helping her forget, for just a little while, that in a few more days, her life was going to shatter like glass.

Across the heads of the crowd, a man's eyes caught hers. *Condor,* she thought instantly. *A dark, swift and unerring predator.* His dark hair was smoothed straight back from his high forehead, not a whisper of curl in it. His eyes were hidden in the shadows, but his blade of a nose caught a gleam of light as did the one high cheekbone that she could see. The angle of his head kept the other side of his face in darkness.

Why aren't you dancing?

The thought came from his mind to hers, as clearly as if he had spoken to her. She turned to look at him more fully. *Why aren't you?*

Because I'm an observer of human nature. Like you.

Just then, he turned a fraction of an inch more, and the light caught him fully. Across the other cheek, the thin trace of a scar angled.

Shock struck her like lightning. Her beer mug slipped through her fingers and crashed on the straw-covered floor.

Heads swiveled in her direction. Hot with embarrassment, Jessica knelt to retrieve the pieces of glass. When she straightened, she felt light-headed, as if all the blood had left her brain. She forced herself to look across the crowd, at that space under the pole where the man had stood. He was gone.

He'd never been there, she thought shakily, walking to the wastebasket to deposit the pieces of glass. She'd been under a strain, and her subconscious mind had manufactured what she'd wanted to see. She'd taken a stranger in a crowd and turned him into Rourke. He was an unlikely choice, that mature male specimen with the prominent nose and the cynical mouth. He had been the right height, she thought, but that was all.

The music stopped. An announcement was made in German, then in English. She caught the words "progressive polka," a free-for-all when interrupted music was a signal to change partners.

As the music started, she saw the dark man again. He'd been plucked from the sidelines and chosen as a dancing partner by a petite blonde.

Jessica watched him move onto the floor with the other woman, place his hand around her waist with old-fashioned courtesy and begin to dance. But over the woman's head, his eyes drifted to her.

She'd seen that kind of byplay between other people, but she'd never been a part of it herself. It wasn't honest, yet she couldn't take her eyes off him. He was, it seemed, equally curious about her.

The man moved with the grace of a cat, making the choppy steps of the dance into a smooth movement that was a pleasure to the eye. His partner looked overwhelmed by her good fortune.

The music stopped...and he loosened his arms around the woman...and turned toward Jessica.

With that grave look on his face, his seriousness was at odds with the gaiety around them. He was waiting for...something.

But what?

The same thing she was waiting for. The courage to walk forward and touch. Her whole being ached with anticipation. She wanted to know what those lean hands would feel like holding hers, how strong the magnetic intensity of his eyes would be when he was looking directly down at her with no one between them. She stood frozen, unable to move, her eyes steady on his, her breath held.

Slowly, he lifted his arms, the invitation for her to step into them shining like a beacon from his eyes. A beacon that was drawing her forward. Unable to do anything else, she went to him.

She'd been right about his eyes. They were a deep wintry blue, a color she'd seen only once before in her life, on the day she'd gone to the shore of Lake Ontario and watched the sun's light glitter on the water. And now, like the water, she felt as if he were...absorbing her.

Jessica took another step toward him, strangely compelled to show him that she wasn't afraid. The music started...and he extended his hand.

Without hesitation, she placed hers in it.

She was enfolded into arms as lithe as a dancer's, brought up gently against a hard, lean body radiating the siren scent of clean male. And how right she felt there! His hand cradled hers as a parent's might a child's, yet he was as sleek and controlled as a leopard. That control gave him the power and strength for gentleness. She knew now how that other woman had felt, being guided around the floor by a man who was so superbly graceful, so adept at holding a woman.

He was wearing a gray suede vest, and a silky shirt in a lighter tone. Where her hand rested on his shoulder she could feel the contrast of velvety softness and sleek material against her palm. Below that, the underlying muscle and bone bespoke solidity... and strength.

She leaned back to look at him. As if he read the after-the-fact wariness in her eyes and was amused by it, his mouth curved and he leaned toward her, bringing his lips to rest against her temple. They were warm and firm... but she didn't want them on her forehead. She ached to feel their strength and pressure on her mouth.

He was a tactile treasure, pleasure wherever she touched. Above the noise of the crowd and the thump of dancing feet, the strange, psychic communication she'd felt with him when he'd looked at her across the heads of other people became more vivid. She seemed to feel his thoughts through the tips of her fingers and all the other parts of her body that touched his. *I'm in touch with him. That's what it is.* Her mind was synchronized with his, and that was why it was possible for her to hear his thoughts.

It's all right. Don't worry. You're safe with me.

I know.

The slight tightening of his grip told her he'd read her thoughts as easily as she'd read his.

The lights, the music, the crowd faded away. There was nothing left but touch and sensation and a drifting floating feeling....

The music stopped. His hands tightened in a refusal to let her go and she found her fingers echoing his reluctance. Someone bumped them, told them they were supposed to change partners. His eyes on Jessica's face mesmerizing her, he shook his head. The music started and they danced. The floor had become more crowded, and they were compressed into a tiny space ... yet to Jessica they were alone on the moon. Nothing penetrated her mind but the feel and scent of this man and a timeless euphoria that wrapped around her like a cloud.

The music ceased again, breaking the mood. Her partner, his eyes on her face, resisted two more efforts to have Jessica wrested from his arms. She was glad he had the strength to act on what she also felt. Her hands tightened fractionally. Her reward was a dark smile that brought a dazzling beauty to the hard bones of his face.

Then, suddenly, the music ended and didn't begin again. The dance was over.

After a moment of holding her in his arms without the excuse of moving to the music, he loosened his hold and she was free.

He bowed his head and then looked up at her, male challenge palpable in his eyes, his face. "Thank you, Jessica."

At the sound of his voice, that rough velvet huskiness so achingly familiar, so totally Rourke's, the room whirled, colors, lights blazing through her head, the way they had that first moment she could see. She'd been dancing with Rourke Caldwell. "What ... are you doing here?"

He made a gesture with his hand. "The same thing you're doing, I presume. Drinking. Eating. Dancing." His eyes were dark, watchful.

Still trying to deal with the shock . . . and the pain, she tried to concentrate on the polite conversation they were having. Polite? She didn't feel polite. She felt...ravaged. In the space of ten minutes, he'd taken her into an intimacy of thought and mind she'd never shared with another man...except him. "What brings you to the city?"

"I'm here to see Scotty." He paused. "I understand you're working here now."

How long? How long was he going to go on saying inane things? And how long was she going to go on following his lead? "Yes. I have a job with Consolidated."

"In Distribution, aren't you?" He shoved his hands into his pants pockets, giving Jessica the feeling that he needed someplace to put them. Other than that, he looked as she had pictured him in her mind, totally at ease. Nothing ever seemed to disconcert him. Certainly she wasn't capable of shaking his innate poise.

Filled with a cool fury that was building, she answered, "Yes. Did Scotty tell you that?"

Rourke nodded, his eyes never leaving hers.

"The information seems to be flowing all one way. He never told me anything about you—"

"No, he didn't. But then—" his eyes stayed locked with hers "—you didn't ask, did you?"

Her chin came up. "I assumed that was what you wanted. You left me without a word of explanation."

His face looked cool, totally self contained. "I assumed that was what *you* wanted."

The sound, the laughter, the music died away. Something in his eyes warned her not to pursue the topic, but she had waited too long, spent too many nights wondering. "How could you possibly think that?"

"Maybe because, when I came looking for you one night that summer, to claim what I thought was mine, I discovered it wasn't mine at all."

"You never came looking for me—"

"Yes." How cool he looked, how self-contained, as if discussing the weather. "I came to the house and Gavin told me you'd gone to a concert. I followed you there." He was quiet for a moment, no hint of emotion in his face. "You seemed to be enjoying yourself rather thoroughly. I realized then that your pretty words of love for me hadn't meant a thing."

"I don't believe you."

"Don't look so stricken, Jess. I recovered. And it appears that you have, too." He dipped his head again, a mocking bow. "Thank you for the dance."

He turned his back to her and melted into the crowd. It was as if he had never been there at all.

The euphoria she'd felt when she was in his arms vanished. She was shaking as if from a physical shock, chilled from head to foot. She brought her arms up and wrapped them around her waist in a futile effort to shake off the cold, then realized it would be much more sensible if she went looking for her jacket.

She found it on a chair, the sleeve half caught under the portly matron ensconced in the next seat, but when she put it on, its wool warmth didn't halt her shivering.

I imagined the whole thing. No man could actually radiate that animal sheen of health, combined with a look in his eyes of having seen too much of the world. And the words he said...the words couldn't be true. He couldn't have been there that night, watching me with Roger. Then

Jessica remembered how Gavin had acted the next day...and she knew Rourke had told the truth.

In her attempt to forget Rourke...she had driven him away.

Now, tonight, he'd walked away from her before she had a chance to explain. Just as he had seven years ago.

Because he didn't want to know the truth then...or now.

ROURKE STEPPED OUTSIDE into the cold air, aware that his body was tight as a coiled spring. He began to pace down the street, skirting the puddles, ignoring the fine mist of rain that was still falling.

He hadn't expected to see Jessica. He'd gone to the festival tent because Scotty had practically ordered him out of the house. "You're as restless as a cat on a tin roof," Scotty had told him bluntly. "Get out of here. Go find some young people who can keep up with your inexhaustible store of energy and leave me in peace."

He couldn't help being restless in Scotty's house. Scotty had retired from the force a few years ago and he'd taken up a new hobby...photography. Scotty's house was filled with pictures of Jessica.

Jessica at eighteen, looking terribly young in her somber black robe as she accepted her high school diploma. Jessica at twenty, in a yellow bridesmaid dress, clinging to her hat as she came down the steps of the church after Anita's wedding, her face so beautiful and young it hurt Rourke to look at the picture. Jessica, at Syracuse University, trying to look sober and mature, accepting her college degree.

Jessica, as she'd looked this fall. She was twenty-four, feminine, beautiful, her slim figure clad in jeans and a T-shirt, leaves mounded at her feet, her hair tossed by the wind, her face alive with life and joy.

He'd picked her out of the crowd tonight instantly...and he'd been watching her for several minutes before she saw him. Even dressed casually as she was, in a silk blouse of a strange color that matched her eyes and wool pants outlining the slender length of her legs, she looked...familiar. She was a woman now, not a girl, but in maturing, the beauty he'd once glimpsed in the young teenager had blossomed fully. How familiar, yet unfamiliar the curve of her mouth was, the moonlit quality of her skin, the sleek slender shape of her. Her eyes were a shock. He'd never seen them as they were tonight, deep, gleaming pools of a strange golden brown color with the sheen of a topaz stone. And so full of intelligence and empathy. And—something else. What was it? Need. The same need he was feeling now.

It had taken him only a few seconds to realize she didn't know who he was...and to make the decision to capitalize on her ignorance. He'd felt like a heel...but he couldn't stop looking at her...and watching her look at him. Anymore than he could stop himself from taking her in his arms.

She'd come to him so willingly. Even knowing that the shy girl she'd been was lost forever, and that she was a woman who, if her willingness to dance with him tonight was any measure, had undoubtedly been held by any number of men. It didn't matter. Nothing mattered. Only touching her had mattered. Even now, after all this time, he still...wanted her. More than ever. But it was insanity. Sheer insanity. Jessica Moore was past history, and she would stay that way. He headed into the cavern of the parking ramp where he'd left his rental car, cursing softly under his breath. For the first time in three years, he felt the old craving for a cigarette.

IN THE FESTIVAL TENT, Todd and Anita, both of them flushed and breathless, appeared on each side of Jessica. Linking their arms in hers, they tugged her along to stand in the line curving around in front of the buffet table.

The strong vinegary smell of the food kept warm over the steam tables made Jessica's stomach lift in protest. She wouldn't be able to eat a thing. But she took a sausage, a spoonful of sauerkraut and a roll on her plate, thinking she might be able to eat a bit of the bread, and trailed after Anita to a small table tucked into a corner of the tent.

Todd and Anita were talking, but she wasn't listening. She was sitting with her back to the tent, facing the crowd, unashamedly looking for Rourke. Had he come to the festival with someone else?

She would never see him again.

Jessica remained at the table for the rest of the evening and when the people began drifting away and a chill penetrated the tent, Todd and Anita drove her home. But when she climbed into bed that night, she lay there thinking about how cruel fate had been.

As the weekend passed, she tormented herself by reliving those few moments at the festival. The rest of the time, she agonized about what Monday morning would bring.

By the time she rolled out of bed to shower and get ready for work, her hands shook with nerves. It took all her concentration to pull on her stockings, fasten the pearl buttons of her imported amber silk blouse and don her most expensive cream wool suit. It took her ten minutes to apply her eyeliner, but when the task was done, she feathered on blusher with a slightly heavier hand than usual. Whatever else, she wasn't going to look like a pale, scared candidate for the guillotine when she walked into Brewster Hilton's office.

Her nerves weren't improved by the phone call that came from Hilton's secretary five minutes after Jessica sat down at her desk, telling her she would be expected to appear in Hilton's office shortly and to wait for another call. Nine o'clock came and went, and the telephone was silent. The bell had not yet tolled for her. Time stretched endlessly. She thought about looking at the computer program again and knew she would learn nothing that she did not already know...that everything tallied. She thought about quitting, just walking out of the building, and knew she couldn't. If she left now, everyone would be convinced she was a treacherous, lying spy who had sold out her own company to another one. No. She would stay, see this through and prove her innocence. Then she'd leave.

When the buzzer finally did sound, her nerves pulsed in an answering jangle.

The walk down the corridor to Brewster's office was endless. Heads lifted as she walked along, eyes darting away from hers, refusing to acknowledge her presence, as if the word was out and she had already been fired.

She pulled open the office door and was told by his secretary, Anne Daggart, a woman far too experienced to show any emotion in her face, to go on in.

Standing for a moment outside the paneled door, her hand on the knob, Jessica tried to take a deep, calming breath, and then another. After that, there was nothing left to do but open the door and walk into the lion's den.

In the grayness of the November morning, the fluorescent lights gave everything an artificial sheen. Brewster's oak desk was as glazed as his eyes. Seated in a semicircle around the desk facing Brewster, were three men, their backs to Jessica.

"Ah, Jessica. Come in." Brewster Hilton had the thin layer of solemnity of a hanging judge at a trial going exactly the way he wished. "This is Mr. Cameron, vice president of sales. He is acting as the president's representative.

She nodded at the short, plump man she knew only by sight. Todd sat in another chair, his face flushed. Beside him, dressed in a gray business suit and looking more darkly attractive than ever... sat Rourke Caldwell.

Slowly, slowly, Jessica knotted her hands and slid them into the pockets of her suit skirt, her stomach churning.

Rourke willed his eyes to stay steadily on hers. She looked pale but composed. The only sign of her unease had been those balled hands going into her pockets.

Empathy rose, swift, sudden. Stunned by the force of his emotions, by the need he felt to protect her, he sat watching her walk gracefully to the chair, her spine straight, her head high. Courage. She still had that same courage.

She'd need it today.

Jessica seated herself and fought to regain emotional control. He'd known. Rourke had known she was going to walk into this room and find him there. But how? And what was he doing here?

Brewster appeared unaware of Jessica's agitation. "As I'm sure you can see, our group has been kept small. The decision has been made to keep our counteraction as discreet as possible."

"Counteraction?" Jessica asked.

"It must be obvious to you by now that what happened with our deliveries wasn't an accident. Someone planned the whole thing very carefully. That someone has to be an employee of this company. In talking with management, the decision was made to hire a consultant trained in dealing with such problems. Over the weekend, inquiries were made of a private agency retaining a roster of people trained in industrial investigation. Quick action on our part is imperative. One of their agents was in the city, since he'd recently flown here to see his family, and he's been assigned to our case. This is Rourke Caldwell and he'll be working with us. I want you to give him one hundred percent of your cooperation. He's to have access to the files, the computers, everything. He's worked with computers and knows machine language, but it will be your job, Jessica, to acquaint Mr. Caldwell with the specifics of your particular program. A desk will be set up for him in your area."

Jessica's cheeks went fiery hot, but her hands and feet were as cold as if they'd been dipped in ice. Her fingers went to the button of her jacket. "I don't see how that would be possible. My area isn't large enough for two people—"

"That can be taken care of very easily. We'll move the dividers back to give you more room. Is there any other problem you foresee in helping Mr. Caldwell with his investigation?"

Jessica met Brewster's eyes across the desk. She hadn't been pronounced guilty yet, but he wanted her as a scapegoat and he was laying the groundwork to come in for the kill. If she made a single protest, she would seem as guilty as Brewster was trying to make her look. "No," she said in a low, throaty voice.

"Fine. I know I can count on you to give him your full cooperation." He looked and sounded as silky as a cat. He was an expert at manipulation, and now he rose, signaling the end of the meeting.

Cameron went around Hilton's desk to shake his hand. "The president will be pleased at the speed with which you've moved on this thing. He was impressed with Mr. Caldwell's record and he's sure this man will have an answer to our questions very soon. See you at the noon luncheon."

Todd rose slowly to his feet and said to Hilton, "What about my current project? Am I supposed to take time off and work on this or..."

"Continue what you're doing but make yourself available to Mr. Caldwell for any questions."

"Yes, of course." Todd met Jessica's eyes briefly. "See you, Jess."

Rourke rose lithely out of the chair, his face expressionless. "Go ahead to your work area, Ms. Moore. I'll catch up with you later. There are one or two points I want to go over with Mr. Hilton."

She met his eyes, a million emotions washing over her, memories and pride and regret all tangled with the feel of a man she'd thought she didn't know who'd held her close and danced with her under a wind-lifted tent.

It's all right. Everything will be all right.

She had to stop imagining that she was hearing his voice inside her head. The idea was ludicrous. If there was ever a man she didn't understand, that man stood in front of her now.

"I'll be waiting for you, Mr. Caldwell," she said, carefully keeping the pain out of her voice and any expression of emotion from her face as she turned to go.

When she walked out the door, Brewster Hilton stood for a moment, his face cool and unreadable. Then his eyes shifted to Rourke, and he sank back in his chair and indicated Rourke should do the same. The older man held a gold case across the desk. "No need to stand on formality now. Have a cigarette, Mr. Caldwell."

"No, thanks. I quit a few years back."

"You must be a man with great willpower. I admire men like you." Brewster looked down at the case as if he were deciding which chocolate to choose from a candy box. "I've tried three times and still can't give them up." He made his choice, put the cigarette lovingly in his mouth and lit it with the desk lighter. He relaxed in his chair, puffing contentedly. "Now. Tell me what's on your mind."

Rourke watched the veil of smoke wreathe the other man's self-satisfied features. In a softly controlled voice, he said, "That wasn't a meeting you held here a minute ago, that was a silent kangaroo court."

Brewster's face didn't change but there was a subtle difference in his body posture. He didn't look quite as relaxed as he had a minute ago. *I hit a nerve,* Rourke thought being careful not to show the sting of pleasure the idea gave him.

"For an industrial spy—" the word was heavy with emphasis "—you are a plain-speaking man, Mr. Caldwell.

"For a businessman—" he mimicked Hilton's tone exactly "—you have a remarkable taste for the jugular."

"Don't let a pretty face fool you. Jessica Moore is smart. She has a mind like a steel trap and she's more than capable of carrying out the whole rotten scheme. Now she's afraid she's going to get caught. You saw how she reacted when I told her who you were."

"She may have other reasons for reacting as she did. How would you feel, walking into a meeting that was already in session, knowing you were the subject under discussion?"

"It wouldn't bother me at all, if my conscience was clear."

"*Is* your conscience clear?"

Hilton stared at Rourke. "My conscience isn't under discussion."

"But you do have security clearance to access those files."

"Yes, of course. But I didn't write the program, she did."

"As I understand it, there are three people with access: Wainwright, Ms. Moore and yourself. Is that correct?"

"Yes." Hilton's eyes narrowed. "Do you consider every person who has access a candidate for suspicion?"

"That seems logical, doesn't it?" Rourke rose to his feet. "Sometimes the most obvious suspect is the one least likely to have done it. I won't keep you any longer, Mr. Hilton. I'm sure you're a busy man."

"Yes," he said, his eyes moving shrewdly over Rourke's lean frame, his fingers stubbing out his cigarette. Rourke had walked across the room and had his hand on the doorknob when Hilton said, "Mr. Caldwell."

Rourke turned slowly, the nuance in Hilton's voice warning him to be wary. "Yes?"

"I can depend on you to remain...neutral?" One eyebrow lifted mockingly.

"Neutral?"

"It's just occurred to me that I've overlooked a rather vital factor."

Rourke waited, refusing to rise to the bait.

"Are you single?" The question was accompanied by a slight lift of the mouth.

"Look it up in my record," Rourke said crisply, and turned to walk out, glad to leave Brewster's innuendos behind him but the man's voice stopped him again.

"Ms. Moore does have a certain charm, and she likes her job. Working with her in such close quarters might lead to a more . . . intimate relationship. If that happens, I'll be forced to ask for your dismissal."

Rourke had learned long ago to control his temper. He looked at Hilton and said coolly, "Then I'll have to work fast and solve the case before Ms. Moore's charm overwhelms me, won't I?"

CHAPTER SEVEN

AT ELEVEN-THIRTY the morning of his confrontation with Brewster Hilton, the decision was made to put Rourke's work station at a forty-five-degree angle to Jessica's, and workmen trundled the extra desk into her area. Any time she lifted her head, she would see him.

What did it matter where his desk was? When she was blind, he'd had only to enter a room and she'd felt his presence. Sighted, she was just as perceptive. In some deep subterranean river of her mind, she had recognized him that night they'd danced. Had he known then he was to be the instrument of her destruction on Monday morning? Perhaps he had and that was why he'd walked away.

She waited anxiously, restlessly, apprehensively. By early afternoon, when it became obvious he wasn't going to appear, Jessica's anxiety turned to anger. He'd already put her through sixty kinds of hell...and he hadn't even bothered to come when he said he would. Was this the first part of his campaign to break her down?

Toward three o'clock in the afternoon, she decided she could no longer wait for Rourke. She would start alone to review the computer program, going back to the beginning and working forward step by step.

After she started, she wished she hadn't. Debugging was tedious and time consuming and tore at her inventive soul. It had been fun creating the program. It was not fun going back over modules step by step, reading the file notations looking for the error, staving off the nagging worry that the basic premise of the program was wrong and that the whole thing would have to be scrapped. By five o'clock, she was glad to quit.

All day, she'd been holding in the tension, controlling the fear. Rounding the corner of her apartment hallway, she was only steps away from the sanctuary of her apartment where she could give vent to her nerves, cry, scream, throw things...when she saw the tall, lean overcoated male with his shoulder butted against her doorframe. His back was to her, but she didn't need to see his face to recognize him.

Jessica thought the morning's meeting had drained the last reserve of pride and poise she had, but she found one more tiny portion of steel to wedge against her backbone. Her head high, she walked toward him.

At the sound of her high heels clipping along the wooden floor, he turned. "Hello, Jessica." He was so gravely polite she wanted to hit him.

Icy fire of long-banked anger flared suddenly. "Hello, Rourke. Working rather late, aren't you?"

He hesitated for a moment as if her remark had caught him on a raw nerve. But when he spoke, his voice was smoothly controlled. "I'm not working right at the moment. I came to talk to you."

She pulled the key from her purse, but now she hesitated, fingering it as she leaned against the wall on the other side of the door, waiting. She had neither the strength nor the desire to engage in small talk with Rourke in the privacy of her apartment. Let him say what he had to say here.

"I'm listening."

"What I have to say to you can't be said out here." The velvet voice took on a touch of granite. "I want to talk to you privately."

"I'd rather not."

He looked unmoved. "This concerns your career, nothing else."

She lost a small portion of her control. Slowly, succinctly, she said, "Then you can talk to me about it tomorrow at work."

"That wouldn't be a good idea."

Her fury exploded. Keeping a tight hold on her anger, she said crisply, "I've been forced to accept your intrusion at work but that doesn't give you a free hand to invade my private life."

He didn't move a muscle. Her tiny dagger of words glanced off him ineffectually. He looked as if he had taken up permanent residence at her door and nothing she could say would move him. "The last thing in the world I want to do is invade your life. But I must talk to you and I want to do it in private."

She looked at him, saw the faint frown lines beginning between his eyes, the tenseness around his mouth. He was a mature man, far removed from the youth she'd once loved. Maybe seeing him and talking to him as an adult was exactly what she needed to pull him out of the fantasy land she'd stored him in since that day in the barn.

"All right. If you insist," she said coolly, missing the smile that lifted his lips as she turned and fit the key into the lock.

Jessica didn't offer to take Rourke's coat and he didn't ask her to take it. Those dark, quick eyes took inventory of the old, high-ceilinged room, roving over the bare wood floors and persistent use of white; white curtains, white walls, a rocker with a white eyelet seat and back. Rainbow-jeweled pillows accented the whiteness of the sofa, a pot of orange and blue plumes in the corner brought out the whiteness of the curtains, a print of Van Gogh's *Sunflowers* blazed bright yellow against the wall. Light from a Tiffany lamp glazed the satiny brown finish of the kidney-shaped teak table in front of the sofa.

Foolishly, she wanted to snatch it all away, the pristine neatness, the color, the light. For he had never been here, and it had been easier to put him out of her mind when she moved here from the farmhouse. Now, that was lost and she had another reason to dislike him. He had no right to take her safety away from her.

For Rourke, it was disquieting to be here, in the sanctuary she'd created for herself. For that was what it was. A bright, brilliant sanctuary that delighted the eye and contained not a single shadow. Obviously, everything in her apartment had been carefully planned to banish those shadows she had once lived with. He couldn't tell her he knew that. He could only say in a casual tone, "Very nice."

"Well within my salary range," she said, her voice sounding deliberately cool.

It was a direct hit. The surprise made him breathe in sharply. He hadn't expected open warfare, possibly because he was still locked in the past, thinking of her as an innocent girl. That could be a mistake. He steeled himself to think of her as any other woman he might have encountered in his work.

She wasn't any other woman. If she were, he wouldn't be here.

Jessica, unbuttoning her coat and hanging it in the closet, had her back turned to him so that she missed seeing his slight intake of breath when he heard her words, the progression of emotion across his face as he registered her meaning. "Would you like anything, a drink, coffee?"

By the time she turned around, years of control made it possible for Rourke to accept her cool animosity without a sign. With quiet courtesy, he said, "Whatever you're having will be fine."

She'd planned on having a quiet glass of white wine in front of the fireplace, and a good cry. Now, with Rourke here, she couldn't relax. The charade had to go on a little longer. "I'll fix coffee. Would you care for a sandwich?"

He examined her face closely to see if her invitation to share a light supper indicated a slight thawing in her attitude. It didn't. The urge to take her up on her parsimonious hospitality warred briefly with his good sense. Good sense was vanquished. "Yes, thank you. I'd like that. As long as you don't plan to put any strychnine in the sandwich."

She was surprised at his frankness and it showed in her face. "I only keep poison around for the rats. But if the shoe fits—"

His low curse warned her but there was no escaping him. In two strides he was within reach. He grasped her rigid shoulders and locked her in front of him, forcing her to look up into his eyes. For the first time, seeing the mocking sardonicism in her face, he lost his superb control. "Is that why you keep baiting me, telling me you can afford this apartment and everything in it, because you think I'm a rat? Dammit, do you think I wanted to take this job, knowing you were involved?"

In those blue eyes, the eyes she had never really seen before, dark storm clouds gathered. "No, I don't suppose you did," she replied. "Why did you?"

He hesitated for a moment longer. "I didn't have much choice but to go to the briefing. They called me Sunday morning and asked me to take the job because the man who was supposed to come from my organization was disabled. I had a Sunday afternoon meeting with Hilton. I was already wary because I knew the problem was in your department, but the moment Hilton told me who he suspected had done the job, I thought of pulling out. But as Hilton kept talking, a sixth sense told me not to. This morning, when you came into his office and I saw how determined he is to pin this thing on you, I was glad I listened to my instincts and stayed." Though it seemed impossible, his grip on her tightened. "Hasn't it occurred to you you're in big trouble? This is more serious than a simple loss of your job. You could be taken to court, fined heavily and barred from the corporate community.

"You need a friend and I didn't see one in that room this morning. Brewster's out to hang you and Cameron is eager to help him. The sooner a scapegoat is tagged, the better Cameron will look to the chief executive officer. Even Anita's boyfriend had nothing to say in your defense."

"Are you saying you believe I'm innocent?" His answer shouldn't have been important to her. But as she stood watching that smooth, male face return to its schooled, carefully impassive expression, she realized how very much she wanted him to believe in her. He was a total stranger...and yet...tension crackled between them, a tension generated by remembrance. Beneath Rourke's lean, cynical countenance and the accumulated experiences of seven years was the memory of what they had shared. Jessica could feel it, as if it were tangible.

"I operate on the theory that everyone is innocent until proved guilty."

He would have said the same to anyone. Hurting, her eyes on his, Jessica said, "What a concession." Her mouth lifted in a mocking smile.

His fingers tightened on her shoulders. "It's a damn sight more than you'll get from any of those jackals who were circling for the kill this morning."

His eyes burned into hers, and suddenly she was overwhelmingly conscious of the strength and maleness of him, of his fingers biting into her flesh. "Take your hands off me."

He relaxed his grip but he didn't release her. Their eyes locked and the wordless communication began again. *Let go of me.*

All right. You're free. His hands slid down over her arms, lingering for just a fraction of a second on top of her wrists before he withdrew.

"I wanted to talk to you, to make sure you didn't jeopardize your situation by asking for my dismissal because we've known each other before."

"I'm not sure we ever *did* know each other. If you'll excuse me, I'll go fix the coffee."

He knew it wouldn't be easy, but he hadn't thought it would be this hard. Yet he couldn't walk away from her now, not this time, not when she needed him. This was going to be a tough case. Unless he missed his bet, which he was sure he hadn't, Hilton needed careful watching. He cursed mentally. Why had he picked this weekend to come and see Scotty?

A few minutes later, Jessica brought out the cups, a glass carafe and sandwiches and napkins on a tray. She set her burden on the coffee table, a nod of her head indicating that he should sit on the sofa. She poured the coffee for him and handed him a sandwich on a small plate the same way she did everything, with an innate grace. Now that he'd been with her a little while, it was easier to see the resemblance between the teenage girl who couldn't see and still moved with the lithe ease of a dancer and this poised, mature woman. But she wasn't the same, she couldn't be, not after seven years. Was this woman capable of living a lie, of hatching a scheme of industrial espionage on a grand scale and having the nerve to bluff her way through afterward with cool poise and righteous indignation? He doubted it. And yet...did he really know Jessica now? He had known a young, untried girl, who was honest and loyal and heartbreakingly naive. Since that afternoon in the barn, Jessica had no doubt learned many things. Had she since learned to lie and cheat and steal?

Looking at her, he would have answered an unqualified no. Unfortunately, he'd learned that avarice and dishonesty could lurk behind the most innocent face. He could trust no one. But neither would he condemn anyone until he'd found the evidence to do so.

Somehow, this was the setting he'd always imagined her in, a bright, beautiful apartment filled with color and light, wearing good clothes, having a successful career. Was it possible she was in financial difficulty and had accepted a bribe?

The thought rocked him badly. The cup rattled in the saucer as he set it on the table. There was one quick, easy way to find out if she was guilty. "If you want me to withdraw from this investigation, Jessica, I will." He raised his eyes to hers. "With so much at stake, you have a right to have an impartial investigator. If you think I'm not capable of conducting a fair inquiry, you have the right to ask for someone else."

How smooth he was. Jessica wanted badly to take his words at face value. She wanted him out of her office, out of her life. But a sixth sense leftover from the days when she had to listen to voices carefully because she had no other clue to a person's emotions, told her not to leap at the easy opportunity he'd given her. She lifted her chin and looked at him steadily. "Do you think you're capable of conducting a fair inquiry?"

Rourke was jolted. She hadn't taken the bait. Instead, she had turned the trap neatly and caught him in it. He had always known Jessica was intelligent, but her quick mind had been partially obscured by her blindness. Now there was nothing to keep him from seeing that here was one cool lady, indeed. And though it galled him to admit it, she was intellectually capable of executing a computer scam. "Knowing you before won't influence me...either way," said Rourke, watching her.

Hands and feet betrayed tension much more easily than facial expressions. The cup in Jessica's hand rattled.

"Then I see no reason to ask for your dismissal."

Were those brave, lying words? Or the truth? For all his training, Rourke couldn't tell. Or were his own emotions getting in the way? "That's your decision?"

"Yes." With great care, she put her cup down on the table, and sat back to look at him. It was an invitation to leave and he knew it. This controlled woman was skilled in all the social graces. Unbidden, a vision flickered through his mind, of an artless teenager running up and down the front steps, greeting him with breathless enthusiasm. He'd lost her, that teenager. A powerful feeling of sadness and regret swept over him.

Rourke rose to his feet. "Thank you for the coffee. I'll see you tomorrow morning."

AT THAT SAME MOMENT, in a public phone booth on the sidewalk of a shopping center in a northern suburb of Rochester, a man dropped three dollars and eighty-five cents' worth of coins into the slot, the exact amount required to call New York City. He listened while the phone made a soft burr in his ear.

After seven rings, just as he was ready to hang up, a male voice answered. "Yeah?"

"What the hell happened?"

There was a silence on the other end. Then the voice said, "It was a crazy mix-up. Nothing went right."

"Where's Johnson?"

The man groaned. "He tripped over a baggage cart in the airport, fell down and broke his arm."

"Why wasn't I contacted?"

"You wanted me to call you at your office?" Heavy with irony, the voice drawled into his ear. "What could I do? You'd convinced the boss you needed somebody by Monday morning. Caldwell was there, Caldwell you got. What's the matter? Don't you like him?"

When the caller clutched the phone and muttered a curse, the other man laughed.

The man in Rochester said, "Is he . . . approachable?"

"No. He'd blow the whistle on you so fast you wouldn't know what hit you. You'd better play it straight and hope you got your rabbit framed extremely well. If you don't, and Caldwell is only half as good as scuttlebutt says he is, he's going to spring your sacrificial lamb. And if he digs around long enough, he might discover the trap you set for her. Sorry things didn't work out the way we planned."

"You're sorry? You may be more than sorry. I want my money back."

There was a brief silence on the other end of the line. "Don't threaten me. I didn't give you a money-back guarantee. You asked for a certain man, I juggled the paperwork and delivered him. It wasn't my fault he didn't get there."

"I want my money back." Said through clenched teeth, the demand became a threat.

The other man laughed, "Call the Better Business Bureau."

IN THE GRAYNESS of the early morning, through a fine mist that bathed his face like cool satin, Rourke jogged a few paces behind Scotty, his sneakered feet pounding along the twisting cement sidewalk. They were running beside the Genesee River, following the sidewalk that began on a high, grassy verge and dipped under the highway bridge on Ridge Road. Even now, at seven o'clock in the morning, rush-hour traffic thundered over their heads.

His breath coming hard, his body warm from the forty-five minutes of exercise he'd already had, Rourke found himself looking down over the shorter wall into the river gorge. A silvery stream of water swirled below. He followed Scotty under the soaring cement arch and came up on the other side. This time, his attention was caught by the wall on his right that served to keep the earthen bank from crumbling. Graffiti and cartoon art covered the stones. A figure of a man was scratched out there, his feet oval loops in front of him. A man waiting to be stepped on. Rourke's sneaker dropped squarely in the middle of a sketched-on sole.

Was he, Rourke, a man waiting to be stepped on, too? No, he couldn't be such a fool. Could he?

In the six years since he'd begun as a corporate investigator, Rourke had never encountered a case quite as sticky as this one. And it was due to get stickier still. Here he was, jogging with his uncle...and trying to think how best to approach him to get the information he needed.

Damn! How could he do it? How could he ask probing questions of the one man he'd ever loved and respected? Yet he had to. For Jessica's sake.

After his evening with Jessica, Rourke hadn't seemed capable of reasonable thought. He'd slept lightly, uneasily, in his hotel bed, and when he awoke, he'd felt as if he hadn't slept at all. All he could think of was how coolly poised she had looked and how different she was from his memory of her. He'd gone to Scotty's house, to the tiny bedroom to change into his jogging clothes, and had tried to piece together the things he knew about this corporate mystery. He'd come up with very little.

Ahead of him, Scotty slowed to a walk. Rourke fell into step beside him.

"Feel any better?"

"Yeah, sure." Rourke said dryly.

"Care to talk about it?" Scotty said, his breath coming hard and heavily from his run.

"No." He couldn't appear eager to discuss Jessica's case. Scotty would smell a rat. Rourke had to be careful. No one was more adept at interrogation than his uncle. Retired or not, the older man was a force to be reckoned with.

Scotty found a tree, leaned back on it and made himself comfortable. "I have a friend who works at Consolidated. I hope your...assignment...doesn't involve her."

Knowing he didn't dare let Scotty see his face, Rourke leaned over and braced his arms against the tree Scotty was leaning on, put his head down and flexed his shoulder and arm muscles.

"Consolidated is a big company," Scotty went on, probing, "and the chances are one in a million that your investigation involves Jessica."

"One in a million," Rourke murmured, his head down between his arms, wishing Scotty would find another topic.

"But she is involved, isn't she?" Rourke's head came up. Scotty went on easily, "Don't bother to deny it. The rhythm of your breathing changed when I mentioned her name."

Rourke gave up the pretense of stretching and propped an elbow against the tree next to his uncle's head. "I keep thinking you're going to lose that acute vision of yours someday but you never do. You go right on seeing more than any one person has a right to see—"

"Is she being accused of embezzling?"

"No. It's more…complicated than that." Rourke left the tree and went to stand on the bluff that overlooked the river. "Her boss believes she sabotaged deliveries to several major retailers and then handed the correct orders over to a competitor so he was able to supply what Consolidated couldn't."

"Sounds like a tricky operation…and a dangerous one."

"It's both. Her boss is sure Jessica did it, and on the surface of things—" he paused, as if the words were difficult to say "—I'm inclined to agree. She designed the program and implemented it. If I thought only about the machine part of the problem, I'd say, yes, she has to be guilty. But in a case like this, it isn't only the information you get from the computer that's important. You have to figure in the human element. And when I do that . . . nothing about the case feels right. Most people who pull a stunt like this either disappear, or have someone else they can blame. They don't sit around with no alibi, waiting to be found, like Jessica is."

Behind Rourke, Scotty was silent.

Rourke turned around. The older man's face was shadowed, expressionless. "You think I'm wrong, don't you?"

"Wrong about what? Wrong to suspect her? Or wrong to believe in her innocence?"

"Dammit, that's just it. Maybe I think she's innocent because I can't believe she's guilty."

A breeze lifted a portion of Scotty's sandy, thinning hair. His sparser head covering was the only change Rourke had seen in Scotty in the past seven years. In a soft voice, Scotty said, "Just make sure you don't decide she's guilty because you're afraid to believe she's innocent."

"I'll believe the truth, whatever that is." Rourke turned back. The river was soundless, too far below them to be heard. The rush of traffic above them filled his ears.

His plan to unobtrusively obtain information from his uncle flitted away in the misty rain. "I need some financial information about her, Scotty."

"Do you now? And you're asking me to do your work for you?"

"Dammit!" He twisted around to look into that bland, much loved face. "I'd rather ask you than have it get around that I'm investigating her finances. One whiff of trouble, and her credit rating could take a nosedive. I've seen it happen."

"I have no information for you, lad. As far as I know, Jess pays her bills on time and doesn't have more of them than any normal young woman who's buying a car and paying rent on a good apartment.''

"Does she gamble? Drink?''

"Gamble? Jess won't even buy a lottery ticket. And as for drinking, I suppose you could say she drinks, if having a glass of wine with an old man on certain special days is your idea of drinking.''

"What about clothes?''

"She probably has the normal amount of clothes—''

"Will you stop telling me how normal she is?''

Scotty gazed at Rourke. "Well, that's what you're looking for, isn't it? Abnormal behavior? You won't find it in Jess . . . unless you're talking about her loyalty to an old man like me . . . or her willingness to spend time with every needy person she can find . . . like those blind children she goes and collects for outings . . . or her troubled friend, Anita . . . or—''

"All right, all right, I get the point. Jessica Moore is a sterling character who does nothing but good deeds and has an unshakable loyalty to her old friends. It isn't possible you're just a wee bit prejudiced?'' Rourke asked, wryly imitating his uncle's brogue.

"It's possible, it's possible.'' Scotty angled a shrewd look at Rourke from under those heavy brows. "I take it you'll be seeing quite a bit of her for the next few weeks?''

Rourke's mouth twisted. "Practically sitting in her lap.''

"You hurt her once,'' Scotty said, his voice deceptively soft. "Don't do it again.''

"If she's guilty, I can't avoid hurting her. . . .''

"That isn't what I meant.''

Rourke stared at his uncle, his eyes dark. Scotty's gaze was level . . . and uncompromising. "Perhaps you'd like to elaborate."

"You walked away from her once . . . but you were young then and hadn't been out of the stable long enough to settle down with any one filly. Jessica, too, was a naive young girl who'd led a very sheltered life. But you're a man now, and Jessica's no longer a sheltered girl. Do you understand me?"

"As you said, she's no longer a girl." Conflicting emotions swirled inside him, like the water below. For the first time in many years, he felt alienated from Scotty. The one man in the world Rourke was sure would trust him in any situation didn't trust him with Jessica. He remembered suddenly how he'd felt, watching her walk around her apartment, seeing the sleek, graceful movements of her woman's body, and a small hard voice within him mocked, *with good reason.*

As if he had read Rourke's mind, Scotty straightened away from the tree. Rourke caught a glimpse of the steel-hard man who once relentlessly tracked and arrested suspected lawbreakers. "Girl or woman, it makes no difference. Don't climb into her bed, lad, unless you mean to stay there."

Uneasy, Rourke moved to the attack. "How protective you are of her."

Not so easily intimidated, Scotty held his ground. "No more protective than you should be. She was a friend to you once when you badly needed one. Now the shoe is on the other foot. Are you going to return the favor?"

Later, in his hotel room, Rourke stripped off his sweatshirt and pants and stepped into the shower, still thinking about his conversation with his uncle. Did he owe Jessica a favor? If he did, he should step out of the job with Consolidated now. The chances of his conducting an unbiased investigation were slim. But if he did step out—and another man was brought in, one Hilton could manipulate more easily—Jessica might be found to be guilty when she was innocent.

Rourke soaped himself, his mouth twisting. If anyone was a match for Hilton, he was. He'd learned long ago how to handle manipulative men. He'd grown up with a master at the game.

The day his mother died, he'd felt the force of his father's will. After months of staying at his mother's bedside, feeling the warmth of her personality encompassing him, giving him strength when she had so little to spare herself, Rourke had been sent to a private boys' school where discipline was a god to be worshipped daily. Rourke had survived, but only after an adjustment period that kept him spending more time in the headmaster's office than he did in the classroom. He remembered it had been hot that fall. He'd walked to classes under the sun's warmth, the sidewalk ahead of him dappled by the shade of tall oak trees, and inside he'd seethed with anger because the trees, the birds, the people around him were alive and his mother was not. The climax had come when he'd finally confided in his roommate about the death of his mother. His roommate had stared at him in surprise. "But she's dead now. She doesn't exist. You can't go on loving a bloody ghost—"

Rourke had gone for the other boy's throat.

Something inside him had died after that. He began to see himself as separate from other people. Until Jessica. That summer on the farm, with her, he'd begun to feel warm inside, almost human, and not nearly so alone.

He'd known it couldn't last. Nothing good ever did. He'd had to leave her and go back to living in the cold again. That year he'd left her to finish his education, he'd known then he wasn't a team player and he'd never be a success in the corporate world in the conventional way. With Scotty's help, he'd found a profession that capitalized on his feeling of isolation and turned it into an asset. He was able to look at his fellow human beings dispassionately, and his detachment made him good at his job. He never got emotionally involved with the people he was investigating.

Till now.

Was he emotionally involved with Jessica? No. That was ridiculous. He didn't have emotions like that. Memory had briefly struck a resonant chord buried deep in his soul, and this morning Scotty had plucked on that same sensitive string, that was all.

Memories were just that, memories. They had no power over Rourke. He told himself he was the same as he had always been, a man trained to discover facts and deal with them logically. He would stay on this case until he discovered the truth, and if that truth showed that Jessica had been involved in corporate espionage, well, that was out of his hands. His job was to find the culprit. The decision about what to do with that person would be made by company lawyers.

Rourke finished dressing and looped his tie around his neck. He hated ties. They were uncomfortable and a nuisance. If Beau Brummell had expired as an infant, he, Rourke, wouldn't be standing here today fastening the damn tie around his neck.

He made a neat Windsor knot, looked at himself in the mirror and grimaced. "It's like putting your head in a damn noose and tightening the knot yourself," he muttered, slicking his hand back over his straight brown hair, not stopping to ask himself why dressing for work on this particular day made him irritable.

CHAPTER EIGHT

IF I'M GOING TO GO, I'll go out in style.

Feeling far less controlled than she wanted to feel, Jessica, in her cream satin teddy and her legs long and silky in nylon hose, plucked a dress the color of caramel from the closet and tossed it onto her bed.

Her job was—or had been—her security, the base from which she operated, the essence of her life. Her work kept her safe from the emotional storms she'd suffered as a teenager. She was older, poised, nothing like that young, heartbroken, blind girl who'd stood at the window feeling betrayed and wishing fiercely that she were someone different.

That girl's dream had come true. She had become someone different. She'd regained the ability to see and she'd become a professional career woman. The only thing she hadn't been able to change was her acute sensitivity.

She could still feel. Too much. And when this investigation was over, there would be new images of Rourke to plague her mind, images of him in places where he had never been before. She'd created a safe world for herself...and Rourke had invaded it again. And brought destruction with him.

By now, everyone in her department had heard what had happened. The sixth floor had a pipeline of information as efficient as a conduit flowing downhill; everything rushed through at the speed of a white-water river. And the other world, the inner private world where she'd learned long ago to keep thoughts of Rourke at bay, that world was crumbling.

A cool shudder passed over her skin. She felt cold because she wasn't dressed, that was all. She slipped into the dress and ran the zipper up the back. *Concentrate on the job at hand,* she told herself. *Do the hot rollers, put on your face, straighten your spine. You'll find that bug in the program and you'll be cleared. And when that happens, Rourke will go away, and you'll be back again in the safe world you created for yourself.*

Safe? How could she ever be safe? In the time before she stood in the festival tent and stared back at the intriguing man who was gazing at her, she'd relegated him to the past. He'd floated in that cloud of gray reserved for the time of her blindness, a faceless male she'd once known who'd faded into a dream. Now she had new memories, memories of being in his arms, moving around the dance floor with an easy grace generated by the powerful muscles of his body, looking at him, seeing his face, his hair, his eyes, feeling his hand on her hip....

Beneath the bodice of her dress, her body tingled, her breasts throbbing with aching fullness. The pearl button she was trying to fasten slipped out of her fingers. Her body turned traitor at the mere thought of him.

Could she hide those traitorous feelings? She had to. He'd pitied her once for her blindness. She couldn't let him pity her now for her emotional reactions to him, reactions he neither wanted nor shared.

Her hair in silky order, her high-heeled pumps shiny, her defenses firmly in place, Jessica walked into the office an hour later. She'd steeled herself for the sight of him, expecting Rourke to be coolly polite, his emotions well-hidden behind his controlled face.

To her surprise, Rourke's armor was awry. His tie was crooked and his straight brown hair was already ruffled, whether from the wind or from a hand thrust through it, she didn't know.

Those astounding blue eyes flashed up at her and in that moment, she knew something had happened to disconcert him. Before she thought, she said, "What's happened? What's wrong?"

If she thought he looked disturbed before, her instant assessment of his state of mind seemed to undo him even more. He scowled, and rather than finding the scowl threatening, she thought the ill-tempered mouth made him look younger, like a boy who'd been pushed about by the playground bully. What on earth had happened to discompose him so thoroughly? "Nothing of any importance. Let's get to work."

His arrogant dismissal of her questions was exactly what she expected. Whatever it was that was bothering him, he wasn't about to share it with her. But his discomposure gave Jessica back a small portion of her poise. She began to go through the program with him, explaining her procedure and reading the file notations.

The first part of the hour went well. But gradually, the strain of controlling every flick of her eyes, every movement of her body, began to tell on her. He'd positioned his chair close beside hers, and with his whole body just beyond her shoulder, her awareness of him sharpened.

Jessica's tension centered in her throat. She went on explaining her work step by step, but she could feel the effort she was expending to keep her voice cool and calm. By eleven o'clock, she was beginning to get hoarse.

Rourke dropped a pencil on the desk, leaned back in his swivel chair and looked at her. What was he thinking? Was he really keeping an open mind? Or was he thinking that they hadn't found any mistakes because she'd planned it that way and that her guilt was causing her voice to tighten?

She kept her eyes steadily on his, knowing he was watching every move she made, every flick of her eyes.

Spending more than half her life not being able to see had given her a keen appreciation of her vision. She saw more than most people did, and at the moment Rourke filled her vision. There was a force about him, a sheer virility she'd never sensed in any other man, a combination of intelligence and sexuality that was as much a part of him as his dark blue eyes.

He would make love to a woman with his mind as well as his body.

The forbidden thought brought a sudden surge of aliveness, a tingle through her bloodstream, an accelerated heartbeat. If she didn't look away, he would see her response to him written on her face. But if she did look away, he'd interpret her inability to meet his gaze as guilt. She wasn't guilty...but any attempt to hide her sexual response to Rourke would make her look that way.

Sexual response. That was what it was, there was no other name for it. She seemed to feel him on her skin: his hands, firm, long-fingered, covered with crisp dark hair, the easy strength of his body, the long muscular thighs encased in gray suit pants. Instead of a suit jacket, he wore a gray leather vest and every time he leaned closer to her the leather creaked softly. It was a conditioning of sorts; the whisper of that leather meant he was moving closer, and by the time they stopped working, her nerves were alive, waiting for that subtle rub of animal skin to bring them springing into frenzied action.

She wouldn't—couldn't—feel this way again. She had to control these nostalgic trips back to yesterday.

This isn't a nostalgic trip back to yesterday. He's here in the present. It's not the memory you're responding to, it's the man.

No. No, she told herself. *Not again!*

Eyes as blue as a rain-washed sky stared back at her. Could he tell what she had been thinking...or was that his own sexual response she saw in the darkening of his pupils? No, it couldn't be. He was indifferent to her, a man with a job to do.

"You look as if you could use some coffee," Rourke said. Prosaic words interjected into the explosive silence gave her some breathing space. Had he meant them to? "Just stay here and relax."

He disappeared in the direction of the coffee machine. Jessica sat in her chair and clenched her hands together. Arrogance she could take. Kindness was something else altogether. She didn't want his kindness...or his sympathy...or his understanding...or anything that might tear down the wall she'd built around her heart.

Julie poked her head in from around the other side of the partition. She was one of the newer programmers, a petite blonde who'd been hired straight out of school last fall. She worked very hard to preserve her image as a bubbly, lighthearted girl. Hilton had wanted to fire her after the first two days but Jessica had forestalled him, telling him that despite being a chatterbox, Julie managed to accomplish a great deal of work.

"He is gone, isn't he?" Julie asked, her eyes searching the work area. "He isn't going to swing around and come back and scare me to death again, I hope. Oh, Jessica, I really goofed."

Jessica smiled. "What did you do that was so terrible?"

"I came in early." There was a wide-eyed, carefully timed pause for reaction that any stand-up comedian would have envied.

"That's hardly grounds for dismissal—"

"The trouble was...he was here before eight o'clock, too. I didn't know it. I was just fooling around, talking to Kristin and—" Julie flushed, and even her high color was endearing "—I was telling Kristin what a hunk he was. I said I'd be glad to confess...but only if he would spend the next several days investigating me. And we both laughed, 'cause Kris thinks he's cute too...and that was when he came out from behind the partition. Lord, I never want to have anybody look at me like that again. Conan the Destroyer on a short leash. He gave us that laser-beam stare of his and said, 'Since you're here, why don't you spend your time working?' which makes it pretty certain he heard me. Do you think he'll have me fired?"

Jessica schooled her features severely to quell the smile that threatened to lift her lips. That was why Rourke had looked so off balance this morning. He'd had his first taste of Julie Ward. "He's a consultant, Julie. He doesn't have that power...unless he finds that you had something to do with our...problem. And—" her voice was carefully light "—he's not going to do that, is he?"

The young woman looked horror-stricken. "Of course not. I wouldn't do a thing like that. I don't have my act together sometimes, but I would never do anything as horrible as selling out the company." Julie's eyes met

Jessica's and the younger woman caught her breath. "And I know you wouldn't, either."

"Thank you for your vote of confidence." Jessica hadn't meant to sound quite so dryly ironic. "At any rate, there's nothing for you to be afraid of. Nobody can fire you for admiring the scenery. You aren't the first woman to do that . . . and you won't be the last. Now go on back to your desk and stop worrying."

Julie, being Julie, didn't obey. "He's not just scenery. He has something . . . extra. He's sexy, sure, but there's more than that. He makes you think that if you ever got lost in a dark tunnel, you could count on him to come in after you, you know what I mean?"

The pain that had been blunted for so many years resurfaced. "Yes, I know exactly what you mean. You're talking about integrity. Mr. Caldwell has it. And on him, it looks very good."

"You don't think I was doing wrong when I . . . admired him?"

"Actually," Jessica said turning away, a gentle hint for the other woman to leave, "I commend you for your excellent taste."

Julie didn't take the hint. She stuck to the ground like the burrs Jessica used to pull from the cornfield on the farm, after she regained her sight. "You don't mind my . . . admiring him?"

"Mind? Why should I mind?" Jessica looked up then and caught that glimpse of intelligence she'd seen once or twice before lurking behind the other woman's light-hearted facade.

"Well, I thought . . . that is, you seemed friendly with him and I thought . . ."

"Mr. Caldwell and my brother were acquainted a long time ago." Jessica gazed at Julie steadily, thinking that of all the things she could have said, this was the least harmful.

"I see." The brown eyes lost their glimmer of shrewdness and became as open and friendly as they had been before. "That explains your knowing him, then." Jessica turned back to the computer, willing Julie to go and take her inquisitive mind with her, but Julie lingered. "You're sure he won't get me fired?"

"I'm positive he won't." Jessica kept her smile in place, but her patience was wearing thin.

Julie's gamine features broke into a smile. "I knew if I told you you'd straighten everything out. Thanks. I really appreciate it."

Jessica watched her go in a swirl of wool plaid skirt, wishing her own problems could be solved as easily.

Quickly, too quickly, Rourke appeared from around the divider. His face was as cool and impassive as ever, but by now Jessica was familiar enough with his profile to know that his jaw looked more set than usual, as if he were clamping his teeth together. Had he heard her extolling his praises? "Are you through giving advice to the lovelorn?"

Jessica was very relieved. He'd probably heard only the last little bit of their conversation, about Julie asking if she was wrong to admire him and Jessica assuring her she had good taste. She sprang to Julie's defense just as she'd done many times before. "Don't be angry. She's very young, that's all."

"This company must have hired half its female staff straight from a nursery school." He handed her her coffee cup, and set his own down on the desk in front of him as he settled into his chair.

"We were all young once." She spoke casually, thinking only of Julie, but when Rourke's eyes met hers over the white plastic cup, the words took on a whole new meaning. Without realizing it, she'd propelled them both into the past where the ground was mine-filled, treacherous.

His eyes focused on her. "I was never that young...and neither were you."

She looked down into her cup, considering his words. He was wrong. She'd certainly been that young once, young enough to believe they had a future together. That was the height of naïveté. But she couldn't tell him that. "Leading the police on a high-speed chase and driving your car through a window comes under the heading of an adult, responsible act?" She glanced up at him, arching an eyebrow, her mouth curved.

Rourke stretched out his legs and thrust a hand into the side pocket of his trousers. The courageous girl had matured into a courageous woman. Here she was, a sitting duck, waiting for him to drop the bomb on her. Any other woman would have avoided any mention of his youthful escapades for fear of offending him. But Jessica, in an attempt to protect a co-worker, hadn't hesitated. He felt the urge to joust with her in the arena she'd chosen. She had opened the subject of their youth. How would she deal with it if he took it a step further? "You haven't forgotten anything...have you?" His legs extended to full length and he placed his booted feet perilously close to her slim ankles.

Jessica had meant to lead their conversation away from the dangerous territory. Rourke had drawn them closer. "I'm not as infallible as all that."

A faint color suffused her cheeks, color that hadn't been there before. Watching her, Rourke picked up his coffee cup, admiring the ambiguity of her answer. Had she forgotten that afternoon in the barn when she'd asked him to make love to her? He supposed she had. Since then she'd no doubt had other lovers, men who'd touched and kissed that silky skin. Something deep inside of him twisted. The coffee that was hot and refreshing a moment ago had taken on a bitter flavor. He'd lost his taste for it . . . and for baiting her, as well.

He was a fool. He should have walked away from this job the minute he heard Jessica's name.

Jessica sat holding her cup, afraid to breathe. Was he going to take the subject any further? He didn't look as if he was. He looked as if he was sorry he'd said as much as he had. The past meant nothing to him . . . and neither did she.

As THE DAYS MELTED into each other, Rourke's feeling that he should have given the job to some other man deepened. On Friday, about two o'clock in the afternoon, after he'd gone over Jessica's program from every angle he could think of, he slammed a pencil on the desk in front of him, startling Jessica. Looking into those strange topaz eyes of hers, widened a little with surprise, he growled, "There isn't a damn thing wrong with this program."

"Should I apologize?" she asked coolly, his anger acting as a catalyst on her tension.

"No. I was just blowing off steam because I had hopes that—" He stopped speaking in midsentence, his gaze drifting warily over her. Then, as if he'd changed his mind about holding back, he said in a softer tone, "I was hoping we'd find some technical bug that would take the pressure off you."

It was these unexpected kindnesses that undermined her determination to treat him coolly. "I was, too. But it seems to be more complicated than that. Where do we go from here?''

"The paperwork is next, I guess." He leaned back in the chair, flexing his legs. "How are the orders recorded? Are they logged into the computer immediately?''

"Yes, if they come over the phone. If the order comes by mail, we log it in and obtain a printout."

"Are the original statements kept?"

"Yes."

"Could you get me the supporting paperwork for . . . say, the Cleveland order?"

"Yes, of course. I'll tell Julie." She rose from her chair.

Rourke frowned. "Can't you call her?"

Jessica shook her head. "It's no trouble. I should be on my feet anyway. Time for our afternoon coffee." They'd established a routine. Rourke went for the coffee in the morning, Jessica made the trip in the afternoon. There were other routines they had established, his moving his chair back to let her in and out of hers, his hanging his coat on the rack first so her lighter cloth coat wouldn't be crushed underneath it, his waiting for her to make her choice at the sandwich machine and then carrying his back to the desk and eating with her.

Other routines Jessica adhered to were not so visible, such as handing him paper carefully to avoid him, leaning forward slightly in her chair to keep from touching his elbow with hers. How much longer would he be sitting next to her in that chair, so close she could hear him breathe?

ROURKE STEPPED into the hotel room and dropped his attaché case onto the bed, thinking this must be the ten thousandth weekend he would spend studying a pile of papers. Feeding fuel to his black mood was the distinct feeling that those papers wouldn't tell him any more than his painstaking perusal of the computer program had. Logic told him they couldn't. Julie hadn't supplied the original order forms, she'd given him the ones generated by the computer. How could they be any different than what was inside the computer?

He sank on the bed and snapped the case open, staring down at the sheaf of papers. In any other investigation, he would have viewed these printouts with anticipation, knowing there was a puzzle to solve, a job to fill the long hours. Tonight the task seemed like a damned nuisance.

There were six bundles of note-size four-inch-wide paper, secured with a jumbo paper clip. He plucked one bunch of notes out and riffled idly through them. He'd never been so stymied before. Usually, after he'd been on an investigation a week, he'd found some anomaly to give him a clue to the vital breakthrough he needed. Not this time.

He tossed the papers back into his open case. Suppose he did find the answer . . . and it led straight to Jessica?

Jessica. Woman. Silky skin, slim body, sweet-smelling hair. Whenever he leaned close to her, his nose tortured him with her delicate, feminine scent. When she moved, the slight rustle of the silk lining of her jacket as it slid against the silky blouse she wore brought a fine line of tension lacing over his arms.

He was developing a need for her. Again.

He'd sworn he'd never be vulnerable to her again. He'd tried to forget her. There had been willing, unattached females at every job he'd had. If he was attracted to a woman and she was not involved in his investigation, he'd ask her to have dinner with him. If, after an initial period of getting acquainted, he received an invitation to spend the night, he usually accepted it. But the women he'd been with were no more than brief interludes in his somewhat solitary life. Never before had a female interfered with his concentration. Now, when he went home at night, he was haunted by the fear that he had subconsciously let the investigation drag on in order to spend more time with Jessica...and that he did not want to be the one to find the culprit if it were her.

The paperwork matched the program, just as he'd thought it would, but Rourke spent most of the next week checking it over again, to be sure. Beside him, Jessica remained as she had been since the first day, so friendly and polite that her real feelings, whatever they were, were well hidden.

It was during this week that the trickle of co-workers into Jessica's cubicle become a steady procession, a situation that was, Rourke decided, closer to Jessica's normal work pattern before his arrival on the scene. Each interruption forced him to stop what he was doing and wait for her. At first, he was annoyed by the constant barrage of interruptions. Then, since he had nothing else to do, he began to watch...and listen. Todd Wainwright's visit was typical.

"The computer terminal is down at warehouse three and Hilton's on my—" Rourke made a move in his chair, and Todd, in a sudden instinctive burst of wisdom, clamped his mouth shut, his eyes on Rourke.

"Go on, Todd," Jessica said, with composure intact.

"He's on...me...to get it fixed. I called the repair service but I get nothing but a big runaround from them. Got any ideas?"

"That terminal was one of the first ones to come on line. I know one of the repairmen who helped install it. Call the service back and tell them you want to talk to this man." Jessica scribbled a name on a scrap of paper. "When you get him on the phone, ask him if he thinks it might be the power source. Tell him you know that if he'll go and check it out for us, he can get it running again."

"That's flattery—"

"Absolutely. Feel free to embellish the dose with as much sugar as you can stand. No threats. They don't work." As he turned to go, she added, "And Todd. Don't forget to use your pass-the-butter voice."

He flashed a boyish grin at her. "Yes, ma'am. Anything you say."

Rourke sat back in his chair, his eyes on Jessica. This was the girl whose social contacts had been so severely limited by her blindness that she hadn't been properly kissed by the age of seventeen. This was the girl who had stood in a dark barn and told him how she felt about him because she didn't know how to lie. Since then, she'd learned all the social graces and business skills. Had she also learned, for fun and profit, to lie and cheat?

THE DAYS, BOUNDED by his work, flowed into each other. Rourke was vaguely aware that it was December. Christmas lights appeared on houses, and once, when he went to the mall to buy himself some socks because that was easier than washing them, he saw children lined up to talk to a plump Santa seated on a throne.

Since his mother's death, Christmas had meant nothing to him. For years it had been a time of acute loneliness, of restlessness and irritability, of not understanding why he felt so out of sorts when everyone around him was flinging Christmas cheer to the four winds. Now that he was older, he knew about holiday anxiety. He hadn't, then. As a child, his feelings at Christmas had been one more thing separating him from the rest of the world. But this year, unless he made an astounding breakthrough that he didn't foresee and he finished up here sooner than he thought, he'd be spending Christmas with Scotty. Perhaps that would be good for both of them.

Hilton, in what Rourke labeled either a rare burst of magnanimity or an attempt to ingratiate himself, had invited Rourke to the office holiday party. Rourke had said he'd rather not be included in the festivities. He knew only those people in Jessica's department, and he didn't want to make her self-conscious with his presence. At least, that was what he'd told himself. Having to watch her attend the party with another man as her escort had nothing to do with his decision to stay away, he reasoned.

Early in the morning on the day of the party Rourke learned by accident that Jessica had an appointment with her boss at four-fifteen in the afternoon.

As the day dragged on, Rourke watched her become increasingly more nervous, even though she tried to hide it. Her lips were bloodless, her cheeks equally pale.

When Jessica returned from her interview with her superior, the sting of nerves turned the skin of her throat a bright pink.

If she had any doubt whether or not her state of mind was written on her face, that doubt was dispelled when she saw Rourke's expression.

No. Not pity. Don't waste your pity on me, she thought. Her head high, and without looking at Rourke, she went to the coatrack to get her coat.

The blaze of pride and pain in her eyes had him clenching his fists. Tension bubbled in him but he rose from the chair lazily, like a man with all the time in the world on his hands. "What happened?"

Jessica turned, her face set in an expression that he was beginning to understand hid pain. "Nothing for you to concern yourself with."

He'd said that to her once. But this was different. She was going to walk out of this building and away from him and he would never know what was tearing her apart.

While he hesitated, he became aware of the silence. Behind the partition, the room was nearly deserted. There had been a tacit signal to leave work early because of the party that night, and the quiet told Rourke he and Jessica were probably the only two people left on the floor.

He reached for her, grabbing her wool-clad elbow. "Tell me what he said to you."

"Believe me, it isn't important. It has nothing to do with the investigation."

"Then what does it have to do with?"

Not looking at him, her voice low, she said, "He wants me to stay away from the party tonight. He feels my presence there would make everyone . . . uncomfortable."

Rourke muttered an obscenity. Jessica lifted her chin, and for the first time since she'd gone to keep her appointment, her eyes locked with his. "Until you find out the truth, he wants everything kept on an even keel."

In Rourke's eyes, a blue flame sprang to life. "Don't let him intimidate you, Jess. You have as much right to be at that party as anyone."

"I wouldn't want to put a damper on anyone's fun."

"But if you don't go, everyone will assume it's because you're guilty."

He felt her body stiffen. "They can believe whatever they like."

"Don't you know what he's doing? He's afraid of you, afraid of your talent and your management skills. He's doing everything he can to alienate you from the people who respect you."

"They won't respect me any less if they don't see me at the party."

Even while Jessica watched, the dark flame in his eyes vanished. All that was left was intelligence and a keen glance that knifed through her soul. His fingers seemed to burn through her coat.

"If you don't want to go alone, Jess, let me go with you."

She looked at him, trying desperately to think logically and ignore how easily he'd slipped into using the old, familiar name. Which was worse, staying home and being thought a thief and a cheat, or spending an entire evening in Rourke's company in a free-and-easy social situation, no longer protected from the force of his attraction by office protocol?

Inexplicably, he relaxed his grip and released her elbow. When she didn't move, he stepped back from her a pace. "I shouldn't be surprised that your pride is more important to you than your reputation for honesty."

"My...reputation doesn't depend on appearing at that party on your arm."

His shoulders drooped, as if the tension had gone out of him. "You're right, it doesn't. I was being selfish, thinking of my empty hotel room and knowing you wouldn't go with me simply because I asked you to." He gazed at her steadily. "I'm as guilty of trying to strong-arm you into doing what I want you to do as Hilton is."

His honesty knocked down the first line of her defenses. She had no armor strong enough to shut out this
Rourke, this strained, brutally honest man. When he
turned his back to her to pluck his coat off the rack, she
stood watching him, knowing his honesty challenged her
to be just as honest. Somehow it was easier to be truthful with him when his back was turned. While he stood
shrugging into his coat, she said to that broad back, "But
for an entirely different reason."

He pivoted around slowly, the collar of his coat turned
up around his neck, creating a backdrop for the subtle
beauty of his hard-boned face. His expression changed
minutely, but it was as unreadable to her as ever. "Don't
be so quick to assign me noble reasons. I wanted to spend
the evening with you and I was willing to say whatever I
had to say to get you to agree." The silence, in a place
normally filled with the sounds of telephones ringing and
voices, was unusually dense, like a heavy weight on Jessica's ears.

Rourke's eyes went to the flushed skin at the base of
her throat. He longed to lay his fingers there to take the
heat from her body into his, to soothe that disturbed skin
and watch it return to its normal pearly hue. Her face was
pink, but a subtler tone, crimson under cream silk. He
was filled with an emotion he couldn't define. "I'll drive
you home."

"That's not necessary."

"Isn't it? You're in no condition to drive. In your
present state of mind, there's a good chance your inat-
tention will involve you in an accident." He hesitated and
then said in that low, velvety voice she remembered well,
"I know you don't want my sympathy. You never did,
even when you were a kid." For a moment, his mouth

lifted in a smile that made her head reel. "But let me do this much for you, at least."

Common sense, reason and the large number of logical brain cells functioning inside her head told her to say no. But another small voice said yes. She pulled her gloves from the pocket of her coat, aware that her hands were shaking. The trouble was, she wasn't quite sure which man had set her trembling, Hilton with his threats...or Rourke with his subtle reference to the summer they had spent together. "I really don't want to end up wrapped around a lamppost."

Rourke's mouth relaxed fractionally. "Doesn't sound like a good idea to me at all." He walked toward her and took her elbow, more lightly this time, like the polite escort he had offered to be. She turned into step beside him as if she had done it a hundred times before.

When Rourke pulled her car up in front of her apartment building, he put the engine in neutral and twisted in his seat to face her. "If you change your mind about the party, give me a call."

"Aren't you afraid you'll be accused of aiding and abetting the enemy?"

In the soft light, his facial skin seemed to tighten over his cheekbones. "*Are* you the enemy?"

"Hilton thinks I am."

Under his breath, Rourke muttered a succinct, earthy word about the validity of Hilton's opinion. Jessica smiled, and Rourke realized suddenly it was the first smile he'd seen on her mouth all day. In the soft light, the feminine curve of her lips invited touching...and kissing.

He balled his right fist and rammed it into the pocket of his coat. Surely he could keep his hands off her for one short evening. "Don't go up in your apartment and brood. Let me take you out to dinner."

His invitation surprised her. It also made his offer to take her to the party much the safer of the two. "If I go anywhere, it should be to the party."

"Then that's where we'll go. I'll pick you up here in what...a half hour? An hour?"

"I can't..." She closed her mouth and searched his face, thinking she couldn't remember when she'd been so neatly manipulated.

"Are you afraid to be seen with me?" His voice was silky.

"No, of course not."

"Good. Shall we compromise on the time and say forty-five minutes?"

CHAPTER NINE

AT THE PARTY, Rourke lounged in his chair, a drink in his hand, his eyes on Jessica. She stood on the dance floor facing her current partner, her hips moving in time to the music, her head thrown back, her hair silky and natural, her mouth lifted in a genuine smile. If anyone was disconcerted by her presence, he was hiding in the kitchen, Rourke thought darkly, watching with a sense of inevitability as yet another man shouldered out Jessica's partner and began a peculiar set of gyrations in front of her.

The man was young, good-looking and agile as an octopus. Rourke felt a flash of irritation, and he must have been stupid enough to let it show on his face. Jessica looked as if she sensed his annoyance and was going to walk off the floor. Rourke felt churlish. He'd brought Jessica here so she could forget her troubles and have a good time; he couldn't begrudge her this moment of enjoyment. He schooled his face to indifference and shook his head, waving his hand at her to indicate she should stay where she was, standing up and gesturing with his glass as if he meant to go to the bar and order another drink.

What was happening at this party tonight was wonderful for Jessica. Consolidated employees in Distribution, stock boys, secretaries, engineers, every living soul who worked on the sixth floor of Building 101, had closed ranks around Jessica. They were doing everything in their power to demonstrate how much they believed in her innocence.

While Rourke applauded their loyalty, he wasn't happy about the result of it. On his feet, walking to a destination he wasn't sure of, he fingered his glass of bourbon, knowing he didn't want anything more to drink. All he wanted was to block out the sight of Jessica dancing with her latest partner.

Turning his back to the dance floor and wondering if there was any truth in the ignorance-is-bliss theory, he strolled toward the glass door that opened onto a brick patio. The party house was on the east side of the city in a hilly section of town, at the bottom of a glen surrounded by evergreens. Looking out the window, he could see that it was snowing, big, fat flakes as delicate as lace. The patio, like most summer places in the wintertime, had a lonely, nostalgic and, under a dusting of snow, incongruous look. A squirrel scampered across the patio and launched himself at a tree, his furry body eerily framed in the middle of Rourke's reflection.

He stared into the darkness a moment longer, thinking he should return to his table on the off chance that Jessica might need him, when the image of a flame-haired woman merged with his in the glass.

Anita.

"What are you doing here?" Her opening salvo was a dead hit and despite the drink she held in her hand, her tone was not friendly.

He turned and leaned back lazily against the frame of the door, his eyes going over her body covered in a simple lime-green sheath that probably cost a month of Jessica's pay, and wondered why this redheaded virago had chosen him as her target. "The same thing you're doing presumably," he countered equably. "Participating in that quaint old American custom known as 'having a good time at the office party no matter how bad it makes me feel.'"

"Oh, Lord. Don't stand there trying to disarm me with your charming cynicism when I've been waiting all evening to give you a piece of my mind. And don't ask me if I can spare it. As many margaritas as I've had on an empty stomach, I probably can't. But I will not be detoured...." She stopped. Apparently the word didn't sound right to her. Gathering herself, she tried again. "Deterred."

"I wouldn't...deter you for the world." For the first time this evening, Rourke felt like smiling.

Anita peered at him, as if not quite sure whether he was mocking her. In fact, he wasn't. He was more than a little curious about what she had to say to him. Her eyes had the glazed look of a woman who'd set herself a task and meant to do it, come hell, high water or a sea full of margaritas.

A long red fingernail came out and aimed for his chest between the narrow opening of his suit jacket. The painted talon landed on his shirt button. Rourke was amazed that her aim was so accurate.

"Don't hurt Jessica...again."

"It's not on my agenda for this evening."

Anita leaned away from him to look up into his face. "You're smooth. Very smooth. I'd almost believe you...except for one thing. I've been watching you trying to keep from looking at her. And watching her trying to keep from looking at you."

Rourke's eyes moved over Anita's mouth, a mouth kissed clean of lipstick. He'd seen her earlier on the dance floor, clinging to Todd and tilting her head up to receive his kisses. Rourke's lips curled upward in a mocking smile. "I'm amazed you found the time."

"If you hurt her again, you'll be . . . you'll be . . ."

"Sorry?" Rourke supplied helpfully.

Anita frowned. "I had in mind something more like—" she paused and concentrated fiercely "—fried in oil. But you're bigger than I remember. I'm not sure you would fit in my . . . hot pot."

"That smacks of cannibalism."

Anita favored him with that concentrated stare again. "Is that supposed to be a joke?"

"I guess not. You aren't laughing."

Her fingernail slipped off his button. He could feel the pointed nail through the silk of his shirt. He pushed aside the languid arm that offered him no resistance, and trying to warn her that the glass she held was about to tip and spill down the side of her designer dress, he said, "Anita . . ." With his free hand, he captured her glass and turned to set it and his own on a small table next to the window.

"She cut off her hair for you."

Arrested, Rourke turned slowly to face Jessica's friend. Eyes glazing, she swayed, as if his taking the drink away from her had thrown her off balance. He grasped her bare shoulders to steady her, afraid she was going to fall over before she explained that extraordinary remark. "What are you talking about?"

"She wanted me to cut it but I wouldn't. So she grabbed the scissors and did it herself. Blind as a bat, but that didn't stop her. She just held up her hair with one hand and the scissors with the other and chopped away." Her gaze leveled, and for a moment she looked sober and very grave. "I don't think I'll ever forget watching her . . . and knowing how much pain drove her to do that."

The graphic picture stunned him. "I'm sorry," he said in a low rasp. "I didn't know."

"You didn't know because you didn't want to know. I knew that. She knew it, too. You were big-time stuff, a rich kid from the city. She was just a little country kid..." Anita stopped and her voice took on a hard emphasis. "And blind. In more ways than one. She didn't see how fast you were going to walk out of her life."

Rourke's fingers tightened on Anita's bare flesh. "I...had my reasons."

"I'll bet you did. I'll bet you had at least ten very good reasons. Well, I'm warning you, mister. Don't hurt her again. She explained how you brought her tonight because you happened to be working together. Just...don't let it get any heavier than that." Glaring up at him, Anita shrugged her shoulders free of his hands and stalked away.

"You forgot your drink," he murmured to her back and then thought it was just as well that she had.

The food appeared about midnight, a buffet table laden with salads, rolls, cheese, ham, spicy pasta and decorated sugar cookies. Someone, he wasn't sure who, brought two plates piled high with food to their table and placed one in front of Jessica and the other in front of him.

"Silverware," a voice said. "They need silverware. And napkins, you Neanderthal." It was Todd's voice, sounding like a first sergeant. Two glasses of champagne, the bubbles still dancing on the top, appeared at the side of the plates.

Jessica glowed, her face flushed with pleasure. She hadn't had much to drink, Rourke knew. She hadn't had time. She'd been too busy dancing. Her slender fingers clasped the glass and she lifted it to her lips, her topaz

eyes sparkling above the wine. She drank, closing her
eyes in pleasure as she savored the taste.

"I'm high," she said setting the glass on the table.

He smiled a lazy, indulgent smile at her. "I noticed."

His smile increased her sense of euphoria. "High on
life, high on people."

Jessica relaxed back and let her arms lie along the arms
of the chair, her posture open, vulnerable. She was
wearing a spangly gold, two-piece dress, the top half cut
in the shape of a butterfly, with a V neck and sleeves that
billowed. The skirt was as molded to her hips as the top
was loose. When she was on the dance floor, the swaying of her smoothly clad bottom under the voluminous
top had been one of the reasons he'd decided to leave
their table and go stand by the patio door.

"I don't need this champagne," she told him, lifting
it to her mouth and drinking.

"No, you don't."

"Have you ever felt this way? As if the world were tied
up with a bow and handed to you on a shiny platter?"

His first impulse was to say no. Then his mind flashed
to the memory of how he'd felt, holding her in his arms
in a dark shadowy barn with the rain pattering over-
head. "Eat something, Jessica."

She sipped her drink and then sat back and turned
those dark, topaz eyes on him. "You've had a boring
time, haven't you?"

She saw too much with those eyes, too damn much.
"It's been . . . educational."

"What did you learn?"

"The same thing you did, I think. How highly thought
of you are in the company."

Jessica looked down at her hands. "I didn't know they
would do this for me."

"'As ye sow, so shall ye reap.'"

"I haven't sown anything...."

"Jessica, I've been sitting on your lap for the past two weeks. I've watched people walk into your office with problems and walk out with solutions. You manage them so skillfully, they don't even know they've been managed. And you do it instinctively, as if you were born knowing how. These people are giving you what you've earned."

She flushed more deeply. "Thank you."

He wished it was that simple. There was more he could have said to her. He could have told her he'd known she was good at her job, but he hadn't really realized what a threat she was to Brewster Hilton until tonight.

Rourke's eyes drifted up and over Jessica's head to the bar area. Hilton was there, a glass in his hand. He'd been there most of the evening, drinking Scotch as if prohibition was going to be reinstated tomorrow, and looking at Jessica as if he wanted to have her for a meal instead of the buffet. Rourke would have given a large sum of money to know what was going on inside that blond head.

When he and Jessica left the party two hours later, it was still snowing kaleidoscope flakes, flakes that sifted down from the sky and nestled in the shiny chestnut strands of Jessica's hair. He put her in the car carefully. She'd had only two glasses of champagne, but she drifted on a cloud of euphoria, more from her state of mind than from alcohol. She was as beautiful as the snowflakes she walked under, one of a kind, delicate...and fragile. Heartbreakingly, crystal-thin fragile. He felt choked with the need to string this night of happiness out for her the way a spider draws out a strand of web.

She laid her head back on the seat beside him, a contented sigh escaping her lips. Even in the darkened car, he could see the white fragility of her throat, exposed by the open collar of her coat and the deeply cut neckline of her dress. The smooth white feminine skin, silky to the touch . . .

He took a tighter grip on the steering wheel and drove Jessica's car through the wintry night. At the late hour, the deserted streets and the drifting snow gave the town a fairyland quality of unreality.

He pulled up in front of her apartment house, parked the car and got out. When he reached her door, she had it open and was swinging her feet down to the ground. "You don't have to walk me to the door."

His mouth tightened. She couldn't wait to get rid of him. "The snow may have made the walk slippery." His hand glided under her elbow while he reached around her to shut the car door.

To Jessica, the sudden warmth and nearness of him was far more intoxicating than the champagne had been. His topcoat made a rustling sound, and his scent was musky, designer expensive, undeniably male. His tall body and dark head cut off the snow and the stars.

She wanted to know what he was thinking. In the dark, she could see only the shadow of his features. As she had once before long ago, she used her sense of touch to tell her what she needed to know about Rourke . . . and lifted her hand to his face.

The air was cold, his skin was warm. When her fingers brushed his cheek, he breathed in sharply, as if she had touched him with an electric wire.

"Jessica." The voice was low, husky, but there was no order for her to stop touching him.

"Your face is…harder than I remember and your jaw is leaner…more…mature."

"Jessica—" The word was a hard rasp of sound filled with an emotion bordering on pain.

"Don't turn away from me, Rourke. Not tonight."

Her fingers trailed down his jaw to linger at his mouth, tracing the bow of his upper lip, the fullness of his lower.

He stood frozen, willing his leaping body to stillness, his mind to reason. The hands that wanted to reach out and touch her hair, her throat, her mouth, he thrust into his pocket and balled into fists. "You're not thinking clearly, Jess."

"I know. Right now, I don't care. I want—I want to feel what it's like to have you kiss me. Again." The last word was a whisper.

Destroyed by that husky murmur that called back the past so vividly, Rourke gathered her feminine warmth into his arms and lowered his head.

Aching warmth flowed everywhere, into cells and nerves atrophied from long disuse. Reaching under her open coat, he lifted her more fully into his body, fitting her hips to his…and his mouth to hers.

It was completion and deprivation, bliss and pain, heaven and hell, to explore the mouth that was undeniably opening to him and generously giving what he wanted before he asked. She tasted so good, smelled so good, felt so good. His senses were on overload, his brain on disconnect. Under her coat, the gold glitter of her dress rubbed against his palm with a sandpaper reality that told him he wasn't dreaming.

Her dress was a barrier between them. He found the gap between the top and skirt and slid his hands up the warm flesh of her back until he encountered the narrow strip of her bra.

Jessica felt as if she were submerging in a warm sensual sea, conscious only of Rourke. His arms enfolded her, his heavy overcoat encircled her and shielded her from the cold. His mouth was welded to hers, his tongue boldly taking what she offered, creating a deep heat within her. He satisfied, only to make her more hungry.

The shock of his hands, hard, masculine, on her bare back sent another shower of feeling through her, a lovely forbidden feeling, a feeling of primitive abandon. This was what she wanted, Rourke's hands on her, his mouth on her, his body on hers....

She felt the clip of her bra give. Her breasts sprang free from their confinement, and satin whispered against skin as his hand glided under the delicate fabric to find that which was his. Had always been his. Flesh swelled against flesh, discovered and found completion. Stinging delight followed and a soft moan escaped her lips. He breathed her name in a harsh rasp, and his other hand anchored her hips against his, the heat and warmth of his arousal burning through her clothes toward the source of the fire smoldering inside her.

"Jessica."

"Don't ask me to stop and think. Not tonight. No thinking...tonight. You've got a snowflake on your cheek. Right below your scar—"

She came up on her toes, and her tongue touched his skin, flicking at the cold crystal. Every nerve in his body tightened with joyous anticipation, imagining that slick, moist warmth touching him in other, more intimate places.

A car went by and turned into the next driveway. Instinctively, she relaxed away from him. As the headlights flashed around in an arc, he caught a brief glimpse of her, lips swollen with the onslaught of his, eyes dark with sensual arousal, hair attractively tousled.

He had started what he could not finish. He couldn't take what she'd offered so generously on a night she was too happy to believe anything could ever go wrong again. He couldn't use her body and walk away, not if he wanted to leave this town possessing the integrity he'd managed to hang on to over the years. Still holding her, he said gently, "We can't, Jess."

She trembled under his hands. "I thought you... wanted me."

Knowing he would be punishing himself as well as her, he lifted her away from him a little. In the faint light of the street lamp, he saw only a shadowed outline of her face, but her body, freed of constraints, was more visible. Under her coat, the gold fabric, lifted, clinging to the crests of her aroused breasts, glittering in the pale light. He picked up a strand of her hair caught on the collar of her coat and remembered what Anita had told him. Jessica had cared for him once, evidently more than he had thought possible. "I do want you. But not enough to hurt you. I did it once before, Jess, but I was young and stupid and too confused about myself to understand what I was doing to you." He paused, and in a lower tone that trembled with intensity said, "I'm no longer too young to know what I'm doing. If I go upstairs with you now, we could be destroying your career... particularly if it turns out you need my defense."

She paused and then her head came up. "It's not my career you're worried about. You're afraid. Afraid I'll want more from you than you're willing to give. Afraid I'll want your heart."

Her words cut more than he ever expected them to. He pushed her away from him a little more, knowing this truth was what was between them...what had always been between them. "I haven't got a heart to give."

A cold wind whipped between them, swirled around Jessica's nylon-clad legs like an icy ghost.

She'd been warned. Scotty had warned her.

Her skin crawled with cold. Bones, muscles, nerves, every cell she possessed longed to be gathered into the shelter of his warm body. While her mind whispered, He doesn't love you. He never has...and he never will.

"You're wrong, Rourke. You have a heart. And someday you'll find the woman with whom you'll want to share it. I just don't happen to be her." In the fingers of light, her throat shone like drawn satin. Her back straightened, her chin came up to a new, proud height.

Watching her wrap herself in the only thing she had left, her pride, tore at his gut. In a dark, throaty voice, he said, "It won't happen."

"Yes, it will. When it does, all those years of loving you've been saving will pour out of you, and you'll make her the happiest woman on earth." She made no attempt to pull her coat together and hide from him what his hands had already possessed. "I envy her with all my heart. Good night, Rourke." She turned, her high heels squeaking with friction against the snow-covered walk. Off balance, she wobbled on her shoes. His arm shot out to catch her elbow and steady her.

Gently, as if she was afraid of harming him, she pulled away from his grasp. "I'm not high anymore. You've brought me down to earth very quickly." Without looking at him again, she walked away into the snowy night.

There must have been other times in his life when he'd felt worse, but they paled into insignificance as he watched Jessica's slender form become a dark shadow behind the veil of snowflakes.

Rourke stood on the sidewalk, unable to move, his world bounded by falling snow…and the pain he'd heard in Jessica's voice.

Slowly, as if he'd suffered a body blow, he climbed back into the car—her car—and started the engine.

Letting himself into his hotel room, Rourke felt as if he were stepping into prison. There was nothing between these sterile four walls to help him forget that for the second time in his life, he'd hurt Jessica badly. And this time—this time he'd felt the warmth of her feminine flesh under his fingers, touched the lovely, aroused peaks that told him her body was readying itself to receive him. He was nearly destroyed by the memory of how she'd stood in that faint light, proud, haunted and so lovely he'd wanted to gather into himself everything she was, had been, would be.

Why had he rejected her? Because he had to. Jessica wasn't the kind of woman a man took to bed casually. He'd known that seven years ago. She was a woman a man took to his heart . . . and loved.

He wanted nothing to do with love. Love was a mirage in the desert, an ephemeral, silvery thing that beckoned and teased . . . until a man walked close. Then it vanished into thin air, lost behind the daily grind of living and working and eating and sleeping.

And illness. Till death do us part hadn't worked for his mother.

He stripped off his coat and his suit jacket, dug his fingers into the knot of his tie, loosening it. The digital alarm he carried with him when he traveled flashed the time. It was twenty minutes to three, but it might as well have been high noon. He wasn't going to sleep, not now, not hurting like this.

His body ached. His skin burned to be pressed next to Jessica's, his hands felt deprived without the touch of her soft roundness.

He was a fool. A man controlled his body with his mind, and with that control, stayed sane. To think of Jessica, to want her, to imagine how it would feel to make love to her, that was a clear path to disaster.

He would maintain control. He would walk away from her a whole man, free of that debilitating force that robbed a man of his good sense and his pride, unchained by that mirage called love.

He stepped into the bathroom, stripped off the rest of his clothes and ducked into the shower.

He stood utterly still, letting the shock of the hot water work its effect on his aroused body, fighting for control with his mind, purposely blanking out all thought. Control. He had long years of practicing control and he would have it now. He'd lost his head with Jessica tonight because she'd pulled old strings, aroused old memories. That was the reason for her extraordinary hold on him. She was old, unfinished business. Hadn't he read somewhere that a woman who wanted to make a man fall in love with her should be elusive enough to give him time to create a fantasy about her? Well, he'd certainly had time to conjure up a hundred fantasies about Jessica. And not one of them, he suspected, was as good as the reality.

Savagely, he twisted the faucet to cold. When he could stand the numbness no longer, he shut off the water.

Cursing and shivering, he stepped out of the shower stall, bringing a puddle of water with him onto the tile floor.

A few minutes later, wrapped in a terry robe, his hair still wet, he went back into the main room, his mind searching for another antidote to his desire. He desperately needed something to keep him from doing what every nerve and cell in his body was urging him to do, get dressed and go back to Jessica. He'd even thought of a reason to return. He had her car.

Gritting his teeth, he cast an eye on the television set. He flicked it on...and saw Fred Astaire bending sinuously over Ginger Rogers in a dance of carefully choreographed sexuality. With a savage energy born of frustration, he twisted the switch and the set went black.

The only other thing that possessed diversion value was his briefcase. He'd kept those printouts of the orders from Cleveland, since it occurred to him he might put them in sequence according to date. They hadn't been that way when he received them, and that fact struck him as odd. He felt the first stirring of relief. Yes, here was a place he could put his mind. Here was something he could concentrate on to banish Jessica from his head.

He pulled from his briefcase a pile of the narrow, note-size papers secured by a paper clip, and sat down at the desk where he'd have room to spread them out. He wasn't even sure what he was looking for. He was acting on instinct, as he often did.

Hitching his robe up around his thighs, he loosened the papers from the clip and laid them on the desk as if they were cards he was laying out in a game of solitaire. With a stern order to himself to concentrate, he began to arrange them in chronological sequence, building a checkerboard, putting orders received in June on the top row, orders received in July in the middle row and orders received in August on the bottom row.

He was nearly finished when something peculiar caught his eye. One of the papers in the upper left-hand corner in the June row had been torn raggedly, leaving a jagged lower edge that looked as if a mouse had nibbled it. Below, in the August row, was the paper with a top border matching it, like the piece of a puzzle. Rourke picked up the slip with the August date, and fitted it top to bottom with the June order.

It matched perfectly.

Stunned, he sat back. If the orders had been processed as they were received, the way they should have been, it was not possible for an order taken in August to follow a June order.

Unless the paperwork was done all at once, at a different time.

But why? Why would anyone do that? The answer came far too easily. *To hide an incorrect change in the computer program.*

The answer to the question of who could have done it came just as easily. Jessica. Jessica would know exactly how to generate a worthless set of papers that looked authentic.

His skin burned, but underneath, his mind was chilled. Was it possible? Was it possible she had created this pile of paper he was looking at?

With a feverish need to know the truth, Rourke worked for another hour, putting the slips in order by matching perforated edges with hands that were showing an alarming tendency to tremble with distress and fury. There were a few he was unsure of, but out of those thirty orders, there were twenty-three that could be fitted together like the pieces of a puzzle, showing the pattern of the printout. And none of those twenty-three orders had consecutive dates. The computer had printed out the orders, not chronologically, but geographically. All the orders were Cleveland orders.

Or were they? No, of course they weren't. They had been processed to look as if they were...but they weren't.

Rourke sat back in the chair, his body chilled, not by the cold shower he had taken but by the clear evidence that someone who knew the computer program and the procedure by which the orders were taken had generated this worthless pile of paperwork merely to confirm the information in the computer.

That someone could have been Jessica.

The woman who'd invited him to spend the night with her...and told him how much she would envy the woman he loved.

He felt as if he were going to explode. Fists clenched, muscles tied in knots, he rose slowly from the desk. He stood in front of that incriminating stack of papers he had been working on for an hour to sort into exactly the right pattern, and for the first time in seven years, he let slip the hard control he'd learned from Scotty. A curse on his lips, in one angry swipe, he swept the papers off the table. They scattered about him, white, drifting, fluttering at his feet like the flakes of snow that had obscured his vision of Jessica. And nowhere in his logical mind did he ask himself why, if he neither wanted nor needed Jessica's love, was he so angry.

ROURKE'S MOUTH WAS DRY, and his feet were cold...and somewhere in the world fairly close to his head, the phone was ringing. Where in God's name was he? He seemed to be lying on his stomach on top of the bed, still wearing his robe.

He came awake slowly. There was something he didn't want to think about, something he didn't want to remember. He couldn't think, didn't want to think...but the phone went on ringing, as if whoever was on the other end of the line knew he was there. He reached out and growled a husky hello into the receiver.

There was silence. Then a feminine voice cool with distant politeness said in his ear, "I'm sorry to disturb you . . . but I need my car."

He'd never heard Jessica's voice on the phone before, but having heard it, he'd never forget it. Every nerve in his body tensed. Why was she calling so early in the morning? Was she afraid he was coming too close to the truth? Working frantically to put the pieces in his head together, he gripped the phone tighter, reaching deep inside his tired brain for control. "How soon do you need it?"

"In half an hour."

"I'll be there in twenty minutes."

He hung up and lay back on the bed, his face dark, thoughtful. The Jessica he'd known would never have called him the next morning after the encounter they'd had the night before. Was this the next step in her scheme to keep him off balance? His heart pounding with a strange excitement, he threw the covers back and went into the shower.

In her apartment, Jessica expelled a long breath, her heart hammering in her chest. She'd crawled out of bed an hour ago, showered and dressed. It was only when she went to her purse to look for her car keys that she realized she didn't have them and remembered where they were.

She'd tried desperately to think of a way to avoid calling him. She'd rung Anita's apartment . . . and gotten no answer. She'd considered calling Scotty and discarded the idea. What explanation could she give that shrewd Scot for not calling Rourke?

She'd spent the next half hour pacing the floor, knowing she couldn't disappoint Michelle, the blind teenager who'd come to depend on Jessica as a lifeline to lighten the darkness of her life.

She knew what it was to wait for people to come and keep promises they had made, wondering if they would, dying a little if they didn't. Nothing, not even Rourke's anger at having her disturb him, would prevent her from keeping her promise to her young friend. Which was why she went to the phone, her hands shaking with anger directed at herself. She had been stupid to let him drive away with her car last night. She should have insisted he leave the vehicle and call a cab.

Rourke was as good as his word. He arrived exactly when he said he would. When she opened the door to him, his hair was still wet from the shower. He was dressed casually in jeans, a turtleneck sweater pulled down over his narrow hips. He looked drawn, as if he hadn't slept, and in his eyes lurked a cool guardedness that made her stiffen with pride. Did he think she was going to seduce him in broad daylight?

"I'm sorry you were inconvenienced."

She'd meant to offer him a cup of coffee, but the look in his eyes warned her not to bother with token civilities. Last night he'd kissed her passionately, touched her intimately. Why did he look as if he hated her this morning? Because she'd come too close to the truth about him? "You can use my phone to call a cab if you like. Just close the door behind you, it's self-locking."

His eyes roved slowly over her denim pants, her cotton shirt, the short fake fur jacket with the ribbed bottom hugging her slender hips. If he remembered last night, it didn't show in his face. He wore a bland, smooth expression that made her want to hit him. "I was hoping that as long as you're going out anyway, perhaps you could give me a ride back to the Consolidated parking lot where my car is.''

She wanted badly to refuse him, until she remembered the reason his car was there. He'd been kind to her, driven her home after her confrontation with Hilton. ''I suppose I could.''

''If you have an . . . appointment, I'd rather not make you late for it.''

''You've already done that,'' she snapped.

At her show of temper, his lips lifted in a humorless smile that turned him into a stranger. Vowing not to give him an opportunity to bait her again, she walked through the door and into the hallway.

Outside, standing beside the car, that same mocking smoothness on his face, Rourke dropped the keys into her gloved hand, inviting her to be the driver. She clamped her teeth together and opened the door on the driver's side, sliding in under the seat, telling herself this was one time she intended to break the speed limit driving to the company building.

He rode beside her without saying anything, and by the time they reached Building 101, she was more than happy to see him get out of the car. ''Wait a minute. I have to get my briefcase out of the back.''

''You're working today?''

Over the open door, he bent down to look at her. ''Anything wrong with that?''

Rourke's words were bland; it was his eyes that were loaded with trouble. ''No, of course not. I just think it's a shame that you're going to work on a beautiful day like today—'' She turned her head and looked through the windshield. The sun had come out and its golden blaze had given the snow-coated world a new lease on life. The blue sky was fresh, sharp, the trees dark and clotted with snow, the air crisp.

"I appreciate your concern."

He'd adopted a faintly mocking drawl, as if he didn't believe she was sincere. Annoyed that she had let him get at her again after she'd spent the whole morning telling herself that after last night, nothing he could say or do would disturb her, she put her hand on the gearshift. "Goodbye."

He stayed where he was, holding the door open, keeping her there. She looked irritated.

"If something comes up that I need to ask you about . . . where can I reach you?"

"I'm afraid you won't be able to."

"No?" It was there again, that touch of mockery, as if she'd given him the exact answer he expected.

"I'm picking up a friend and we're going ice skating and then out for lunch. We haven't planned exactly where."

Rourke fought to control his temper. Sometime during last evening, when she'd been dancing and smiling with her co-workers, she'd made a date with another man. Was that before or after she'd decided to ask him to stay the night? She'd played him for a fool. "Where will you be skating?"

Rourke's face had gone hard, taut. Why? What had she done to offend him? Surely he should have been flattered by her admission that she wanted him, not offended. Feeling the heat come into her face, she considered telling him it was none of his damn business. But she couldn't. Because this was business, and had nothing to do with their personal lives. If she didn't tell him, he would no doubt, in his present state of mind, jump to the asinine conclusion that she was trying to hide something.

Rourke waited, watching her, sure she wasn't going to answer him.

"It's a rink not far from Lake Ontario." She gave him the name of the rink and the street address. "I'm sure you could have me paged there if it's absolutely necessary."

"I'm sure I could," he murmured. "Goodbye, Jessica." He pushed the door shut, leaving her sitting alone behind the wheel of the car, feeling as though, if he had prodded her one more time, she would have gotten out of the car and strangled him.

ROURKE SHOT A CURT HELLO to the security guard, shunned the elevator and began the hike up the five flights of stairs. He was breathing faster when he walked into the now-familiar office area, but he knew the exercise had been good for him, cleared his head of thoughts about the softness of Jessica's skin . . . and the possibility that she was the best actress in western New York.

He went straight to the rotary file that sat on Jessica's desk and flipped it around, looking for Julie's home number.

The phone rang repeatedly. He was about to hang up when a groggy voice said, "Hello?"

She'd slept late after the party, he thought, his lips twisting, and he'd disturbed her rest. Right now, he didn't particularly care.

"Julie, Rourke Caldwell here. I'm looking for the original invoices for the Cleveland orders. Where are they?"

There was silence, as if his question had stunned her. Then the feminine voice, no longer groggy, said timorously into his ear, "I . . . don't know."

"You don't know? I was given to understand you were in charge of filing them."

"I am. But I . . . that was the first thing Jessica wanted to see when the trouble started. But we . . . couldn't find them."

"You couldn't find them. They just disappeared?"

Another long pause punctuated by the sound of Julie's quickened breathing. "I know I filed them . . . that is, I'm pretty sure I did. But they're just not there. The folders are empty. We looked everywhere for them but . . . we couldn't find them. Jessica was afraid they had somehow gotten into the pile of junk papers and thrown away by accident."

"Some accident. Why didn't you tell me this?"

Again, the young woman hesitated. Finally she said, "Jessica told me not to. I'm on probation as it is, and she knew if I said anything I'd be fired. She said not to worry, that we had verification of the orders in the computer printout."

"I see."

"I suppose . . . I'd better start looking for another job."

"No, Julie. Not yet. It's possible you didn't do anything wrong. You may have filed those papers exactly where they belonged."

"But if I did, why aren't they there?"

"I don't know," Rourke said slowly, knowing he had to be careful what he said to this frightened young woman who thought the world revolved around Jessica Moore. "But I intend to find out."

CHAPTER TEN

GLIDING AROUND inside the covered ice rink with Michelle hanging on to her back pocket, Jessica thought of Rourke. The shouts of the other children echoed inside the cavernous building, and the constant scrape of her skates reminded her she should keep her mind on maintaining the smooth rhythm that made it easy for Michelle to skate along. It seemed as if nothing could dispel her mood. She'd lain awake most of the night, wishing she'd found a way to tell him the truth, that she loved him and always had. But how could she? He thought she'd lied to him once. With the investigation underway, any declaration of her true feeling for him would be more suspect than ever.

The air was crisp, heavy with that mixture of scents peculiar to indoor ice skating rinks: artificially cooled water, wet concrete, wool socks. Michelle clung to Jessica like a barnacle. She was a slim girl, but the centrifugal force as they rounded a turn made Jessica hope that denim was as tough as it was supposed to be.

Behind her, Michelle laughed. "Faster, Jessica, faster."

Jessica pushed thoughts of Rourke out of her head and strained to take the girl at a faster pace as they wove through the other skaters. Those hands in her pockets jiggled up and down. "Giddap, horsey."

This was childish behavior for a fifteen-year-old, but Michelle was showing off. Mike was in the spectator's pen. Michelle had refused his overtures of friendship for the past three weeks, but she wasn't above showing off for him.

Jessica knew the feeling. It was so long since she'd thrown herself up and down seven steps to prove she was capable of doing anything a sighted person could do, for Rourke's sake.

In seven years, nothing had changed. Last night, when his hands had taken the intimacies she'd wanted him to take, she had felt whole...and so had he...she knew he had. Whether he could admit it or not, he'd been moved.

But when he'd returned this morning, he'd looked as if he had never known her at all...and never wanted to know her.

IT WAS JESSICA'S HAIR that caught Rourke's eye first, that glorious hair, with a color between blond and brown that was hers alone. Unfettered and flying around her shoulders, it looked like molten, tawny sunlight. Then he saw the girl skating behind her. The girl's head was thrown back and she was laughing. Her hair, too, was loose and free, a cocoa shade of brown. Jessica skated by Rourke, too intent on keeping her balance to see him. But the girl turned her head to laugh at the spectators, as if she were taunting someone who stood there...and Rourke saw the girl's eyes.

He swore softly. He had assumed Jessica was meeting a man. Instead, here she was, giving a precious portion of her free time to a teenager who needed her.

Had she really been protecting Julie and not herself when she withheld the information about the missing order forms? He wanted to believe it...needed to believe it. But was he allowing his personal feelings to jeopardize his investigation?

Or was he allowing his investigation to jeopardize his personal feelings?

He was beginning to wonder if he could think straight at all. He'd walked into this rink, bracing himself to watch Jessica moving around the ice in the arms of another man. When he saw she wasn't, he was filled with a relief so intense he knew it no longer made any difference whether she was a liar or a cheat. Whatever she was, he wanted her. Wanted her as he'd never wanted another woman in his life. And somewhere, between last night and this morning, he'd lost the inclination to be noble.

Jessica came off the rink, Michelle behind her. Together, they banged into the protective barrier separating the rink from the area where tables had been set up next to a snack bar. Mike appeared at Michelle's side, his smile pathetically eager, his hands holding out two bottles of soft drink.

Jessica smiled back at Michelle's would-be swain and took one. She liked the gangly sixteen-year-old, liked the shy regard for the young girl in Mike's eyes...mixed with a gleam of determination. Mike didn't know how to get past that barrier Michelle had built around herself, but he wasn't about to give up. The girl refused his offer of a soft drink and was standing on the other side of Jessica with her head turned away.

"Keep trying," Jessica mouthed silently to him.

"Forget it, Jessica." He shook his head and a flash of bitterness crossed his face. He raised his voice and looked at Michelle. "I'm just not good enough for her."

Jessica looked up to shake her head at Mike...and saw Rourke leaning his tall, elegantly graceful body against the corner of the snack counter.

Her stomach tightened. Just what she needed. Mike and Michelle in a confrontation, and Rourke, bringing bad news. "Stay with Mike a minute, Michelle. There's someone I have to see."

Michelle reached out to grab her. "Don't leave me with him."

Jessica ignored the feigned desperation in the girl's voice, transferred Michelle's death grip to Mike's arm and set the soft drink down on a table. "I'll only be gone a minute."

Mike covered Michelle's hand with his other one, his face cool. "You can stop acting as if this was the supreme torture of your life. I'm not going to hurt you." Jessica left them, Mike looking annoyed, Michelle's body stiff with anger.

Walking toward Rourke on her skates, Jessica tried to read his expression. She couldn't. He didn't look as if he had made a horrendous discovery, but he rarely let anything show on his face.

"What is it? What's wrong?"

He gave her a bland look. "Why are you assuming something is wrong?"

"You wouldn't be here if it weren't."

"Wouldn't I?" His eyes drifted over her. She was still wearing the fur jacket, and now, with the extra inches the skates gave her, she was nearly as tall as he was. She looked all long legs, eyes and floating hair. He had never wanted her more. "You've grown taller."

It was a delaying tactic and she knew it. "You've shrunk," she shot back. "What is it, Rourke. Have you found something?"

His eyes roved over her face. "The invoices are missing. But you already knew that, didn't you?"

Her eyes didn't waver from his. "Of course. How...did you find out?"

"Julie told me."

"I told her not to—"

"It's a good thing she disobeyed your instructions or you'd be in more trouble than you already are."

"Is that possible?" she said dryly.

"It would be, if I decided to include in my report that you were withholding information from me."

"It isn't important information. All the orders are there in the computer-generated printouts."

Rourke watched her carefully. Was she saying that with the confidence of a person who actually believed it, or the bravado of a practiced liar? "That match the data in the computer."

"Of course they match—" At the expression in his eyes, she stopped.

Was that genuine surprise he saw in her face? If it wasn't, she deserved an Academy Award. "You're taking a lot for granted, aren't you?" he drawled, his eyes lazy on her face. "The originals might not have matched at all."

"That's impossible."

"Is it? Well, we'll know for sure Monday when I start calling customers and checking on their orders."

He looked for the panic to appear in her eyes. It didn't. She looked puzzled, but not frightened. "I don't understand how that's going to help you find out who tampered with the program."

She was either very clever...or innocent. He would have given all he had to know which. "In an investigation like this, the direct path is not always the right one. It's the little detours that often give you the answer you're looking for."

"If missing invoices are all you've discovered, and Julie told you I knew, why are you here?"

To Jessica, sensitive to his every mood, it seemed impossible that Rourke's silence was changing before her eyes from cool detachment to sexual invitation. But it was. There was a subtle change in his body posture, a tensing of his hands, a tautening of his jaw. Those blue eyes sought out the sensitive places in her face, her cheekbones, her mouth, and lingered. A response flared deep within her. Under the fur jacket, her body leaped to awareness to sensations remembered, to the touch she yearned to feel again.

"As I said, it's the detours that can turn out to be most . . . interesting." When she shook her head, he said quickly, "I was a fool last night, Jessica. Will you forgive me?"

There in the cold arena, her color heightened. She might not have forgiven him, but she could never be indifferent to him. "What are you saying, Rourke?"

Carefully choosing his words, he said, "I'm saying we should give ourselves a chance to spend time together . . . away from the office."

Time together. A phrase fraught with promise. She thought she knew this dark, enigmatic man, but after his refusal of her last night, never in her wildest dreams had she imagined he would be standing in front of her the next morning pouring promises of heaven over her with those darkly intense eyes. Did he know what she was feeling, how anticipation was warming her spine like a well-stoked fire?

"How much longer do you plan to say here?" he asked, his eyes watchful, the question too direct to give her a chance to reject him.

She cast an anxious look away from him, back over her charges, looking like an adorably errant chaperon. "I can't leave now, not when Michelle has just taken her first step toward getting back into the world.'' The girl was talking to Mike, actually talking to him.

"Is that what it is?'' He nodded at the couple standing where Jessica had left them.

"For her, yes. She lost her sight six months ago in an accident, and she hasn't allowed anyone her own age to get close to her since.''

"Quite a project you've taken on. If you'd rather not leave now, how about if I come back in an hour and a half and join you for lunch?''

Her heart accelerating, Jessica toyed with the idea of refusing him ... and knew she couldn't do it. "I suppose we could ask Mike to come if he's free, to even out the numbers.''

"I like even numbers,'' Rourke said softly. Jessica turned away, her head spinning.

As she suspected he would be, Mike was free. By the time Rourke returned, Mike had worked a minor miracle and talked Michelle into skating with him. Their truce held through lunch. The hamburger shop was warm and welcoming, casual and clean. They bundled into a booth together, Mike and Michelle on one side, Jessica and Rourke on the other. Conversation was easy, and her sandwich tasted good to Jessica after her morning of exercise. Did Rourke plan to stay with her for the rest of the day? And what would the night bring?

When Mike asked about his work, Rourke was strangely indulgent. Investigative work was nine parts tedium and one part excitement, he told the boy, then turned the conversation away from himself. Before Mike knew it, Rourke had the boy talking about his interests in school, his position as editor of the school paper.

The talk flowed around Jessica and drifted away. She wasn't concentrating on words. Other sensations were much more real to her, Rourke's shoulder wedged into the booth against hers, the low, velvety sound of his voice, the scent he wore.

Rourke had always been a skilled conversationalist, and he hadn't lost that ability. Age and experience had heightened his skill in drawing out others and putting them at ease. Yet he had deliberately chosen a profession that kept him from making life-long friends. Why?

He was a man alone. She had recognized that quality about him the first time they met. And even though she hadn't known who he was that night in the festival tent when they'd met again, she'd recognized it in him once more. Recognized... and absorbed the fact empathetically. She knew what it was to be alone. That first summer, Rourke's loneliness had drawn her like a magnet. She'd wanted to enter his world... and take away his loneliness.

Today, she acknowledged the truth. She still did. No matter what risk was involved.

When the bill came, Rourke offered to pay... and was promptly voted down. Coins and bills were piled on the table, each person paying his own share.

Outside, Mike looked at Michelle standing across from him. "We can't go home yet. It's only two o'clock. Let's go to the park and build a snowman."

Jessica waited, expecting to hear some polite phrase from Rourke that would hasten his departure. He wasn't dressed to spend an hour packing snow. He was wearing a sweater, but his leather jacket was designed for style, not warmth. The hip-length coat had the malleability and bronze color of an old saddle, and a broad lapel lay open to the winter breeze. His smooth dark denims were just as impractical and he wore no gloves.

In the brilliant sunlight, his hair took on the deep brown cast of a seal's coat, his blue eyes traveling over her face. "I'm game if you are."

"Come and ride with me, Michelle." Young Mike was braced, waiting for her refusal. But Michelle was hesitating.

"If you'd like to ride with him, go ahead," Jessica said softly.

Michelle waited for a moment more, then responded with a nonchalant, "Okay." Mike took a step toward Michelle, but Jessica shook her head, warning the boy not to help her when it wasn't necessary. The few steps between them were smooth and bare. Michelle walked alone. No one moved.

Michelle took a tentative step toward Mike and then another and another. Next to him, she held out her hand. He grasped it as if it were a lifeline. "My car's over here. I'll lead the way," he called back over his shoulder.

They drove in a car caravan toward the park, Mike leading, turning through the park entrance. Now the road was winding and narrow, wandering up hill and down. Mike passed several parking areas until Jessica began to wonder if he knew where he was going. At last, he pulled off the road and Jessica followed. A glance in the rearview mirror told her Rourke was doing the same.

When they got out of their cars and approached a snow-encrusted clearing, they were alone together in another world. The only sound was the tall swish of the pine trees ringing the glen, their needles rubbing against each other in the breeze.

"This is perfect. Our snowmen will be safe here," Mike announced. It was then that Jessica understood why Mike had been so particular about the area of the park he'd chosen as their destination. Here, there was a wide open space with no tables or trees as obstacles for Michelle to fall over. She could range freely over the bottom of the glen without tripping over anything.

Moved by his thoughtfulness, Jessica nodded to him, her eyes silently thanking him. Mike colored, looked at Michelle as if afraid she, too, sensed what he'd done. "Well, what's it gonna be. A contest? The old folks against the kids?"

"Old folks?" Rourke said in a challenging tone. He was pulling on a pair of gloves slowly and steadily, as if readying himself for battle. "Look to your laurels, young man. Those of us with experience are about to show you how it's done." He lifted his eyes to Jessica, their dark blue depths carrying a double meaning that made her breath catch in her throat.

If only he wasn't so damnably good-looking, she thought. He hadn't buttoned his leather jacket, and the blue wool sweater he wore accented his dark eyes and brown hair. He was going to freeze, Jessica thought, wishing she had the courage to go to him and button up that jacket for him.

Strangely enough, it didn't feel cold in the protected glen.

The snow was wet and heavy at a temperature just above freezing, ideal for sculpting snowmen. When she and Rourke anchored the first ball in place with more snow, it lost its round shape entirely and took on the flare of a nineteenth-century woman's skirt. Rourke recognized the shape more quickly than she did and when he lifted the second ball on top of the first and began, with conspicuous expertise, to smooth the snow into the contour of a woman's bosom, Jessica stood back, her hands on her hips. "Some snowman."

Rourke looked at her as if she'd lost her senses, then at his handiwork. "I'm thinking creatively," he said, his eyes going from the bustline he'd just created to hers.

"I've never heard it called that before."

"Michelangelo chipped away the marble to find the statue that was inside, how can I do any less? Stop standing there making like an art critic and start a snow-ball for the head."

"I'll roll a snowball for you," she said, reaching down, scooping up a heavy wet blob, stretching her arm back to take aim at his head. When she saw he was braced and ready to duck, she whirled and threw the snowball at his snowwoman, neatly spoiling the careful curve of her bustline.

"Despoiling a work of art. That calls for severe pun-ishment." Rourke advanced on her, all mock male aggression. Laughing, Jessica backed away, but he caught her and held her while he reached down for a handful of snow. Purposely, she leaned against him, nudging her knees with his to throw him off balance.

They went down together, Rourke heavy on her. Above, the sky was blue, his eyes were blue... and the world spun out a vivid reel of color and sensation she could hardly absorb. He lay on top of her, warm, scented man, snow-wet tangled legs.

He looked down at her, and his complacency van-ished. He was breathing faster, and against her thigh she felt his reaction to their locked limbs. He lowered his head toward her, his velvety blue eyes absorbing her. "Lying in the snow like this can bring on hypothermia. It's an extremely dangerous condition, with symptoms of confusion—" here, his lips brushed hers "—and a leth-argy that makes it difficult to breathe."

"I have it already," she murmured, lifting her arms to his neck. "Is there any hope for me?"

"Possibly, but only if you make instant contact with someone not so severely afflicted, someone willing to share his warmth with you." Rourke took her mouth gently, tasting with exquisite care, his hand moving up to cup her jaw and steady her for the deeper, more disturbing intimacies his tongue was taking.

The clear trill of Michelle's laughter brought Jessica's hands up to push against him. Rourke didn't move. She said his name and pushed at him again. Reluctantly, he raised his head. "We're setting a bad example for them," said Jessica.

"Not yet, we aren't," he growled. "But given a little time, I might work up to it."

"Let me up."

He leaned across her, supporting his weight on his palms, but keeping her trapped inside his arms. "I rather like you this way, your hair spread out on the snow. Your cheeks have roses in them." He touched her face with a cold, wet fingertip.

"Rourke—"

"Hey, anything wrong?" Mike's voice inquired, from around the other side of the not-yet-headed snow lady. "Yes," Rourke muttered under his breath, pushing himself to his feet and tugging Jessica to hers before Mike rounded the snow sculpture. "It's too damn crowded here."

"What?"

"Nothing's wrong," Jessica said nonchalantly, brushing the snow from her jeans.

A half hour later, the snow lady got her head and an elaborate hairdo that resembled Mount Fuji's symmetrical peak. Not to be outdone, Mike and Michelle turned their snowman into an arrogant Napoleon Bonaparte, complete with a hand tucked inside his jacket. Jessica wasn't exactly sure when Mike started chasing Michelle, but even though she ran in circles around the park, she lost, as she was fated to do. Mike snatched her coat from behind and caught her. To proclaim his victory, he picked her off her feet and whirled her around in the air, giving her a violent case of the giggles.

"Maybe I should take lessons from him."

"Maybe you should," Jessica said lightly, amazed at her own temerity.

Rourke caught her arm and turned her toward him. "Am I forgiven for last night?"

In the clear, crisp air, the layered order of his hair was awry and damp with frosty snow. His cheeks were bright with the cold that touched hers, but he seemed unaware of the chilly temperature. His entire attention was focused on her, as if she were the sole source of his energy. "Yes," she said, and turned away, not wanting him to see the love that shone in her eyes for him.

She'd told him yes, but she hadn't met his gaze. Rourke was filled with a strange turbulence. Had she forgiven him? Or had she simply mouthed the polite answer she knew he wanted to hear? How long had it been since he'd ached for a woman like this? He was not sorry when Jessica expressed concern about the cold wetness of Michelle's clothes and suggested they call it an afternoon.

They trooped through the snow toward their cars, leaving Napoleon and Madame Pompadour to stand in lonely splendor in the clearing. Michelle climbed in beside Mike, and Jessica stood outside the car telling Michelle goodbye. Mike drove away, and the clearing was suddenly very still. Her last defense was gone. This was the moment she had both longed for and dreaded. They were alone.

Rourke leaned against his car, waiting for her. Her boots seemed stuck in the snow, making it difficult for her to take the next step, for each one brought her closer to him. And breathing had become impossible.

He watched her come toward him, knowing that he was through playing games. It was time for a strong dose of honesty. "Are you going to invite me back to your apartment?"

He waited for her response. Her head came up, and it seemed to him her breathing quickened. He wanted her to be disturbed. He wanted her to share the need, the ache. Did she? Or had her invitation to him last night been an impulse, one she could easily deny?

In the quiet, Rourke's voice held a deep velvety tone that resounded in Jessica's ears. He was asking for more than a simple invitation to come in for a chat and she knew it. His body was still and he looked relaxed, but his eyes had darkened and his face held that look of control she was beginning to recognize concealed a strong emotion. But what emotion? Love and caring? Or fleeting sexual need? Did she have courage enough to take whatever he felt for her and give in return all the love she'd always had for him?

She straightened her spine and looked at those vibrant eyes that waited for her answer. She loved this dark, complicated man and she always would. And for the first time since they met, he was willing to acknowledge his physical need for her. "Yes, I'm inviting you."

He made no sign that her answer pleased him. He simply stretched out his hand in a silent invitation for her to climb into her car.

All the way back, watching his car trailing behind hers on the snow-covered streets, Jessica kept a tight grip on the wheel. She was a mature woman and she knew what she was doing. But she also knew that, after she made love with him, Rourke would be deeper in her soul than ever. If he walked away this time, she would be destroyed. She was taking a chance. A wonderful, terrible chance.

At her apartment, Rourke got out of his car, followed her inside the building and up the stairs. Outside her door, before she could move, he bent and picked her up effortlessly in his arms.

Warmth swept through her, followed by hot, flowing need. "Rourke, put me down. You—"

"What's the matter? Isn't this right? It must be. I watched Mike and this is the way he did it. Open the door, Jess."

She obeyed and then buried her face in his shoulder and the wonderful, undeniably masculine feel of his cold leather jacket against her cheek was the stuff of dreams.

It wasn't like him to play the gallant knight and he knew it. He was feeding her romantic fantasy, something he'd never done with a woman before. But he found himself enjoying her feminine submission, the feel of her face pressed against his body. Soon, he would know all of her softness pressed against him. A surge of hunger for her, deep and urgent, swept over him.

She made one last attempt to bring them both back to sanity. In a low, husky voice, she said, "I'm not sure this is the right thing to do. We might be...jeopardizing your career as well as mine."

Rourke looked down at her, his eyes capturing hers. "Not if you're innocent. You *are* innocent, aren't you?"

There was a long echoing silence as he stood holding her in the threshold of the door. She met his gaze steadily. ''Yes.''

''Then we have nothing to worry about.'' Carrying her, he strode through the entrance to her apartment and kicked the door shut behind him.

CHAPTER ELEVEN

ROURKE'S HARD LEAN BODY rubbed against Jessica's as he let her slide down the length of him and set her on her feet. Her flesh stung with pleasure, her head reeled. Glad for something to do that gave her an excuse to move away from his masculine warmth, she went to hang both their coats in the bathroom to dry. When she returned to the room, he stood quietly at ease...waiting. "Have you decided what you'd like to have, coffee or cocoa?"

His eyes met hers, his mouth lifting. "I'll have—" in the moment of quiet, as he paused, her heart found a faster rate "—whatever you're having."

"I'm having coffee." Her look, her tone, answered his subtle sensual probing.

The gleam in his eyes told her he would allow her to stall...for now.

He followed her out into the kitchen and leaned against the refrigerator, watching her while she worked. When she had loaded the coffee maker, there was nothing left to do but turn and face him. "It will be ready in a few moments."

Unmoving, he stood with his arms folded, that blue gaze roving over her face. "And what shall we do in the meantime, is that what you're wondering? I have a suggestion."

He studied her with a combination of boldness, sheer stark courage and a rare, rare, vulnerability.

It was the vulnerability that undid her. She loved him, this lone wolf of a man, and she would always love him. He was the special combination of qualities that matched her like lock to key. More complicated, more subtle than he was seven years ago, he was still hers. And this time, she recognized her feelings for what they were, a love that had grown far beyond a youthful yearning. This love was a mature acceptance of Rourke for what he was. There was only one thing wrong. He didn't love her...and probably never would.

She turned away to pull the mugs from the cupboard and pour the coffee with a careful concentration meant to combat the tendency her hands had to shake. Indicating the padded swivel chairs around the circular table, she set the mugs out and asked him to sit down. He hesitated for a moment and before he could move toward her, she slipped into her chair.

It was a ritual, lifting the mug to her lips, the quietness, the guarded glances. After a time that seemed like a microsecond and an eternity, he set his cup down, china clicking against wood. "Shouldn't we be getting out of these wet clothes?"

"I...suppose we should." She made no move.

"Have you changed your mind, Jessica?"

"About what?" She lifted her head and met his gaze head on.

A faint smile lifted his lips. He relaxed back in the chair and there was in his expression the recklessness and determination of a pirate captain rigging his ship for a storm. "About finishing what we started seven years ago."

"We can't go back, Rourke."

"No," he said softly, "but we can go forward."

"Is that what you want...to go forward?" She lifted her head. "I'd like to be very clear about this. You've already rejected me twice and I'm not sure I care to chance it a third time."

Nothing in his face changed, but he came to her and pulled her onto her feet and into his arms. "Do you think I would hurt you that way deliberately? The first time...the first time, you were a child, a sweet, adoring child. I wanted to leave you the way I found you...innocent, untouched. The second time you were on an emotional high, not thinking clearly. Both times, I had to fight every minute to keep my hands off you."

She gazed at him steadily. "I'm no longer a child—"

"Thank God for that."

"And I'm not high."

"Aren't you? I was sure one of us was. It must be me." He held her anchored against him, a hand at her back, the other curved around her ribs, under her breast. "Do you know how good it feels just to hold you?"

"Only because I know how good it feels to be held." She raised a hand to caress his cheek. His muscled body pressing against her soft curves, he lowered his head, but he didn't kiss her. He created a little distance between them and bent to fit his mouth in the soft hollow of her throat, as if to tell her that this time he meant to share much more than a few chaste kisses with her. At the thought of what he was asking and what she was answering, a shudder raked her. With a low sound of satisfaction, he dragged his lips upward along skin gone ultrasensitive, bringing a heated warmth flowing up through her.

"I wasn't rejecting you, Jessica. I was keeping you safe. But this time—this time it's up to you to decide

who's going to stay safe and who's going to go hungry.''
He sounded as agonized as she felt.

His mouth, heated, passionate, closed over hers, and
what he hadn't taken before, he took now. What she
hadn't given before, she gave in full measure. She offered him her mouth to explore, pressed the pliant softness of her body against his, easing his loneliness by
telling him of hers with the urgency of her hands and the
eagerness of her mouth.

He broke away from her and looked down into her
face. ''Jessica. Are you very sure this is what you want?''

Pride urged her to take the lifeline he'd thrown her and
pull away from him. A burning hunger nourished over
long years of loneliness made denial of the truth impossible. She raised her head and let him read the message of
surrender in her eyes.

He lifted her off her feet and into his arms. Again, he
looked down at her for that microsecond of time, giving
her one last chance to rescind her unspoken affirmation.
When she didn't, he carried her out of the kitchen,
through the living room and into the hall. Her bedroom
door was open, and in the light that filtered through from
the other room, he made his way to her bed. As easily as
if he had been there a dozen times, he deposited her
gently in the cloud of pillows, sat down beside her and
reached to turn on the small lamp on her night table.

Rocked by how quickly everything was happening,
Jessica looked at him for reassurance. His gentle smile
told her he knew exactly what she was feeling. He
smoothed a tendril of hair from her forehead with a hand
that wasn't quite steady and, as if he couldn't stop himself, leaned over and looked down at her.

His face was as dark and unrevealing as ever, but in his eyes lay that strange, unfamiliar vulnerability. He needed her reassurance as much as she needed his.

Sweet, undeniable longing for him surged through her. "You're too far away." She raised her hands to catch his head and bring his lips down to hers. "Much too far away..."

Her mouth anticipated his with a sweet heaviness, and, as if he knew what she was feeling, he brushed her lightly with his lips, teasing her, prolonging the waiting, heightening the pleasure, giving her time. But she didn't want time. She wanted his mouth on hers, blotting out thoughts, fears, dreams.

Instinctively sensing her hunger, he kissed her erotically, deep thrusts of his tongue bringing knots of fire to the pit of her stomach.

A pillow tumbled in over his head. He plucked it off, his mouth lifting with amusement. "Did anyone ever tell you you have too damn many of these things?"

"No," she said, her eyes on his. "No one ever did."

He looked down at her, his face serious, gentle. "I wasn't asking if you've had other lovers. I don't have that right."

"And I don't have the right to ask you about other women you've... been with."

When she most wanted to see his face, he turned his head and with a careless flick of his hand, tossed a heart-shaped pillow to the floor. Whatever thoughts he was having, he wasn't going to share with her. When he turned back to her again, his face told her nothing.

"From the moment I met you, you've been the only thing that's real to me. And you're the only thing that's real to me now. Lift, Jess," he ordered her and pulled the delicate white eyelet spread out from under her. He deposited her back between the sheets, threading his hand through her hair, and she saw the desire she felt reflected in his face. "Real, warm, feminine," he murmured, "this is what I was seeing when we were in the snow. Your hair spread over a pillow, your eyes darkening and changing when I touch you..." He closed his eyes, a long sweep of dark lashes against his cheek, then opened them again. "I've thought about this for so long—so damned long—"

"Once you were real to me, too. You let me touch you, remember?" she murmured. "Like this—" She caught his hand and brought it up to place it on her cheek. He cupped her jaw and kissed her, a light, lovely kiss full of promise. His hands wandered down, discovering the softness of her throat, the smoothness of her skin, the fullness of her still-covered breasts. His touch was sweet, so sweet, yet its very gentleness fueled the flame of her desire and when he began to rub the cotton material of her shirt against her nipples in slow, mind-destroying circles, watching her, watching the effect his hands had on her, she writhed with tormented impatience.

She struggled to stop her responses, but an intense burning began deep inside her and her hips moved in inevitable, instinctive invitation. He smiled, a smile she'd seen for the first time tonight, an unfamiliar lift of the lips, yet one she already knew too well, with the tiny scar moving over his cheekbone. Knew, and had waited for. Forever.

She reached for him, wanting, needing to touch him. He dodged away, moving his hands lower, rubbing first her abdomen and then her thighs in a seductive circle.

When her skin was so sensitized that she felt as if she were on fire, he unbuttoned her blouse and brushed it off her shoulders, his long fingers cool against her heated flesh.

He tugged the cotton lower, and light spilled over her, gleaming on her creamy curves, shadowing the hollow between.

His hands stayed on her arms, where the cotton was folded. He cherished her with his eyes, only his eyes. When he had drunk his fill of her visually, he stripped her blouse away and his fingers moved over her naked midriff slowly, sensuously, warm against her skin. Her denims were unzipped and pulled down over her, his fingers caressing her thighs and calves in the same agonizingly delightful way. Her last garment went the way of her other clothes. She lay on the bed naked under his smoky gaze, and felt cool and shivery and heated and molten.

If she'd thought his touch was soul-destroying while she was still in her clothes, his fingertips grazing lightly over her naked body were ten times more devastating. Like the drops of rain sliding down a windowpane his fingers skimmed from throat to breast, from waist to thigh, lingering lightly here, teasing there.

"You don't . . . play fair."

"An old lesson," he murmured, his mouth against her throat. "Well learned from you." His mouth followed his hands, bringing damp coolness and stinging life to every inch of her. Below the indentation of her waist, he teased her navel with his tongue, flicking it lightly, while his hand found the heated, guarded place of her femininity.

His touch was unfamiliar and familiar, part of the tender light and the warmth of the room and the rustle of the covers at his back, part of the giving of herself, the accepting of him. He was strange, yet so well known, a hard, tough, lean man, and yet his touch was infinitely gentle. That gentleness created a violence in her, a violence fed by endless days and empty nights. The hunger went bone deep, drove away any thought of his unfamiliarity, his long absence. She was a wanton, fears and thoughts of caution, reason, restraint gone, banished forever. "Rourke—"

He leaned closer. "Undress me, Jessica."

The soft demand in his words was like water disturbed in a pond. Jessica shuddered. Watching him, she took her time, lingering over the lifting of the ribbed bottom of his sweater, letting her hands glide up his bare chest to tangle in that dark nest of hair, pulling his head free, dropping her hands to circle his wrist under the sleeve he still wore, and all the while, savoring each delicious intimacy. New intimacies, new discoveries. The strength of his bones, the tendons of his hands. Tendons she'd once had to touch to learn of his strength and gentleness. Now she touched them because she could do nothing else. Her fingers sought him with an intelligence of their own.

She tossed the sweater away and she could see him now, the breadth of his shoulders, the taut, smooth skin, the hard muscles of his arms and chest.

What she was feeling must have shown in her eyes. Rourke leaned forward and brushed his mouth over her throat, down to the poised and hardened tip of her breast. He sucked on her nipple lightly, moistening it with the warmth of his lips, the damp silk of his tongue. She hadn't known pleasure could be so intense, so all encompassing. A soft moan escaped her. Her hands closed over his shoulders and she held him, knowing he was both the danger and the haven.

He rose to his feet to finish undressing and as the hard strength of his body emerged from his clothes, she thought she had never seen anything more beautiful than the fluidity and grace of his hands, his torso, his thighs.

When he stretched his muscled length down on the bed beside her, he was more than grace, more than beauty. He was life itself, the other half of her.

And now that he was beside her, warm and real, Jessica was afraid to claim him. She couldn't be lying here, feeling the touch of this vital man whose fingers glided over her with a curious combination of reverence and hungry possessiveness that echoed her own state of mind. It couldn't be she with her hands buried in the silk of Rourke's hair, feeling his warm mouth everywhere. It couldn't be she touching, reaching, pleading for him to ease the blinding heat he was creating with his lips and tongue.

Yet it was, and when he moved over her and she lifted to meet him, his low, muffled groan told her he'd discovered the truth, that there had been no other men in her life.

Her pain was sharp, fleeting. He groaned, "Ah, Jess, you..." Rourke stroked her hair and his eyes were filled with such tenderness that he set her shimmering with the brilliance of love. Her body closed around him and whatever he meant to say was lost in the agonized sound of passion torn from his throat.

A sheen of perspiration gleamed on his coppery shoulders and his eyes were closed, his head thrown back. He fought to retain control, and when he succeeded he opened his eyes and looked down at her.

"Jessica. All this time... and you were still—"

"Waiting," she told him. "Waiting for you." She held her breath, not knowing how he would react. She wanted so badly to tell him she loved him.

"I feel... as if I've never made love to a woman before."

The warmth, the depth, the huskiness in his voice, the brilliance in his blue eyes swept away Jessica's doubts. She reached up to touch his face. "Before, when I couldn't see, I thought you were beautiful. Now I can see how right I was."

He looked down at her, his eyes heated, his face sensual. "You are the one who's beautiful, my warm, silky, wonderful woman."

"I'm not beautiful—"

"You don't believe me?" His mouth curved, his eyes shone with his new knowledge of her. "Then I'll have to spend the rest of the night convincing you."

His mouth on hers exploded skyrockets of feeling inside her, and the rhythm of his body made her feel more beautiful than words ever could. With infinite care, he loved her, his mouth and hands exploring, teasing, stroking, soothing and enticing, until her own heated need flamed higher and higher and rose to meet his.

SHE LAY CURVED into his body, her back to his chest. One of his arms was tucked under her shoulder, the other draped over her waist. His fingers found her hipbone and as if, in the aftermath of their lovemaking he meant to keep possession of her, his fingers closed round it. In silent reply, her hand found the hard muscle of his thigh and her fingertips slid up and down the hair-crisp skin. He might be feeling possessive, but so was she.

"What is it?" He leaned closer, his lips in her hair, his voice husky, commanding. "Tell me."

How did he know she was disturbed with no more than the touch of her hands betraying her state of mind? "It's nothing."

His hand closed over her hip, claiming her. "You're thinking about work."

She turned in his arms and pressed her mouth against the soft hollow of his throat. "I…" She wanted, needed desperately to tell him that she loved him. Instead she whispered, "You don't know how much it means to me…your…trusting me."

He stiffened slightly, then relaxed. "How could I do anything else?"

Still languid from the aftermath of loving, she smiled up at him, her mouth curved, sensual. Her eyes roved over his tanned nakedness. "My irresistible charm convinced you I'm not a criminal?"

He kissed her eyes, her cheeks, brushed her mouth lightly with his lips. "Among…other things." He traced a hand down the smooth skin of the valley between her breasts, then leaned over and kissed the bud he'd been caressing.

Arousal arrowed through her love-induced lethargy, making her aware that this was only a respite, not the ending. "Rourke—" His hand dropped lower, stroked the triangle of tawny, warm softness. She breathed in sharply.

"Is something wrong?" he asked imperturbably, his hand circling lazily.

"I can't…think when you're doing that."

"I'm the one who's supposed to be thinking," he murmured, covering her mouth with hers. "At the moment, you're only required to feel. And in that department everything seems to be in perfect working order." The gentle teasing of his hands became an onslaught. "But maybe, just to be sure, we should check…"

With his eyes savoring the long, silken length of her with a gaze in the blue depths that held the promise of a return to rapture, he trailed a finger around her ear, down her neck and over her shoulder. "Let's see. Yes," he said, watching the shivers ripple under her skin in response to his touch, "subcutaneous reactions seem to be normal, perhaps slightly elevated."

"Rourke—"

He wasn't listening. He was dedicated totally to her, single-mindedly pursuing his exploration of her body. "The fingers bend, the knees flex, the toes... Ah. I seem to have found an acute sensitivity in the toes—" his fingers traveled with the speed of light upward "—and in the breasts...." Satisfaction in his eyes, he watched the rosy peaks tighten and lift to his touch. "Yes, everything seems to be in working order... and... made to order." His mouth sought and found hers and her body welcomed him with new passion, learned from him... and gloried in her deepening love.

"WE HAVEN'T HAD any dinner, you know."

"Are you hungry?" Rourke stroked a finger down between her breasts.

"A little." Jessica looked up at him in the darkening twilight, her eyes full of the love she couldn't express. "All that fresh air and... exercise."

"So." He flopped over on his back, looking very complacent. "What are you going to fix?"

"What am I going to fix? I thought we might share the honors."

"My menu's a little limited. I do make a mean cucumber sandwich."

"Cucumber sandwich?" Her tawny eyebrows arched in surprised disdain.

"Yes. I'll even share my recipe. Two slices of bread, six slices of cucumber and a dollop of mayonnaise."

"Please." She shuddered delicately.

Rourke looked at her as if she were quite mad. "You don't like cucumber sandwiches? Mine are sheer magic."

"It would take a strong dose of black magic, plus hypnotism, to get me to eat one."

"Well, that's it then. The end of a beautiful love affair." He rolled over on her and kissed her, as if he were giving her a goodbye salutation.

Before he could move away, she caught his bare shoulders and held his face inches away from hers. "Wait a minute. Let's talk about this. Maybe we can work out a compromise."

"You want to compromise me?" The devil lurked in his blue eyes.

"I make a mean peanut butter and chocolate chip sandwich."

Now it was his turn to shudder and he did, with great enthusiasm. "Peanut butter and chocolate chips? I've fallen into bed with a lunatic."

The insult didn't bother her. Even while he said it, his fingers stroked her hair lazily, possessively, and his eyes played just as lazily and possessively over her face. "I use crackers instead of bread," she told him.

"You *are* crackers, crazy, gone...and not to be allowed in the kitchen alone. Do you have a robe I can wear?"

She did, an Oriental unisex garment that Anita had brought her as a gift from Hong Kong. Made of an electric-blue stressed silk, it had enough material in it to go around Jessica twice, and huge dripping sleeves. Belted, it fit Rourke rather well. The sensual garment gave him the air of a supremely confident potentate lounging in his tent after a major victory on the battlefield.

Jessica picked up the terry sarong wrap she used when she came out of the shower, and wrapped her sensitive body into it, glad her shoulders were bare. She felt warm, alive, vibrant . . . real.

In the kitchen, she fought valiantly to concoct a tray of goodies that would take away the empty spaces inside both of them, but Rourke was behind her every step, lamenting her lack of creativity and the vast wasteland of her vegetable drawer, which contained not a single cucumber. She sliced cheese, found grapes and arranged crackers on a plate. There was a bottle of wine tucked in the back of the refrigerator she'd been saving for a special occasion. Knowing there would never be an occasion more special than this one, she brought the wine out for Rourke to open.

They took the Roman feast back to bed. Feeling like a candle those Romans were famous for, Jessica centered the tray in the middle of the bed and sat. Rourke settled in on the opposite side, crossing his legs in front of him and eyeing the food with more enthusiasm than he'd shown in the kitchen.

Sometime after the first pangs of hunger were satisfied, she found herself leaning back against the headboard, all the pillows propping her up, Rourke leaning over her like an adoring slave, plucking grapes from the bunch and pressing them to her lips. His robe was open to the waist, his eyes infinitely tender, his face more relaxed than she had ever seen it. When he brought another cool, fleshy fruit to her lips, she shook her head. "No more. I've had enough."

"Have you?" Her sarong had one snap at the top and Rourke had already scouted out its location. One tiny tug and it parted. He brushed aside the edges and treated himself to another feast, caressing her with his eyes. "Have you really? Funny. I still seem to be hungry...for you.'' He bent to her, taking the already peaked crest of her breast into his mouth.

THE NIGHT WAS FILLED with a dozen Rourkes, a tender Rourke, a teasing Rourke, a passionate Rourke. He took and gave, made love to her and dozed with her, murmured to her and woke her again to love her with a wild passion. And for every facet of his marvelous inventiveness, she found an answering wantonness in herself, a primitive ability to give and take, to express her love in a thousand, mind-destroying ways that pleasured him... and her as well.

In the morning, she found herself in the shower with him, learning new ways to please him, guiding him in new ways to please her.

She was standing in the kitchen, dressed in her robe and making the coffee when he stepped behind her and cupped her breasts. She discovered a new, stinging awareness of her body. ''Rourke—''

He bent his head, buried his mouth in the soft, sweet-smelling mass of her hair and murmured, ''I think you've turned me into a sex maniac.''

His words sent a shivery thrill up her spine. He wanted her, and it was thrilling, yet he'd said nothing of caring for her...or of staying. She wriggled under his grasp and turned around to lift her face to his. ''We can always hope.''

He cupped her chin and held her head to look at her soberly, his eyes roaming over her face. ''How are you feeling this morning?''

Crazily, she felt shy. In one night, he'd learned so much about her. He'd learned that wherever he led, she was ready to follow. ''Physically or mentally?'' She kept her eyes on his, challenging him to back down and look away. He didn't.

"Both." His eyes changed fractionally, the blue darkening, flashing a message of hungry intensity that his cool face didn't reveal.

"I'm fine." And she would be. As soon as he moved away. At the moment, she felt as sensitive as a finely tuned violin. The hard bones of his hips fit against hers, and his thighs were inserted between hers as if the intimacy their bodies had shared still acted like a magnet, drawing them together irresistibly. He was doing the impossible, making her remember what they had experienced together even while he generated a new, heated need.

"I don't want to stop touching you."

"I . . . don't want you to stop."

"I don't intend to."

He leaned down and kissed her, a teasing, good-morning kiss that held a wealth of sensuality. He'd used her soap in the shower, but on him, it smelled undeniably masculine. His hands threaded up through her hair, lifting the tawny strands away from her neck. A drifting coolness settled around her throat and shoulders, even while his tongue brought a hot, honeyed warmth to her mouth. She clung to him, her arms around his waist.

His eyes dark, unreadable, he released her. "Maybe we need to sober up on that coffee you made."

He drew away and her body cooled and her mind reeled. He seemed to be traveling through a labyrinth of emotion she couldn't follow. He was openly ready to touch her physically. But he wasn't ready to share what was in his mind.

She poured coffee for him, and then set about preparing the scrambled eggs and toast he said would be fine with him, intensely aware of him as he leaned against the counter and watched her. He wore only his jeans, and it was hard to keep her eyes on the food she was preparing and away from that expanse of broad chest with its sprinkling of crisp brown hair. There was a male unself-consciousness about the way he stood, and his relaxation added to her tension. She managed to finish preparing the food, and after she dished out the eggs and sliced the toast, she invited him to bring his mug of coffee and sit down.

They spent the day in lazy togetherness, Jessica wondering when Rourke would mouth a polite phrase and leave her.

But he didn't leave her. He helped her cook supper, and together they cleared and washed the dishes, Jessica aware of a breathless waiting and a new, unfamiliar ache that she now knew exactly how to ease....

Rourke's second night with her was like the first, and yet different. She was learning how to love him, how to use her mouth and her hands to bring him to an agonized ecstasy that matched her own. When, long after midnight, he dressed and left her, the apartment had never before seemed so empty.

CHAPTER TWELVE

DURING THAT WEEKEND, Jessica and Rourke had created their own world. But on Monday morning, they were forced to meet each other in the real world, the world where they were antagonists. Nonetheless, Jessica crossed the sixth floor with an eagerness she'd never felt before, coming to work, knowing in a matter of seconds she would be seeing him.

When she stepped around the barrier, Rourke was there, seated at his desk, waiting for her. For a breathless moment, she wondered if she had imagined it all, the intimacy, the love. Then he lifted his head from the paperwork to gaze at her... and she knew she hadn't imagined a thing. Rourke's eyes were not the eyes of an industrial investigator. They were the eyes of a lover.

Knowing her cheeks were warming from that darkly intimate look, she walked around him to hang her coat up. For two people who needed to hide their response to each other, they were off to a disastrous start.

How could she stop looking at him? His lean face wore the look of sensual fatigue that her loving had given him. The faint circles under his eyes, the relaxed curve of his mouth suited him. He had the complacent air of a satisfied male. Did she have that same look of sexual satisfaction? She'd covered the darkness under her eyes with makeup and used a paler color of lipstick on her well-kissed mouth, but she had the feeling the signs of exhaustive lovemaking were there for anyone who cared to look. And Rourke was looking.

"Behave yourself," she said softly as she sat down within touching distance of him.

His chair creaked with his weight as he leaned back. Deliberately, he unbuttoned his gray suit jacket and clasped his hands behind his head, stretching his body to full extension. Unable to do anything else, she took inventory, letting her eyes follow that lean line of body she knew far better than she had two days ago.

"Practicing what you preach?" he taunted lightly.

That set the tone for the rest of the day. It became a battle to the finish, Rourke much more skilled at acting than she. He touched her hand, brushed her knee, inciting her senses to riot every chance he could, all the while looking as bland and unfriendly as he ever had, covertly watching to see if he'd cracked her thinly stretched control. Did Tom, when he came into her cubicle to ask a question on his current project, see how she struggled to keep her eyes directed away from Rourke? Did Julie notice the heat that rose in her face when Rourke passed her a sheaf of papers and deliberately touched her hand? It was almost as if he wanted people to know he was her lover.

Once, during the afternoon, when they were alone and he asked her a question, she answered him as impersonally as she would have any other business associate, and got a mocking look of amusement in return. She felt a flash of irritation. How could he make this a game? It was as important for his position as it was for hers that they maintain their office formality. Yet she knew that the situation appealed to Rourke's offbeat sense of humor. He kept up the pressure all day, even though he was on the phone most of the time, calling customers to ask for duplicate orders.

As the clock neared five, Jessica found herself cheering its snail's pace on. She needed—desperately needed—a respite.

When the building began to empty, Rourke helped her on with her coat and said in a low voice, close to her ear, "Pizza, later, around nine? I'll buy."

He looked blandly sure of himself. After the day he'd put her through, she should tell him to go fly a kite off the nearest bank of the Genesee. "With or without cucumbers?"

"Without."

"Are you sure?"

"I'm sure." His dark eyes were warm, caressing.

On the way home, she stopped to buy another bottle of wine. Christmas lights twinkled everywhere, along the streets, on trees, inside her. Never, never had there been a day like this, a week like this, a life like this.

Whistling an off-key rendition of "White Christmas," she parked the car, snatched up the bottle of wine and the candles she'd gotten as a last-minute inspiration and walked into her apartment building.

Anita was waiting by her door. It was too late to disguise the joy radiating from her face, too late to hide the wine and the candles behind her back as she childishly wanted to do.

"You look like Christmas," Anita said dryly.

"It's a nice night and I was enjoying the lights." She took her keys from her purse, avoiding Anita's eyes. "I'd ask you to stay for dinner but I'm expecting company later."

"I suspected that. I didn't come for a meal. I just came to give you this." Anita brought a brightly wrapped package out from under her arm. "Put it under your tree and don't open it till Christmas."

Guilt washed over her. She had Anita's gift bought but she didn't have it wrapped. She was behind with her holiday shopping and wrapping, preoccupied as she was with Rourke. "You can come in for a minute, can't you?"

"If you can spare the time."

Jessica opened the door...and knew she was in trouble. A pillow Rourke had thrown at her lay on the floor. In the kitchen, the tray sat where she'd left it, two wineglasses beside it.

Anita took in everything with one turn of her head. "In all the years I've known you, I've never seen your living space disordered. What happened to my neat friend?" Dark green eyes examined Jessica. "Or do I even need to ask?" She shed her coat and dropped it carelessly on the couch. "I assume the bed is appropriately rumpled?"

Telling herself Anita was not her mother, Jessica walked into the kitchen, deposited the candles on the table and put the wine in the refrigerator to cool. Turning, she met Anita's shrewd gaze head-on. "Have you come to rain on my parade?"

"I came to offer words of wisdom. It looks," Anita said, leaning against the doorway, "as if I might be just the tiniest bit late."

"I know what I'm doing."

"No, you don't." The blunt words were said with warmth, with love. "You think you're going to pull off a miracle here, that Rourke Caldwell is going to fall madly in love with you and stay with you forever, just as you always dreamed he would." She looked bleak, as if she didn't enjoy saying the words any more than Jessica enjoyed hearing them. "Honey, I'd move heaven and earth if I thought it would happen that way for you. I'd even stand up at your wedding. But it won't. Men don't change. They just get...more so." Her shoulders drooped, and the silence in the apartment was deafening. "Well, that's it. End of lecture. If I stay any longer, I'll get maudlin." Anita shrugged into her coat. "You know where I am if you need me." At the door she turned, then impulsively, she went to Jessica and put her arms around her. "Merry Christmas, Jess. God bless. Call me if you need...anything."

The familiar scent of Anita's Parisian perfume drifted to Jessica's nose. The nerves in her stomach tightened. She felt as if Anita was telling her goodbye. Perhaps in a sense, she was. Jessica was no longer the bumbling girl who needed her. She was an adult, responsible for her own life. "Merry Christmas, Anita."

THE NEXT MORNING, Rourke rose from his bed and pulled on his robe, his mind in such high gear that the ringing of the phone hardly registered. When it did, he muttered a word. Who could be calling him at seven o'clock in the morning? Unless it was Jessica. His face changed to lazy anticipation as he went to the phone.

A male voice said in his ear, "Rourke? This is Gavin Moore." The caller paused. "Sorry to bother you this early in the morning...but you don't seem to answer your phone in the evenings."

The bland words were loaded with meaning. His senses telling him to be wary, Rourke sat down on the bed and relaxed against the headboard, outwardly at ease, inwardly on guard. "What's on your mind?"

"That's what I called to ask you."

Rourke was silent for a moment. A master at the game, he turned the rapier neatly back. "In regard to what?"

Gavin wasn't in the mood to fence lightly. "Anita told me you've been spending your nights with Jessica . . . but I didn't want to believe it."

Rourke hesitated. He didn't want to hurt Gavin. "How Jessica and I spend our nights must be our business, surely."

"Don't hurt her."

"I have no intention of hurting her."

"You did it once before."

"She was a child then and blind. Now she's all grown up . . . and she can see."

"No, she can't. She'll always be blind where you're concerned. You aren't planning to marry her, are you?"

Obviously, the idea of Rourke as a brother-in-law didn't thrill Gavin. Rourke dealt with pain he hadn't expected to feel. "The subject hasn't come up."

"Then stay away from her."

Rourke ran a finger down the tie of his robe. "Are you speaking for Jessica . . . or for yourself?" Where had that absurd thought come from? Jessica would never break off a relationship with him that way.

"I'm talking for myself. Are you going to stop seeing her?"

"No." The flat, rock-hard finality in his own voice surprised him.

"I'm sorry." Gavin didn't sound it. "I hoped I could reason with you. Since I can't . . . you force me to take action."

"What kind of action?" He was amused. Threatening people was not Gavin's forte.

"If I have to . . . I'll tell her what you've done . . . what you are."

"She knows a great deal about me." His voice was silky. "What could you possibly tell her that she doesn't already know?"

"I may surprise you, Caldwell." The phone clicked in Rourke's ear.

Don't hurt Jessica. Over and over Rourke turned those three words in his mind. He'd never wanted to hurt Jessica. And he wasn't going to hurt her again. She was a grown woman with a mind of her own . . . and a wonderful, beautiful, responsive body to match. He'd made love to her in every way he knew, and she'd met his passion with a joyousness and a growing sense of her own sexuality he found more erotically exciting than the tricks of experienced women. She'd learned to meet his passion and give him more pleasure than he dreamed it was possible to have with a woman. He was going to go on making love to her, pleasuring her in every way he knew. He hadn't known she was a virgin, nothing in their preliminary lovemaking had warned him, but even if he had known . . . his mouth twisted . . . it wouldn't have made any difference. He'd wanted her for seven long years and when he walked into her apartment that night, he'd been driven by one goal.

He wanted her. He wanted her pliant and loving in his arms, totally aware of him and no other man. He wanted Jessica to know the reality that was his body, his mind. But marriage? Marriage led to boredom and, inevitably, betrayal.

He stripped off his robe, showered, dried himself off and wrapped his lower body in the towel, thinking time was growing short. He'd been given till the fifteenth of January. After that, whether he'd discovered the culprit or not, he was through at Consolidated. And when it was over, he'd pack his case and walk out of her life. Again.

He got into his clothes, donning the gray three-piece suit that was the classic civilized garb of the twentieth-century businessman. He might look civilized, but he wasn't. What he was doing to Jessica was primitive and ruthless and unconscionable. And he could no more stop it than he could stop breathing. He wanted to possess her totally in the time he had before he left.

And he would leave.

For if he stayed . . . he'd be committed. Committed to the biggest farce life had to offer. Love.

Nothing lasted a lifetime, least of all a fragile, ephemeral emotion like love. He ought to know. He'd thought he felt it once . . . for her. And he'd thought she'd felt it for him. She hadn't. It had been sexual attraction, just as it was now, a fire that flared up and then died. When it did, he would walk out of her life . . . and she'd find another man, just as she had the first time.

Love never lasted. It hadn't lasted for his father and mother under the stress of her failing health. It didn't last for his father and his second wife even though they'd had everything: money, status, intelligence. Ill-health, too much money, not enough money, whatever happened in the outside world made no difference. Love didn't last.

But while it burned—oh, yes, while it burned—he would go as close to the flame as he dared. He would take whatever Jessica had to give . . . because he had to. He had to walk close to the fire and warm himself, just this once. When it was over, he would pack, call a taxi and get on the next flight out.

From the bright, lighted warmth of the hotel into the snowy dark of the morning, he stepped into his car to drive to the office, knowing the thought of leaving Jessica brought on a bleakness of heart and mind he hadn't felt in a long, long time.

AT THE END of the day, alone in her apartment, Jessica hung up her coat, kicked off her shoes and sank down into the couch, threading a hand through her tawny hair. She thanked heaven the day was over. There had been no game today. This time, it was Rourke who withdrew his hand to avoid touching her, Rourke who kept his chair a careful distance away from hers.

She ached with loneliness for him. Had Anita been right? Was Rourke already regretting his relationship with her and looking for a way to end it? Hurting, Jessica padded barefoot into her bedroom, unhooking her skirt and sliding it down her nyloned legs. She felt raw, as vulnerable as she had felt when she'd been a blind teenager and had met Rourke for the first time.

She slipped into her jeans and pulled on a T-shirt, avoiding the sight of her unmade bed. Had it been only last night they'd made love and then, surrounded by pillows and sheets tangled with their lovemaking, drunk the wine and eaten the pizza Rourke had brought? Had he really spilled wine on her bare body accidentally... and then, not so accidentally, had he taken off the residue with careful, spine-tingling strokes of his tongue? And had she actually reciprocated, going back again and again to taste the salty tang of his skin until he'd groaned and told her she was driving him out of his mind?

He had, and she had. They'd been thoroughly, determinedly decadent, and in the morning she hadn't suffered one single pang of regret. She'd felt good, so good. She'd suffered no ill effects from the food or the alcohol... and she knew why. She was in love, and nothing could hurt her. Nothing, except Rourke.

Long ago, the girl she'd been had vowed never to fall in love again. The woman she'd become was brave enough to risk everything.

A knock on the door brought her to her feet. It wasn't Rourke, for she knew his knock. Perhaps it was Anita.

"Hello, Jess. May I come in?"

Her brother looked strangely vulnerable. Lines of weariness around his eyes made him appear older than he was. He stepped inside and stood looking around. She knew what he was looking for. Evidence of Rourke's presence. There wasn't any, not in here, not at the moment. But if he looked in her bedroom...

Avoiding his eyes, she extended a hand. "May I take your coat?"

Gavin made a restless movement with his shoulders. "I'm not sure I'm staying here that long." He seemed to brace himself. "I came to...talk to you."

This time, she met his gaze, her shoulders thrown back, her chin high. She was a woman now, no longer the kid sister he had once guided through the labyrinth of life. "About what?"

Gavin thrust a hand through his hair, around the back of his neck. "I got a call from Anita."

"So you came to play big brother."

He looked tortured. "I owe you that much, don't you think?"

"I don't need a big brother anymore, I need a friend."

"You need more than a friend." He walked to a window, flicked aside a curtain, turned around and cast a glance over the room. "You have a knack for creating peace. I've always liked that about you, Jess."

He was retreating a little, and they both knew it. Jessica sat down and braced herself.

"When you regained your sight, the folks were worried. They were afraid you'd...go crazy, do all the things you hadn't been able to do before. When you didn't, they were relieved." He straightened and looked at her. "I know you're old enough now to live your own life...but...this is crazy. You're living the fantasy you created with a man I brought into the house at a time you were the most vulnerable." His face twisted. "It's no good, can't you see that? Rourke's not like you and me. He was a rich orphan, a hell-raiser, a boy growing up without anyone to love or discipline him."

"He's a man now—"

"When I brought him into the house, he didn't have a friend in the world who cared about him...except Scotty. Then he meets you," Gavin went on, as if she hadn't spoken, "and a few months later, his father performs an operation on you that restores your sight."

"He told me he had talked to his father—"

Gavin looked like a man on the rack. His fingers went up to his hair again. "Did he also tell you he bargained away his inheritance to finance your operation?"

The shock was all the more fierce because it was so unexpected. "That can't be true."

"Well, it is. I found it out when the folks came to me for help about their financial situation." He sighed, then looked as if he were bracing himself. "Rourke took back a mortgage on the farm and they thought they had finished paying it off. When they went to make the final payment, they discovered he hadn't cashed one of their checks. He'd set up a special account and when the last payment was made the account reverted to them along with the land. They couldn't believe it.

"They asked me to look into it and when I got started, one thing led to another. Through a friend who does legal work for our agency, I talked to the lawyer who wrote up the original contract. He thought I already knew about Rourke's bargain with his father. Rourke gave up his inheritance in exchange for Alcott's agreement to perform the operation on you.''

It couldn't be true, Jessica thought. Rourke couldn't have given up so much for her seven years ago... when she meant so little to him that he had walked away from her without looking back. "I don't believe you. You must be mistaken.'' She felt chilled, icy.

"It's the truth. The folks gave me orders to keep my mouth shut about the mortgage, but they didn't know about the inheritance. Neither did I till two weeks ago.'' He rose and paced to the window again. "My question is... what kind of a guy does a thing like that?'' Gavin turned. "What kind of a guy gives away everything he has and then just walks away? I could only come up with one answer, Jess. He never wanted that money in the first place...because it would have tied him down. He's never had anything permanent in his life...and he still doesn't want anything permanent.'' Something in his face changed, and his eyes darkened, as if he were feeling regret or remorse. He shook his head. "A guy like that doesn't care for one damn thing. And he'll never care for you the way you care for him.''

She looked at him, her eyes clear, her gaze unwavering. "You have no way of knowing that's true.''

He turned on her, fierce, intent. "He hasn't changed, Jess. And the trouble is...neither have you.'' His eyes moved over her, infinitely compassionate, infinitely sad. "Say you'll stop seeing him.''

Aware of a coldness creeping along her arms, she wrapped them around her middle. "I...can't do that.''

He stared at her for a long interval and shook his head. "I should have known better than to ask. You're as stubborn as he is—''

"You went to him? You asked him to stop seeing me?" Her topaz eyes darkened. Gavin groaned. "I've really put my foot in it, haven't I? As a father figure, I'm a failure." He put his hands on his knees and stood. Jessica caught his arm. "What . . . did he say?"

"He refused. No, don't look pleased. It's a matter of pride with him, nothing more. He's not about to let someone else tell him what to do." His eyes met hers. "In that, you're his equal."

"Gavin, I know you care for me and I care for you. But I'm in love with Rourke." Never before had she said the words aloud. It was a relief to know she could articulate them.

"Well. There's nothing more for me to say then. Is he . . . coming here tonight?"

"I . . . don't know."

"He hasn't moved in with you."

"No."

"Jess, listen, I . . ." At the look in her eyes, the words died. "If it hadn't been for me you would never have met him. I feel responsible."

"You needn't. What Rourke and I feel for each other now has gone far beyond what happened seven years ago."

"I see. All right. I'll say good-night then." But at the door, he paused. "We will be seeing you for Christmas, won't we?"

"Yes, of course."

He turned, and then swung back again. "Jessica. Don't . . . bring Rourke with you to the farm."

She met his eyes steadily. "He's spending the day with Scotty."

"Well, that's good. He won't be alone." He said goodbye, and went out the door, before she had time to ask why he cared if Rourke was alone on Christmas.

When Jessica was a child, her poor eyesight had made her dependent on others. When she regained her sight, she'd regained her independence as well. It had been a long, slow journey, But now to discover that she never could have done it at all if it hadn't been for Rourke... And at such a cost to him.

Why had he done it? Why? Why had he given up so much for her... and then walked away?

Gavin's voice echoed in her ears. *He doesn't want anything permanent... anything permanent....*

A half hour later, the phone rang. It was Rourke.

"I'd like to see you. Are you free this evening?"

Every instinct for self-preservation told her to say no. "Yes."

"I'll be over in about an hour. Have you eaten?"

"No."

If he heard the coolness in her voice, he wasn't reacting to it. "Do you like Chinese food?"

She told him she did. "Good. I'll bring some. Without cucumbers."

Acting on instinct rather than intellect, knowing that tonight she was leaving all the childish dreams behind her and becoming a woman in charge of her own life, she donned a Chinese robe. It was a form-fitting tube of silk in a hot rose color, the side closings and narrow mandarin collar decorated with white piping, the body of the robe sleek and fitted, the sleeves billowing.

She fastened all the buttons at the high neck, wrapped her hair up into a tight knot at the top of her head and knew what she'd felt instinctively was true, that silk covering her body from head to toe and her hair tied up in a knot on top of her head made her look infinitely more provocative than she might in a lacy negligee. She looked smooth, controlled, all woman, a package to be opened with great relish.

When Rourke came into the apartment an hour later, he cast a glance over her and his eyes narrowed. "Hello." He took off his coat and tossed it over the back of the couch, moving as he always did, with the same fluid ease, but his eyes held hers all the while. He was still for a moment, then he strode to the kitchen, deposited the carryout containers filled with food and turned back to her. "You look...quite...devastating. The problem is...I'm not sure whether the message is an invitation or a declaration of war."

She stared at him, saying nothing.

"Ah. War, is it? I wonder why? What is it I've done, Jessica?"

While she stood there trying to sort out her own conflicting emotions, he cupped her jaw with his hand. "What is that old adage about love thine enemy? You make that impossible task quite...easy." He leaned over to kiss her lightly on the lips, and that tenderness, that control destroyed every urge she had to hurt him.

Gently, he pulled her closer. "Jess. Tell me what's wrong."

"There's nothing wrong."

It was a lie, and that tilt of his lips told her he knew it. His other hand slid down to her hip, and he made a satisfied sound when he discovered she wore no undergarment. "I'm glad there's nothing wrong. I concur. Everything seems to be very...right." There was warmth in his voice and a hint of amusement. His hand cupped her buttock, sliding silk against skin in a thoroughly expert way.

"Rourke, I . . . must talk to you."

He didn't move a muscle. "That's why you're dressed like this . . . to talk?" He sounded amused. She made a move to escape him, but he turned her and pressed her into the wall, keeping her trapped against the wood, leaving his hands free to begin to undo the very top button under her chin. At that first brush of his knuckles against her throat, she was powerless to move away. The button at the base of her throat gave while his blue eyes held hers steadily, watching her for reaction . . . or protest.

Cool air wafted over her heated skin. Letting him begin to undress her in the living room was a tiny liberty; she'd granted him so many others during the course of their time together, yet then she hadn't known he'd given up the whole of his inheritance for her. She hadn't known she owed him everything, her ability to see, her independence, her life.

"I'm dressed like this because I thought that you should have what you paid for wrapped in a pretty package."

His fingers stilled on her flesh. He lifted his head and his eyes were dark with controlled anger. "So Gavin made good on his threat. And I thought he was harmless."

"Sometimes people can surprise you with their ability to hurt. How much was your inheritance, Rourke? How much did you give away to give me my sight?"

He met her eyes fearlessly. "I can't tell you that."

Even while she felt furious, ready to tear at him, she couldn't help admiring his unflinching honesty, his refusal to lie. "You must. You—"

He shook his head impatiently. "Even if I wanted to, I couldn't. It's an indeterminate amount based on investments made over the past ten years. There's no way I could put a numerical value on it. Nor would I want to.'' He caught her chin and tilted her face up to his. ''Jessica. You had nothing to do with the bargain I made with my father. It was the best thing that could have happened to me.''

''That's ridiculous. You can't possibly believe that.''

''I do. I'm sorry if that stretches your credulity, but I see no reason for me to stand here and argue about the logic of something I did seven years ago. At the moment, there's something much more interesting to do....'' He was on fire for her, wanting her as he never had. She was all delicious womanhood, scented and silked just for him, and he intended to take what was his. He caught her shoulders, and then, watching her face, he let his hands glide down her arms, creating a delicious friction of silk against skin.

She shuddered and when she would have moved away, he caught her hands. ''What do you want from me, Jessica? Should I beg your humble pardon because I gave you the gift of sight?''

''I want you to work out a repayment schedule.''

His face turned to stone. ''I had a feeling this idyllic existence of ours was made of fragile stuff. Well, maybe I don't give a damn what you want. If you think I'm going to let a few threats from your brother or your own enlarged sense of pride drive me out of your life, you're wrong.''

Jessica stared at him, unable to believe what he was telling her. He looked dangerous, a man who'd seen the dark side, a man not to be toyed with. She should have been afraid. She wasn't. Instead, a wildly flaring hope flashed through her.

As if he realized he'd said too much, he swung away from her and went to the couch to pick up his jacket, easing down to perch on the low back of the couch. "So now that we've seen just how constant your love is . . . suppose I tell you I don't want to 'work out a re-payment schedule,' nor do I want to leave. What would you say to that?"

His hand lay along his thigh, relaxed, brown, supple, a hand that had brought her delight she hadn't known was possible. But there was a tension in those relaxed fingers that told her he cared about her answer. Cared more than he wanted her to see.

"I'd say you're very intent on having everything your own way."

Rourke watched her, letting her see only the bland expression he'd schooled himself to show her. Inside, he felt as if he'd been ripped apart. He wanted to let his hands flow over that silk thing; he wanted to slide his fingers up into her hair and take it down strand by strand. Why had she done this? Why had she dressed so entic-ingly and then put distance between them, physically and mentally? He thought he knew her, but he didn't. Like a fool, he hadn't taken Gavin's threats seriously. He'd thought his secret was safe.

"If I had my way . . . we'd be in the bedroom right now."

"We can't . . . go on together. Not unless we come to some agreement."

He dropped the jacket to the back of the couch and folded his arms. "Things are exactly the same as they were last night. Nothing has changed."

Some part of his brain looked at what he was doing with amazement. He'd never fought to stay with a woman before. At the first sign a woman gave that she expected more than a fleeting affair, he'd walked out the door and hadn't looked back. Now Jessica had given him the opportunity to go... and he hadn't taken it. He was crossing a barrier he'd never crossed before... starting down a road he'd never traveled. And nothing on this God's earth could make him turn back.

"Everything has changed."

"Including," he said, in a soft, controlled tone, "your feeling about having me here?"

"I want you to stay but—"

"On your terms," he said in an even tone.

"There are no terms. I'm merely asking for a reasonable way to release me from this... obligation to you."

"There is no reasonable way," he snapped, his control breaking. He unfolded his arms and braced his hands on the back of the couch next to his thighs. "There are things you don't understand, things I can't explain. My father wanted my inheritance for other reasons. He wanted me out of his life and I wanted to go. The bargain suited us both."

"It doesn't suit me."

"I'm sorry. I wanted to leave behind something positive for you. There was no need for you to know, and I assumed you never would." He seemed to relax a little and that slow, devastating smile lifted his lips. "As far as I'm concerned, the debt has gone beyond the statute of limitations."

With a quiet resolve, she said, "I'm going to make out a check to you... and I want you to take it and cash it. I'll repay you... if it takes me the rest of my life."

He gave her a look that told her his mind was already leagues ahead of her. "And if I don't agree to your terms, I can leave tonight?"

She felt as if she couldn't breathe. "Yes."

He gazed at her with a look that bordered on cool disinterest. "I could lie and say I'd take the check and then tear it up in the morning."

"Yes, you could do that. But you won't."

"You know me better than I thought you did." He sat very, very still. "You leave me no alternative." He got up, and very deliberately, he picked up his suit jacket and put it on. "Goodbye, Jessica."

Regret washed over her, regret and an overwhelming urge to give in to him, to tell him that the money didn't matter, that nothing mattered but his staying.

"Well, how shall we end it? It was fun while it lasted? So long and no hard feelings?" The dark pain in his voice caught her by surprise. It matched the agony she felt.

"Rourke. Please. Don't go."

The look in her eyes arrested him. She had swallowed her pride and asked him to stay and she'd done it without blinking an eye. A deep surge of emotion swelled within Rourke. He saw, more clearly than he had ever seen before, how bleak his life would be without her. "I don't want a check, Jess. I didn't take your parents' money...and I won't take yours. I don't want your money...any more than I want your gratitude."

"Gratitude isn't what I'm feeling at the moment." She stepped closer to him.

"No more talk about checks?"

"No more...talk." Boldly, she slid her hands under his jacket.

His eyes darkened with wicked satisfaction. With exquisite care, he cupped her chin and brought his mouth down to hers. When he'd finished kissing her with such tenderness she felt as if her soul were lifted out of her body, he smiled down at her. "Thanks for not missing your cue."

"You . . . never intended to go at all, did you?"

Watching her, his eyes dark with an emotion she could only guess at, he said, "No."

"Then why did you put your suit coat on?"

His eyes were dark, arresting, as he said, "So you could help me take it—" the lips moved in a slow smile "—off."

MUCH LATER, after they had reheated the Chinese food, eaten and returned to bed for some much-needed sleep, Rourke lay beside Jessica, listening to the slow rhythmic sigh of her breathing.

Warm fingers reached out and caught his arm. "What is it?"

"Nothing," he said.

"You're not sleeping."

"Not yet. I will. It's all right. Go back to sleep."

She turned toward him in the darkness, waiting for the kiss the warm breath on her cheek told her she was going to receive.

Rourke knew he shouldn't be kissing her like this if he expected to get any sleep tonight. His hands reached to capture the silkiness of her hair, but he was the one who was trapped. Under his lips, the smooth skin of her temple felt like satin. He wanted, needed, to press his lips to more of that wonderfully textured skin. Jessica was his haven, his home, the home he'd never had.

She moved as if to press closer to him. Unable to refuse the sweet temptation she offered, he lowered his mouth to hers and drank from her, savoring the sweetness that she gave so generously.

The room faded. He was back, back in the stable once more, and he was kissing Jess, sweet, untouchable Jess, and there was no time, no world, no separateness. She moved drowsily, opening her arms and mouth to him, inviting him to touch, to take. He found her sweetness, her moist readiness. Before he could stop himself, he moved over her and matched his body with hers. Then he was one with her and the elation was unbearable.

CHAPTER THIRTEEN

ON CHRISTMAS DAY Rourke stood with Scotty in the kitchen, leaning against the counter, holding a tiny liqueur glass half full of peach-flavored schnapps. The dinner was over, and Rourke felt pleasantly sated and content. There was no other place in the world he'd rather be at the moment. And yet... watching Scotty's spoon swirl the warm chocolate in the pan, Rourke thought of the lady who put chocolate chips in her peanut butter sandwiches and wished Jessica were here, standing beside him. She could have been... if he'd had the courage to ask. Scotty would have been delighted to have her. But Jessica had planned to go to the farm and be with her family, and Rourke hadn't wanted to ask her to change her plans. Later on tonight, he would go to her apartment and deliver the small parcel he carried in his pocket and they'd celebrate Christmas together then. At the thought of that private celebration, his body warmed.

Dragging his mind back to the present, he raised his tiny glass to Scotty. "My compliments to the cook. The dinner was excellent."

"I do what's easy. Ham that some kindly person in a factory has already cooked, potatoes that do nothing but sit in the oven in their foil. The women, they make a lot of fuss, you know, but there's nothing to cooking if you keep your dishes simple."

Rourke gazed at the melting chocolate and the long-stemmed cherries Scotty had taken out of the jar and set in neat rows on a paper towel to drain. "I don't think I can eat another thing."

Scotty smiled. "That's what I always told Fran. And she always said, 'you'll eat just one chocolate-covered cherry, Scotty McDonald, or you'll not be sleeping in my bed tonight.' And of course, I always ate just one." Scotty's smile was very male, very adult.

It was a Christmas ritual at Scotty's house, the cherry dipping after Christmas dinner, just before the gifts were opened. It was also the way Scotty paid homage to the woman who had been his wife. Rourke remembered Fran McDonald as a short, plump woman with boundless energy. She didn't walk, she bustled. She didn't hug, she surrounded. Her sudden death just a year before his mother's had saddened Rourke ... and nearly destroyed Scotty.

Scotty lifted the spoon to let the chocolate spin a sweet, cocoa-brown thread down into the pan. "Your father called. He wants to see you."

Rourke stood stock-still, absorbing the shock of Scotty's words, knowing his canny uncle had waited until now, when Rourke, mellowed by good food, good talk and good liqueur, would be most receptive. "What a strange thing for him to want," he drawled, his eyes on Scotty's face. "I wonder what brought that about."

"He heard you were in town." Scotty kept his tone casual and moved the spoon around the pan. "It's past time you made your peace with him."

"You're my true father, Scotty. You always have been."

Scotty stopped stirring and looked up at Rourke. "I'm pleased you think of me that way, my boy. I regard you as my son, and nothing will ever change that. So as father to son, I'm saying, exchanging a few civil sentences with Alcott won't hurt you. It might do you a world of good."

"We have nothing to say to each other."

As if he hadn't heard, Scotty went on in the same even tone, "Can't imagine what this day must be like for him. His wife celebrating her divorce in her own apartment, his butler retiring...that big house must seem very empty."

Rourke raised dark blue eyes to Scotty's lighter ones. "How is that any different than it ever was?"

"He's made the first move, son. Think what a large dose of humble pie he had to eat just to pick up the phone and call here."

"He should have called me."

"He knows you well enough to know what you'd have said."

"And he knows you well enough to know you'd plead his case."

Scotty's eyes sparkled with love...and wisdom. "Not doing too good a job, am I? Promise me you'll think about it?"

Rourke wanted to say no. But here in Scotty's kitchen, surrounded by the warm smell of chocolate mingling with Scotty's affection, he couldn't be churlish. "I'll think about it."

It wasn't much of a concession, but it was a concession, and the look on Scotty's face told Rourke his answer had pleased the older man. Rourke realized he'd always waited for and savored that look of approbation on Scotty's face.

The chocolate was ready. One by one, Scotty dipped the cherries in by their stems and set them on a buttered

tray. When he finished, the delicacies went into the refrigerator and the pan was set in the sink to soak.

"Now, to the presents." Scotty wiped his hands on a
towel and clapped Rourke on the shoulder. "Come, boy.
Let's see what Santa Claus has brought you."

Sitting cross-legged beside Scotty's Christmas tree,
Rourke opened the small box with his name on it. Inside, nestled in cotton, was an old-fashioned gold pocket
watch. He raised dark eyes to Scotty.

"It belonged to my father, your grandfather. I had it
cleaned and repaired for you. It's in good working order."

Rourke held the watch in the palm of his hand, looking down at it, feeling emotions of a dozen different
kinds wash through him. Here was a gift far beyond its
intrinsic value. Scotty was giving him the family torch,
the flame, a part of Scotty's own past to carry into the
future.

"It's a railroad watch. You have to hold the body of
the watch in one hand and get a firm grip on the stem
with the other in order to set it. Your grandfather worked
as a conductor on the Buffalo and Erie railroad for forty
years." Rourke looked up and found Scotty watching
him. "He was a constant man, a good man—" Scotty
paused "—a faithful man. His blood runs through your
veins, too, you know, along with mine. Your father isn't
your only ancestor. When you look at the watch...
remember that."

A constant man. A good man. A faithful man. His
grandfather. The surge of emotion that coursed through
Rourke was nearly uncontrollable. His eyes dark, he
raised his head to gaze at Scotty. "I'll remember."

THE DAY AFTER CHRISTMAS, shortly after ten o'clock in the morning, Jessica collected the presents she'd received from Gavin and her parents and packed her case to leave the farm. The roads were snowy and it took her a little longer than the usual hour to drive back to her apartment.

Time didn't matter. It was Friday, a company-designated floating holiday, a day on which she could do anything she wanted to do. In the hallway, she set down her case to fish for her keys and open the door, when she saw the slip of white paper wedged in the crack of the frame. Her heart pounding, she unfolded it, and recognized Rourke's strong, slashing script.

Thought you were coming back tonight. Waited as long as I could but found it isn't true that only horses can sleep standing up. Call me. R.

She let herself into the apartment, tossed keys, coat and case on the floor by the couch and headed for the telephone.

He sounded drowsy, as if he'd just woke up. How long had he waited last night outside her apartment, falling asleep on his feet?

"I'm sorry I missed you," she told him.

"I wanted to wish you a Merry Christmas."

"It isn't too late."

He hesitated. She said quickly, "Come over for dinner. We'll have something simple."

"Are you sure it isn't too much trouble?"

His formality pleased her. Despite the intimacies they had shared, he regarded her as someone worthy of his best manners.

"It won't be any trouble."

"What time would you like me?"

His formality had vanished like the wind. The husky tone told her he'd used the provocative turn of phrase with precise intent.

She wanted to say, immediately. Instead she said, "How does five-thirty sound?"

"Five-thirty sounds good."

She hung up the phone and the world twisted, turned, became bright as a burning star. Her day at the farm had been flat. She'd tried desperately to hide her disappointment that Rourke hadn't made any attempt to arrange a way to be with her on Christmas. At the farm, she'd felt Gavin watching her as they opened the presents, and later, as they stuffed themselves with turkey and trimmings and gathered around the piano to sing Christmas carols. She'd wanted to tell him she hadn't complied with his request to exclude Rourke from her visit to the farm, that the reason Rourke wasn't with her was because he hadn't wanted to be. But she didn't want to spoil the day for her brother or her parents, so she'd said nothing. But for her, there was no sparkle in the day. Later in the afternoon, saying she needed the exercise to walk off all the food she'd eaten, she put on her coat and boots and went out to the barn, hoping that there, she would feel closer to him.

She didn't. The barn was nothing but a creaking, empty building that looked as if it should have been torn down years ago. Her father had sold the cows when Gavin went away to school, and the horses the year she'd left. There was nothing here now but wisps of hay, shadows and memories. She reached into the horses' feeding bunk for a spear of hay, twisting it between her gloved fingers. Seven years ago, she hadn't been able to see the duskiness, the cracked boards, the broken pieces of harness. But Rourke had. And it hadn't made any difference. He'd still taken her in his arms and kissed her. Was her love like this barn, out of date? Was she clinging to something that should have been destroyed years ago?

Jessica had returned to the house, shaken. She hadn't slept well that night, and in the morning she'd been anxious to return to the city, where her memories of Rourke were recent and the loving they'd shared was not a child's fantasy, but real . . . and adult.

Jessica stood in her apartment and shook her head as if to free her mind of her thoughts of the day before, of the insecurity she'd felt when Rourke hadn't called, of the aching need for him to be there with her, of the foreboding sense of anxiety she had about what would happen when his work was done and it was time for him to go. She couldn't think about tomorrow. Today was what counted. He was going to be there with her tonight and she had a million things to do to prepare.

By the time Rourke knocked, she flew to the door, too anxious to see him to wait, too much in love to hide her feelings. When he stepped inside, he took one look at her face and opened his arms.

She went into them joyously, burrowing into the soft wool of his open overcoat, smelling the crisp coldness of winter air that clung to him. Underneath, like a sensuous invitation, his expensive scent beckoned, reminding her of his maleness . . . and his desirability.

She leaned into him, her body seeking contact with his. He took her slender weight with ease, his arms folding around her, one hand coming up to cup the back of her head.

"Yes," he breathed into her hair. "That's exactly how I feel. Hungry. So hungry for you . . ." His hands moved down to her hips and he lifted her into the cradle of his body, letting her feel his desire for her.

She breathed in sharply, unable to hide her response. He lifted her off her feet and into his arms. "Did you leave anything on the stove that will burn?"

"Everything is on low."

"Not quite—" here, his mouth lifted in a slow, sensual smile "—everything."

ROURKE SLIPPED out of the bed, waking Jessica from her doze. He was back before she had made the decision to climb out of bed and see what he was doing. "Merry Christmas," he said. In the soft light of the lamp beside the bed, she caught the glimmer of a gold chain. He raised her hand and clasped the delicate bracelet around her wrist. Dangling from one link was an exquisitely sculpted horse.

She closed her fingers over it, tears in her eyes. He remembered. He remembered everything, just as she did.

"Merry Christmas, Jess."

"It's beautiful. Thank you. I . . . your present is out under my tree."

"I'll get it later." He lifted her hand and kissed the sensitive skin just below the strand of gold.

With her other hand, she threaded her fingers through the crisply dark, curling hair on his chest and said daringly, "Happy New Year . . . my love."

As she had half suspected it might, that simple mention of the future destroyed the rapport between them. Bare as Rourke was, the sheet draped casually over his hips, his head propped on his elbow, his breath warming her temple, the tension that arrowed through his body was as evident to her as if it had shot through her own. He lowered his arm and lay back on the pillow as if he didn't want to look at her. Instinctively, needing to touch him to stave off his thoughts as well as her own, her fingers brushed over his chest, encountering, almost by accident, the hard nub of his male nipple hidden in the nest of hair. His body's reaction was instantaneous. Needing this sign that she could affect him physically if not emotionally, she caressed that nub, feeling it lift and harden under her fingers. His face still wore that smooth bland look she knew he used to hide his emotions, but there was no denying the response of his body... or of his willingness to submit to her caresses. He lay like a statue in the glow of the lamplight, looking bare and male and infinitely desirable. She trailed her hand down the deep curve of his abdomen, paused at his navel, and then slowly, found the velvet richness of him.

It took all the control he had to lie unmoving under those softly delicate, wildly exciting hands of hers. He accomplished it only by stern force of will. Yet there was added titillation in disciplining his body to stillness under her hands. His quiet acceptance encouraged her to take new, more daring paths with her fingers. She wandered, discovering textures, smoothness, hardness, softness. Under lids drooping with sensual pleasure, he watched the look of intense sexual delight flush her cheeks, darken her eyes.

She was more skilled now in the tactile language of lovers, and the tension of his body and the ripple of his skin revealed to her what his face concealed, that he shared the pleasure she was feeling. He was controlled now... but how long would he retain that control? A deep womanly instinct told her it would only be a matter of time... and touch. Her fingers drifted over him, lightly at first, then more possessively.

He breathed in sharply...and as suddenly as it had begun the battle was over. She had won.

He grabbed her wrist but he didn't pull her hand away. "Jessica—"

"Do you want me to stop?" She was wide-eyed, innocent, a seductive Lorelei.

This was dangerous territory and he knew it. Never had he allowed a woman to wield such sure, feminine power over him. He felt as if he were sinking deep into the heart of her and there was no way to stop.

Control. He must regain control. Catching her hand and pulling it out of the way, he lunged on top of her, pinning her down with his weight and shackling her wrists with his hands. "What do you think?" he said, and looked down into her eyes, and knew that, at this moment, his regaining control had been an illusion. For he was hers, and the power he thought he'd held so securely in his grasp had slipped to the woman who looked up at him with heated invitation in her eyes.

DRESSED IN SOFT GRAY PANTS, his chest and feet bare, he leaned against the counter, watching her as she worked in the kitchen, telling himself he was a fool. He'd made love to other women and walked away from them, and it hadn't mattered. Now, suddenly, it mattered. He should get dressed and walk out the door before...what? Before he hurt her any more?

The damage was already done. But even while he stood there, his body sated with her lovemaking, he wanted to reach out and touch her. He wasn't going anywhere, and he knew it.

She hadn't bothered to dress, she'd merely pulled on a peach silk robe and tied it tightly around her waist. The garment moved seductively around her legs as she walked, taking the tossed salad she'd prepared ahead of time out of the refrigerator and dishing it out into wooden bowls, spooning the beef tips in wine she'd had simmering in the oven onto their plates. She retrieved the wine bottle from the freezer where she'd put it to chill quickly and handed it to him to open.

There was something in the silent way he watched Jessica that both excited and chilled her. What was he thinking? She would have given the world to know. Yet she did know. He was thinking about leaving. Shaken by the thought, she leaned back against the counter.

Rourke extracted the cork efficiently with an expertise she'd come to expect from him, but his mind wasn't on it, she could see that. He didn't need to concentrate to do things handily. He was lean, elegant and graceful as he poured the wine into the glasses she'd set out, equally deft as he replaced the bottle in the ice bucket.

When he took the chair opposite hers, she wrapped her pride around her like a mantle, lifted bright topaz eyes to him and picked up her glass. ''Shall we drink to the New Year...or would you rather continue to deny its existence?''

This was his opening, he knew it. He also knew, after one look into her eyes, that she had given it to him purposely.

He leaned back in his chair, fighting to control the tenseness threatening to tighten muscles relaxed from Jessica's lovemaking. ''My contract ends on the fifteenth of January.''

The sudden tremor of her fingers made the glass tilt fractionally. She steadied her hand and didn't spill a drop. It was what she had expected to hear; why should it come as a shock that he could coolly sit across from her and recite the date of his departure as if he'd been counting the days? "I know that."

Jessica drank the wine, which was cool, crisp and clear. How was it possible to taste anything when the world was crumbling around her? She set the glass carefully on the table. "You're going to leave when your contract is done."

She was making it easy for him. Never had a woman made it so simple for him to tell her he was leaving. Then why did it feel as if she were twisting a knife in his gut? "There was never a question of my doing anything else."

Her throat felt full and thick. She tried to remember the things Scotty had told her about Rourke's home life, about his mother's lingering sickness and his loss of her at an impressionable age, about the lack of attention . . . and then, at the onset of his maturity and good looks, too much attention from the wrong kind of women. Rourke's cynicism was bone deep.

Jessica knew all that. She also knew that she was looking at the man whose body she knew as well as her own. Knowing he planned to cold-bloodedly walk out of her life when his job ended, made her hurt as she had never hurt before in her life.

"Did I ever give you the impression it would be otherwise?" He twisted the knife a little deeper, all the while looking blandly unmoved by what he was doing to her.

"No."

"Would you like me to leave?"

Not a flicker of expression crossed his face. Pride screamed, telling her to say yes. Something far deeper and more basic ordered her to say, "No."

The meal she'd prepared that had seemed delicious a moment ago was like ashes in Rourke's mouth. He'd asked her to make a choice between her pride and him, and within the space of a breath, she'd made it. She'd swallowed her pride...and given him an example of courage he couldn't match.

He flung the fork down against the plate, and the crack of the utensil against china echoed through the room like a gunshot. Pushing back his chair, he went round to her and grasped her shoulders, pulling her up to him.

"I...watched...love die once. I won't do it again."

His eyes crackled with emotion. Hers matched his, bright, sharp, knowing. At long last, she'd penetrated the barrier. "Whose love do you think will die? Mine? Or yours? Are you afraid I'll grow tired of you? Or that you'll grow tired of me? I've loved you for seven years, Rourke—"

"You don't love me—you never loved me."

"Do you think if you keep telling yourself that long enough," she said coolly, "you'll finally begin to believe it?"

His eyes moved over her face, their blue sharpness a pain slicing her flesh. "Jessica." Her name was dragged from him, a hoarse sound of agony. "Don't try to...make this any more than it is. We're having an affair...the affair we should have had seven years ago. But when it's over, that's all we'll have."

"You don't believe that any more than I do. During these past few days, you've shown me what depth of feeling you're capable of."

Rourke's face twisted into a harsh, agonized expression. "Don't tell me what I am...what I feel. Let go of me, Jess. Just...let go."

The pain in his eyes mirrored her own but when she spoke, her voice was quiet, composed. "You're the one who's holding me."

His hands tightened once, spasmodically, as if his body was fighting his mind, and then his hands slid down her arms and she was free.

He went into the bedroom, and when he came out, fully dressed with his coat on, she knew she had lost. Rourke stood across the living room from her, the same man she had greeted so joyously only a few hours ago, a cool stranger with a cool face, his suit and overcoat in immaculate order, all traces of her loving erased from his body...and from his mind. At the door, he turned. "It was good with you, Jess. Damn good."

He went out quickly. Blindly, she reached out, her hands closing around a delicate vase she'd searched for hours to find. The long search only seemed to heighten her pleasure at lifting that vase and heaving it at the door with all her might. The crash of china against wood gave her an immense satisfaction...and made her realize with a sudden, intense clarity that Rourke was more blind than she had ever been. She collapsed on the couch and buried her face in her hands, rediscovering the pain and tears she'd thought were gone forever.

JESSICA HAD A WEEK'S VACATION left. She'd been saving it for a getaway winter vacation in January, since the company allowed its employees to carry over days into the first quarter, but on Monday morning, she called Brewster Hilton and told him that since she wasn't going to be allowed to start on a new project until the problem was found in the program she'd designed, she was taking off the days between Christmas and New Year's.

If he was surprised, he hid it. "I have no problem with that. Perhaps it's a wise idea, Jessica. We'll see you on the following Monday."

She wasn't a coward, but she knew she couldn't face going in to the office during those three days between Christmas and New Year's Day. Many people used their vacation time to extend the holidays, and the office would be nearly deserted. She and Rourke would be, for all intents and purposes, alone. And she did not want to be alone with him, not until she'd had some time to recover... and think.

She thought best while she was cleaning, and so, on Monday, after a bleak weekend when she'd done little but pick up the vase shards from the carpet so she could open and close her apartment door, she cleaned. She started in the bedroom first. There were crumbs in the bed and on the floor. She ripped away the sheets, carrying them to the washing machine tucked behind folding doors in her bathroom. She dusted her bedroom furniture, vacuumed the floor. And all the while, the tiny horse dangled against her wrist, reminding her that she was back exactly where she had been seven years ago. She loved Rourke, and he was going to walk out of her life again. The only difference was, this time, he'd given her advance notice.

Everyone was right. Anita was right, Gavin was right. They'd all been right about him. She moved the vacuum over the floor with a vicious energy born of frustration. She'd been so sure they were wrong.

A need to get out of the apartment swept over her. With the same energy with which she'd begun to clean, she put the vacuum cleaner away, showered and dressed.

Climbing into the car, she told herself she didn't know where she was going, she was just going to drive. But she guided the car out onto the highway that ringed the city and led north to the park where she and Rourke had once laughed and played together.

It was close to noon when she reached the secluded spot where they'd built the snowmen. She stopped the car and got out, scuffing her boots through the new layer of snow that covered the ground. Had she expected to see their snow sculptures still standing? Foolishly, she had.

Madame Pompadour hadn't melted, she'd been knocked down by careless hands more interested in destroying than creating. Bits and pieces of her lay on the ground, pieces that had been molded by her lover's hands. Jessica looked at the snow mounds and felt as if she had been ripped apart, just as the snow lady had.

A strange, energetic fury swept over Jessica. "Stop lying there falling apart all over the place," she told the various parts of the aristocratic snow lady as she walked around surveying the damage. "Where's your backbone? Where's your spine? Don't you have any more sense than to let other people come along and tear you into little pieces?"

Feverishly, Jessica began packing a snowball, talking while she worked. "I'm surprised at you, falling apart this way. I thought you had more class." Turning, she clapped the snowball on the stump of the skirt that was left. Bit by bit, she began to rebuild the snow lady on a smaller scale.

How long she worked, she wasn't sure. When she finished, the lady was a foot shorter and her bustline wasn't as expertly sculpted as when Rourke's hands had molded her, but her head was on and her hairdo nearly restored to its former glorious height.

Jessica stood back to admire her handiwork.

The snow lady stood there, mocking her. *You're no better than I am. You let people rip you apart. Go put yourself together. You know you need him, love him, want him. You know he's happy when he's with you and*

*that he's good for you...and you're good for him. Yet
you're out here in the forest with me instead of fighting
for him. You're letting him walk away from you without
a single protest. You're saving face instead of saving your
love. You're acting like the scared teenager you were
seven years ago instead of the adult woman you are. Stop
hiding behind your pride and do something.*

Dazed, Jessica asked, "What can I do?"

Fight for him.

"How? How can I fight for him?"

The snow lady gave her a mocking look. *You're the one
with the brain and two capable hands, you figure it out.*

"My man tossed me away, Madame Pompadour."

An imperious, icy look was the only answer.

"He said he'd watched love die once and he didn't
want to do it again."

Whose love? asked Madame Pompadour.

"Whose love? Why, ours."

*Your love? Your love is alive and well. Whose love did
he watch die the first time? Was it his parents' love for
each other?*

Jessica stood stunned. "I don't know."

Then find out.

"How?"

The answer echoed inside her head. *Scotty. Scotty
would know.*

Filled with the same joyous elation she felt when she
had solved a technical problem in a program, she
snatched off her wool cap and tossed it in the air. Catching it, Jessica turned, made a waist-deep bow to the imperious snow lady and raced back to the car.

It seemed to take forever to reach Scotty's house. She
made a screeching turn into the driveway and ran up the

steps to pound on the door. He answered it, surprise and then pleasure creasing his face. "Hello, lass."

The sight of him brought her down to earth. "Scotty? I...I need to talk to you."

"Do you now, lass? And what seems to be the problem?"

"I'm going to lose him...unless you can help me."

He was silent for a moment, his eyes patient. "What is it you think I can do?"

There were questions from Scotty, no admonitions. Just acceptance. He was a marvelous man. She loved him almost as much as she did Rourke. "You can...tell me about Rourke's father. You've never told me about his father."

There was another little pause. "I had to wait until you loved the lad enough to ask." His eyes brightened with welcome. "Come in, lass. I'll put the teakettle on and we'll have a cup of tea, a chocolate cherry or two...and a long overdue talk about Rourke's father."

In JESSICA'S CUBICLE at Consolidated, seated at his desk, Rourke grasped the receiver and tried to hang on to the fragment of his temper that he still had left. "I don't care how many people are on vacation or who you're missing. I want those invoices out here tomorrow."

Rourke didn't bother to listen to the other speaker's excuses. "You have heard of express mail, I presume." Icily polite, he waited, sardonically arching an eyebrow. "Good. Then use it." Stalling the final attempt at procrastination, Rourke said roughly, "You'll be reimbursed," and dropped the phone.

"That's hardly the way to win friends and influence customers."

Rourke turned in the padded chair to find Brewster Hilton standing just inside the blue barrier. When had he come in? The man was like a damn ghost, moving up behind people on those rubber-soled shoes. His jacket was off and his shirt sleeves rolled back, a concession to the informality of the quiet floor and the small crew of people remaining at work on the Monday before New Year's.

Rourke leaned back in his chair. "They're your customers, not mine." He let his eyes drift over Brewster's tall frame. "If I could get hold of someone other than peons who don't know anything, or executives who don't know anything, I wouldn't need to apply the pressure."

"I assume that, as executives who don't know anything, you are excluding present company?"

Rourke stretched his long legs and pulled at the crease of his pants. "Why should I? It seems to me, if you had known your job, you would have tested this system before you put it into use."

"It was tested," Hilton said, his tone bland.

"When?" Rourke said the word in exactly the same tone that Hilton had used.

"A week before it was put into service. And again, on the day before."

"Did you oversee the test?"

"Yes."

Rourke kept his eyes on Hilton steadily, calling on all the lessons of control he'd learned over the years. "And you consider yourself knowledgeable enough about the system to certify that, when you ran the tests, it was working in good order?"

Hilton's eyes narrowed. "Am I being interrogated?"

Rourke swung his chair away from Hilton and faced the computer, as if he were no longer interested in the man's presence. "I was just curious. Would you say you're as familiar with the system as Jessica is?"

It was quiet enough on the floor for Rourke to hear Hilton's breathing. "Of course I am."

"You're conversant in the language the program was written in, PL1?"

"It was my job to learn it—"

"Ah. A conscientious man. Most commendable." Rourke swung away from the computer to face Hilton again. "Then perhaps you won't mind if I get on with my work?"

I've made a mistake, Rourke thought, as Hilton turned without another word and stalked away. It was stupid to put the man on guard more than he already was. Rourke's head ached and he couldn't concentrate, but that was no reason to make a mistake that he probably couldn't undo.

He'd called the office in New York City and asked them to run a financial check on Hilton, but because of the holidays, work was backlogged and he hadn't received the report. He would have given all the money he had in his pocket to have that report in front of him right now.

He dragged his eyes away from the computer screen to look out the window. Jessica's philodendron, Brunhilda, dangled from the curtain rod looking complacent . . . and dry. Somebody ought to water that plant.

Considerate dude, aren't you, Caldwell? Worrying about your lady's plants, even though you know the reason she took unscheduled vacation these three days was because she couldn't face you. What a Galahad you are.

His mouth twisting, he rose from his chair and went to get a cupful of water.

'When he returned to the cubicle, Todd Wainwright stood there, shifting his weight from one foot to the other and looking around nervously, as if he expected Rourke to jump out from behind one of the desks. "Oh. There you are."

"Yes," Rourke murmured, "here I am."

Wainwright looked at the cup in the other man's hand and then up at his face, as if he couldn't understand why Rourke was going to drink plain, unadulterated water. "This came express for you. I signed for it and thought I'd better wait until I could give it to you directly." Wainwright handed Rourke a bulky yellow envelope. Rourke tossed it onto the desk and turned his back to Wainwright. His attention on the plant, he emptied the cup of water over it. When he swung around again, he saw Wainwright hadn't moved. The younger man's eyes were going from the monitor to the yellow envelope Rourke had thrown onto the desk.

"Have you found anything yet?"

Something clicked inside Rourke's head. He hadn't seriously suspected Wainwright as having anything to do with the plot to undermine the company's business, but now the man stood there looking nervous. Had he been wrong about Hilton?

"Not yet." He hesitated, then, with great care, set the cup on the desk. "But if I'm lucky, that package you brought might give me a part of the solution."

Todd looked up at Rourke, swallowed once and said, "Jessica didn't do it."

Rourke's eyes narrowed. "Do you have any proof to substantiate your statement?"

Wainwright's chin came up. He looked like an errant boy facing his teacher. "She couldn't have done it. She's too proud of her job here. She just received an award a little while ago.''

This was news to Rourke. "A cash award?"

Todd nodded. "You didn't know that, did you?"

"No," Rourke admitted. "Jessica didn't mention it."

"She wouldn't. She's too modest. That's why Anita thought—" his eyes lifted to Rourke's "—why *I* thought I should mention it to you."

So. Anita had primed Wainwright to initiate this confrontation. Rourke remembered Anita's defense of Jessica at the Christmas party. The woman might be a bit of a flake, but she was a loyal flake. Jessica was lucky. But if it was Wainwright rather than Hilton who tampered with the computer, Ms. Adams had put her lover in a damn difficult position. It might be wise to probe just a little deeper. "It's possible Jessica felt the money she got wasn't a large enough sum and decided to augment it with—"

"You *are* a bastard," Todd said, his face brightening with color.

Rourke relaxed, his hip against the edge of the desk, his smile bland. "I have it on quite good authority that my mother and my father were married before I was born."

"That's not what I mean and you know it. Anita warned me, but I didn't believe it. I said you were a reasonable man, that you'd listen to what I had to say—"

"And I have listened," Rourke said softly, steel in his voice. "Now, if you've completed the assignment Anita gave you, I suggest you get back to work." It was hard to look at the man and realize it was Anita's courage and loyalty that had moved Todd Wainwright to spring to Jessica's defense, not his own. Rourke had seen Jessica soothing and solving Todd's problems along with everyone else's. Didn't the man have any guts?

Todd's face turned a darker red, as if he had picked up the tenor of the other man's thoughts. "If you pin this on Jessica, it will be a frame, a deal you worked out with Hilton."

Rourke's face turned wintry with barely contained anger. "I don't work out deals."

Wainwright's eyes were bright with tension. "That had better be true."

His back stiff, Wainwright dodged around a barrier and left Rourke alone with nothing moving in the room but the pulsing cursor on the screen and Brunhilda's gentle swaying against the window.

Sitting down, Rourke took up the yellow packet. It contained the invoices he'd been waiting for from Cleveland. With them, he constructed a fairly accurate picture of that particular order.

He expected it to be a tedious job to locate the corresponding order among those cataloged by the computer. It was surprisingly simple. So was the problem. The Cleveland order had been loaded on a truck headed for San Diego.

Rourke sat back in his chair, staring at the computer screen. The orders hadn't been changed . . . but the destinations had. It was so simple. So neat, clean and orderly. The one small key was like the Rosetta Stone, the breakthrough to the puzzle that had been incomprehensible hieroglyphics a moment ago. All the destinations had been changed. He didn't know what the exact combination was, but he didn't need that information. All he needed to know was how the change had been made in the program . . . and who had made it.

It had obviously been done by someone with a passion for neat, clean orderly changes.

No. He couldn't think that way. Not yet.

You won't have to, his mind whispered. Any change will be logged in by the person who made it.

Rourke scrolled back in to the part of the program where the destinations had been determined . . . and saw immediately what had happened.

The pointers had been changed.

The changes were logged in on the computer's clock, giving the time and date. And the name of the person who had made the changes was filed below.

Jessica Moore.

Rourke sat very still, absorbing the blow. Jessica had changed the destinations.

His mind cast around desperately for other possibilities. There were none. To go on line and work on the program, Jessica had to enter her password and her name and the computer had recorded it. There could be no mistake.

How could she have done this and thought she wouldn't be found out? It was so obvious. If it hadn't been for the holidays, and the slowness of response to his request for the orders from Cleveland, he would have discovered this a week ago. Surely she'd known when he received the invoices from one supplier, he would know the truth.

She had known. She had taken him into her arms, her bed, her life. She'd professed her love, even though she'd known he wouldn't reciprocate. She'd been far more clever than he'd ever dreamed she could be.

She'd made a fool of him.

He fought for control, but he couldn't control that clench of his stomach, that cold clamminess crawling up

cursor...and the file notations he'd been reading slid over a notch.

Arrested, he moved the cursor again. Again, the file notations slid over. They were out of alignment. Whoever had made the change had forgotten to reinsert the tab that would keep those file notations lined up with the others.

Every nerve in his body tingling, he scrolled through other parts of the module. Changes had been made, most of them by Jessica. Not a single one was missing the tab. Neat, orderly Jessica, who'd spent her first years in shadowy darkness, had a fetish for order.

She wouldn't have forgotten the tab.

Stunned, he returned to the part of the program where the problem was, moving the cursor around again. Again, the file notations slid over a space, indicating that the tab had not been replaced.

Someone else had made the change...and logged in Jessica's name.

But in order to do that, the operator would have had to know Jessica's password.

"Having any luck?"

The hair on the back of Rourke's neck prickled in alarmed surprise, and he whirled around in his chair. Brewster Hilton stood there, looking down at him.

"Not yet," Rourke said, calling on every single skill he had to control his expression. If Hilton could creep up on him that way, he could certainly have done the same to Jessica. And he would have been able to see her typing out her password. "I'm sure I'll find something soon."

In the afternoon, Rourke went back to Jessica's apartment.

He hadn't expected a warm welcome...but her icy greeting pricked his conscience more than he had expected. So did her gray, drawn face. If she'd slept last night, there was no evidence of it.

And why shouldn't she have lain awake? Hadn't he threatened her with a jail sentence?

Torn between the agonizing need to pull her into his arms and the necessity of finding out the truth from her, he said, "It's possible there's been a mistake."

Jessica's head reeled. What kind of cruel game was he playing with her? First he accused her of committing the crime, then he offered her hope.

"A mistake? What kind of mistake?"

"I'm not sure," he said slowly, watching her. "That's what I came to find out."

"Computers don't make mistakes like that."

"But people do."

A measure of her control snapped. "Don't you mean *I* made the mistakes?"

"The changes could have been made by someone else...someone who knew your password. I came here to ask you some questions that I hope will give me the right answer."

"You already have your answer...the one your *proof* gave you."

"Stop it!" He stepped forward and grasped her shoulders. "If you don't help me...I can't help you."

She flung her head up to stare at him through eyes dark with anguish. "Last night you were ready to arrest me and tonight you want to help me?"

"Don't you understand? The changes were made with your password, logged to your name. Unless we can figure out how it was done, I don't have a hope in hell of clearing you."

"You believe in me? You don't think I used you sexually or enticed you to cover up my guilt?"

His face changed subtly. He gazed at her, his eyes moving over her face and up to her hair. She had it pinned up, as if she were cleaning. "Let's say I'm suspending judgment."

Rourke caught the faint scent of lemon oil furniture polish. Superneat Jessica had been cleaning an apartment that was already spotless. The conviction grew that he had done her a great wrong. "There are shadows under your eyes. Haven't you been sleeping well?"

To Jessica, his presence in her apartment where she'd spent twenty-four hours in torment was just another form of torture. One straight strand of hair had fallen over his forehead, something that happened very rarely and his eyes were full of her reflection. He was warm and close, his male scent achingly familiar. "No, I haven't been sleeping well. I . . . would you please take your hands off me?"

For the second time since he'd stepped into her apartment, he felt a stab of pain. "Of course," he said, knowing he'd been taking an unkind advantage, putting his hands on her. He'd needed to touch her. "Is there any way Hilton would have had access to your password? Did he ever ask you for it?"

She moved a careful distance away from him. "No."

"Do you remember what word you were using at that time?"

Jessica shook her head. It was an effort for her to think, he could see that. Still, he couldn't stop probing, not if he was going to get at the truth. "Not exactly, but since we change our codes every month, I could probably work my way back to it. When was the change logged in?"

"October the fifth. Four-forty p.m."

"The day before we started sending the information out to the terminals. Clever of . . . whoever."

"The code, Jessica."

"I think, at that time, I was using my initials. Jam."

Rourke looked at Jessica. "Jam?"

"I know it isn't very sophisticated—"

"Jam?" he repeated, like a man possessed.

"I'm sorry it isn't something more exotic—"

"You should be," he said roughly, but he was smiling at her oddly, as if she were a child who'd given him the right answer. "On the keyboard that would be written with your index finger, little finger, index finger in lower rows of letters. A word incredibly easy to figure out if someone was watching over your shoulder. Did Hilton ever come and look over your shoulder while you worked?"

"No . . . not that I can remember . . ." she said.

"A thing like that would be hard to remember. Try. Did you ever turn around and find he'd wandered in and was standing behind you?"

"No—yes! Yes, he did that more than once. I'd forgotten about it. At the time, I thought it was just another phase in his campaign to unnerve me."

"All right. We have opportunity, now all we need is motive. And I'm working on that." He went to the door, looking like a restless tiger who'd grown impatient in the confines of his cage. Then he turned back.

She was pale, vulnerable. His fists clenched at his sides. He ached to stay . . . but he was equally driven by the need to extricate her from the dangerous situation she was in. If he was going to succeed in clearing her, he had a night of work ahead of him. "As soon as I have anything concrete, I'll call you."

"I'll be waiting to hear," she said, looking at him, her eyes guarded.

Trust me. He didn't say the words, but they were so strong in his mind that he thought she must have heard them. *Trust me one more time.*

Rourke sat at the desk in his suite, muttered a dark curse and leaned back in the chair, staring at the dispatch he'd gotten from his company. He'd never known his colleague, Mark Tranyor, to be slipshod about compiling material, but this sheet had a thin feel to it, as if he'd done the minimum work required. Rourke lifted the phone and dialed the New York City number.

The woman on the switchboard sounded new. He didn't recognize her voice. "Mark Tranyor, please."

"Tranyor here."

"Mark, this is Rourke. I'm calling about the financial report you did on Brewster Hilton. I wondered if—"

"Brewster Hilton? I didn't do any report on a Brewster Hilton."

Rourke sat very still, staring at the sheet that had Tranyor's signature on the bottom. "Are you sure?"

"Sure, I'm sure. I would remember a name like that one."

Rourke felt the muscles in his stomach clench. "You better let me talk to Loring. I think we might have some internal problems."

It was almost an hour later when he hung up the phone. He paced the suite with impatience, knowing he had to wait until Wainwright left work and headed for home. By six o'clock, he was seething with nerves.

Anita answered the phone. He identified himself and asked to speak to Todd. Wainwright came on the line, his defensiveness evident even in his greeting.

Rourke wasn't in the mood to humor him. "I need some information. What made you think Hilton and I might be entering into a liaison?"

There was a long, ringing silence. "Hilton needs money."

"Why?" Rourke rapped out the word. "Does he keep a woman on the side, fly to Las Vegas, play the ponies?"

"Bingo on number three."

"He bets the horses?"

"There's an indoor track at Batavia. Sulky racing. He can't be bothered to watch the race being run on the track. He stays on the lower floor and watches it on closed circuit TV while he stays close to the cash. He's a real compulsive bettor."

"Bingo, indeed," Rourke murmured. "Thanks, Wainwright. I owe you one."

Knowing where to look, it was simple to find the answers . . . and the proof he needed. After a long evening spent waiting, Rourke's patience was rewarded. Just before midnight, the call from Loring came, confirming the chain of bribery that had begun with Hilton and spread out in a pool until it reached an employee in Rourke's firm. After talking to Rourke, Loring had held Cavenaugh in the office building through the afternoon and evening, applying pressure. At eleven-thirty, knowing his wife would be frantic, wondering where he was, Cavenaugh broke down and admitted the truth.

Rourke spent the rest of the night compiling his papers and writing his report. It was almost five in the morning before he fell into bed, knowing he'd only get two hours of rest before the alarm went off.

He woke feeling groggy and disoriented. He crawled into the shower, hoping the water would help him wake up. It did. Or was it his thoughts of what this day would mean to Jessica that brought his mind into alertness?

Rourke dressed and tied his tie, his hands not as steady as they should have been. He blamed the late hours of the night before...and knew he was a liar. Jessica's career was at stake and if he'd make some mistake, left some loophole open for Hilton to crawl through, she could be badly hurt.

He resisted the urge to go over the material one more time, collected it all, piled it into his briefcase and shrugged into his coat.

At ten o'clock exactly, Rourke walked into Brewster Hilton's office and found the people there he had told Hilton to assemble. Wainwright slouched in a corner chair, his long legs stretched out in front of him, as if he'd come into Hilton's office to relax. Cameron looked eager. And Jessica...Jessica looked frightened...but wonderful.

Barricaded behind his desk in his comfortable chair, Hilton wore the complacent expression of a successful hunter. "You have the results of your investigation?"

"Yes."

"Well, then, sit down, sit down." He bubbled like a water fountain. "We're all anxious to hear what you have to say."

"Are you indeed?" Rourke murmured silkily, and tossed a paper on the desk. Only one numerical figure was on the paper—$55,422.00. The amount was marked paid as of October 24, the previous autumn.

Hilton blanched. "Where did you get this? And—" he was scrambling now, trying to think "—what does it have to do with me?"

"You know the answer to that as well as I do."

"See here, Caldwell, what's on that paper?"

"The amount of Hilton's gambling debt. He paid it with the money he received as a bribe from your rival. He sabotaged the computer program directing the trucks with your Christmas orders."

Hilton clenched his fist in anger and his face regained some color. He rose from his chair, leaning over his desk, as if he would like to crawl over it and throttle Rourke. "You can't prove that—"

"He also bribed a man from my organization, a man named Richard Cavenaugh." Just as Rourke had hoped he would, Hilton reacted visibly to the man's name. "The original plan was for Cavenaugh to send an investigator who knew the scheme and would implicate Jessica, just as Hilton wanted. When a mishap kept that man from taking the job, I was chosen as his replacement. That left both Cavenaugh and Hilton in a weakened position. All they could do was hope I'd find the false trail of evidence they'd planted for me and implicate Jessica. I found the evidence...but I also found something Hilton had overlooked. In Hilton's haste to change the program, he neglected to replace a tab, something Jessica would never have done. As a result, the file notations had moved over a space. And that space—" Rourke looked at Cameron "—tells me that Jessica did not make the change.

"We think of computers as being impersonal machines, but a software program can be as characteristic as a thumbprint. File notations can be added carelessly, or neatly, with articulate care, or so sparsely they're almost unnecessary. But those file notations carry an imprint of the programmer. Jessica, because of her childhood blindness, has learned to keep things neat and orderly. Other changes in the program were logged to her name, and none of them—" he paused, looking at Hilton "—not one of them lacked the tab."

"If she was in a hurry—" Hilton said, his face a fiery red.

"No. She wasn't in a hurry." He shot a look at Jessica. Her face was cool, expressionless. What was she thinking? Did she care that he'd spent all of last night preparing this case in her defense? She didn't look as if she did. She looked . . . numb. Rourke returned to the attack, his eyes flashing to Hilton. "You were the one who was in a hurry. What did you do, send her to another part of the building to give you access to the computer so that the changes would be logged in on the clock during regular working hours?"

Hilton sank back into his chair. "You're framing me. You're framing me to save her."

At Cameron's anxious glance, Rourke drew a large envelope from his briefcase and passed it over. "The only piece of evidence I don't have is the name of the man who was Brewster's contact from the rival company. I expect to have that by this afternoon."

"It's a lie—" Hilton tried again, one last desperate denial.

Cameron's head snapped up, his dark eyes bright and hard. Rourke had banked on the shrewd intelligence he'd seen in the man's face during that first meeting. "I knew you played the ponies, but I didn't think you were stupid enough to let it go this far." He slid the papers back into the envelope with no more than the briefest of glances. To Rourke, he said, "I assume that there is enough evidence here to have a warrant sworn out for his arrest?"

"Yes."

"Then consider it done." Cameron got to his feet. "I'll call security. Don't try anything foolish, Brewster. It will only make things worse for you." Cameron's shrewd eyes moved to Jessica. "I'm sure you, like I, am very grateful to Mr. Caldwell, for discovering the truth."

"Yes," said Jessica. "Very grateful." Her eyes met Rourke's but there was nothing, absolutely no emotion in them. "Am I free to go? This is a vacation day for me."

"Of course, of course. Go home. I'm sure you'll want to go out and celebrate New Year's Eve. You have two things to celebrate, right? The beginning of a new year and your good reputation restored, thanks to Mr. Caldwell." He was so effusive he was nearly purring.

"Yes," Jessica said, and turning, left the room.

By the time Rourke had had his hand shaken two more times and heard Cameron tell him what a clever man he was, ten minutes had gone by before he could return to his desk, clear it and pack his briefcase. By that time, Jessica's coat was gone . . . and so was Jessica.

He went to his hotel room and called her apartment. There was no answer. He wondered if she was ignoring her phone.

He put his coat on again and drove around to her apartment. Her car wasn't there. He went back to the hotel and called Anita.

"I'm sorry," Jessica's friend said, sounding gratified that Rourke was reduced to calling her to find Jessica. "I don't know where she is."

Gavin delivered essentially the same message with only slightly less animosity. Thrusting his hands through his hair in anguished frustration, Rourke sank down on the bed in a hotel room that echoed with silence. Where was Jessica?

CHAPTER FIFTEEN

ACTING ON INSTINCT, Rourke drove to the farm, making the one-hour drive in a record forty minutes. He got out of the car, slammed the door and started to walk to the house... when he saw a forkful of hay sail out the barn door. Through his lawyer, he'd kept track of Jessica's parents, and he knew it had been years since Mr. Moore had done any farm work.

He tracked through the crunchy snow and entered the shadowy warmth of the barn. Jessica was there, wearing an old plaid coat that looked as if it belonged to her father and boots big enough for Gavin's feet. A forkful of hay came flying in his direction. He did a side step and cried, "Hey. Watch out."

Jessica looked up, registered his presence... and returned to her work. Another clump of hay came sailing toward him.

"Is that the thanks I get for saving your hide?"

Slowly, Jessica buried the fork tines in the hay at her feet. "I thought you didn't want my gratitude."

"Well, maybe just a small word of thanks would be in order... or, barring that, an explanation about why you took off without a word."

She lifted dark topaz eyes to him. "I didn't want to see you."

"So you came here to hide... and clean. Typical."

She gave him a mocking look. "It seemed a fitting end to the day. More or less...keeping things in perspective."

The pain was still there. She hadn't forgiven him for not trusting her. "Cameron wanted to commend you for your forbearance with Hilton. He even plans to put his money where his mouth is. You're getting a raise and two weeks' vacation whenever you want to take it. I think he's frightened to death you'll quit...or file suit."

"Was that what you came to tell me?"

"Partially, yes."

"Good. You've delivered your message. Now move. You're in my way."

"Jessica, for Pete's sake— There's something I want to say, and you're making it damn difficult."

"Good."

"I came to say I'm sorry."

"Fine. You've said it." The fork plunged into the hay. He took a step toward her. "Dammit, Jessica. Will you stop that?" He grabbed at the fork but she jerked it out of his reach, and the first tiny gleam of interest came into her eyes. She said, "I seem to remember playing this game with you before. But you had a decided advantage over me then. You could see."

"And now I'm blind. Is that what you want me to say? Will it help if I admit how blind and stupid I was?"

"It would be a beginning."

He took a step closer. "Would it make you say yes when I ask you to marry me?"

She looked up at him then, but in the dim light, he had no idea what lay in those topaz eyes. "No."

"No, it wouldn't be a start? Or no you won't marry me?"

"Yes, it wouldn't be a start, and yes, I won't marry you."

"Well, that seems clear...I think. Or is that a definite maybe?"

"Go away, Rourke. Is that definite enough for you?"

Rourke stood still, looking around. "It started here, didn't it, Jess? Is that why you came here? Knowing this was where it should end?"

She propped the fork in the hay. "Goodbye, Rourke."

He took a step closer. "If I touched you—if I touched you the way you touched me that day—we'd be down in that hay in two minutes. And this time...this time, I wouldn't be so damn self-sacrificing."

The humor was there, lurking just below the surface. It tantalized Jessica, asked for a response. She steeled herself to say what had to be said. "I want you to go."

"There's a ticket in my pocket to New York. Shall I use it?"

She hesitated, her eyes dark, heated. "That's entirely up to you."

ROURKE DIDN'T GO to the airport. Instead, he drove back to Rochester. Outside his father's house, a huge Christmas wreath hung on the door he hadn't stepped through in seven years. Steeling himself, Rourke put his finger to the bell.

The door opened, and expecting to see the butler, Rourke looked up...and found he was face-to-face with Alcott.

Rourke wished he'd had more time to prepare himself for this meeting. Alcott looked older. Older than seven years could possibly account for. "Scotty said you wanted to see me."

"Rourke? It is you, isn't it? Come in."

He stepped back, moving like a much older man. Rourke followed him into a hallway that was as frigid as an ice house. It was as if his home had grown old along with Alcott. "Come into the study. I've shut off some of the heat in the rest of the house to save on the fuel bill."

His father practicing economy was a rare experience for Rourke. He kept his coat buttoned and followed Alcott down the hall. Impossible not to notice the dusty condition of the house, the marred beauty of wood floors that hadn't been waxed recently.

His father had recovered from the shock of seeing him. Rourke could almost see the man who had sired him rallying his pride, straightening his spine. "Sit down, my boy, sit down. Would you care for a drink?"

Rourke looked at the bottle already standing on his father's desk. "Whatever you're having will be fine."

Memories washed over him. He remembered sitting here in this book-lined study, pleading Jessica's case, knowing he would never again ask Alcott for anything.

Alcott poured a splash of Scotch into a glass, and as he bent to hand Rourke the glass, Rourke noticed the way his father's hair had thinned on top. Sinking in the chair Alcott indicated for him, Rourke watched his father settle into the swivel chair behind the desk.

"So. How have you been, my boy?"

Rourke twirled the alcohol around in his glass. "Maybe a better question is how have you been?"

Alcott's eyes flickered away to a point somewhere beyond Rourke and his face softened. It was then Rourke realized this wasn't Alcott's first drink of the day.

"Life is a damnable thing, my boy. You go along thinking the world is a fine place to be…and then it…all slips away from you." He raised blue eyes to Rourke. "Scotty didn't tell you about the malpractice suit."

"No," Rourke said softly, "he didn't."

A look of fierceness brought Alcott's brows together. "I won the damn thing... but does that make any difference? No. All the public remembers is some damn fool accused me of blinding him. That's what they remember." Raising the glass to his lips, Alcott drank deeply.

Rourke watched, knowing that even with the years of animosity between them, he would never have wished this for Alcott. Of all things, Alcott was most proud of his ability as a surgeon. To be questioned in a court of law about that ability must have hurt him deeply. "I'm sorry," Rourke said softly.

Alcott lowered the glass, and pinned his uncoordinated gaze on his son. "Are you? Are you? Well, damn it, don't be. If there's anything I don't want, it's your pity."

This was the Alcott Rourke knew of old, the Alcott who had lashed out at his son. Yet now, sitting here, Rourke waited for the old resentment and fear to surface...and felt...nothing. Somewhere along the path toward falling in love with Jessica, he'd lost his hatred of his father. And his losing that hatred had stripped Alcott of his power over his son.

Almost as if he knew what was going on in Rourke's mind, Alcott narrowed his eyes and studied Rourke over the desk top. Rourke accepted his visual assessment, wondering if there were spears of hay sticking in his lapel. How ironic it would be if there were.

A shrewdness came into Alcott's eyes. If Rourke had needed any confirmation of his final unshackling from his father, it was there. Alcott had evaluated him...and deemed him to be a worthy opponent. "You've... changed. You're a man."

The acknowledgment was made almost grudgingly. Rourke fought the urge to smile. "Time does that for boys."

Alcott snorted. "Not always. So. You're working on a big case in town."

"I finished it today." Rourke waited, watching those shrewd eyes take their measure of him. His father had something on his mind.

Alcott cleared his throat, looked down at his glass, then up at Rourke. "Some of the members of the board have heard about your investigative work and your reputation as a corporate troubleshooter. They wonder why you didn't come in with us two years ago when you were supposed to. I told them you had other interests but they insisted you be approached. They've heard about how knowledgeable you are about the workings of industry."

"I see." He waited, knowing there was more.

Alcott drank again and very carefully, set the glass on the table. "They're unhappy with the adverse publicity I got because of the trial. They pressed for my resignation." Alcott looked at Rourke. "I told them I might convince you to join us if they allow me to stay in an advisory capacity."

Rourke sat for a moment, absorbing the sense of Alcott's words. "You can't be serious."

"I'd hardly joke about a thing like this." His father's hands trembled on the glass. "I need you, Rourke."

It was, he supposed, the final revenge. After years of neglect, Alcott needed his son. Rourke sat gazing into the face of the man he'd hated for so many years, waiting for the surge of satisfaction, and felt nothing but pity and a wish that fate had been kinder to his father. "I see. And if I refuse—"

"I'll be eased off. Gently. But eased off, nevertheless."

Alcott met Rourke's eyes, saw nothing encouraging there. His hand trembling, he lifted the glass to his lips again. Rourke, watching, felt an urge to smash the glass away. "Would my... position require my giving up my other job and staying here in the city?"

Hope played across Alcott's face like a ray of light. "Yes. They want you full-time. I'd be glad to pay any relocation costs you might incur—"

"I can pay my own moving expenses."

"Then you'll consider it?"

There was no urge to make his father suffer as Rourke lifted his glass. He simply needed time to think. If he said yes, and Jessica continued to reject his offer of marriage, he would be trapped here in the same city with her, watching her go out with other men. If he said yes, he would be staking everything he had on himself and on Jessica. He would be making a decision that would be, for the most part, irrevocable. He had no reason to think Jessica might forgive him in the near future...or at least, forgive him before she found another man. Could he take that chance?

Could he do anything else?

He lowered his glass and looked into his father's eyes. "How soon would they want me?"

"You... accept?"

Rourke hesitated, feeling the coldness of the glass under his fingers. If he was making a mistake, it was the mistake of a lifetime. "I accept."

"I... thank you."

Rourke stood up, knowing he wanted to end this quickly, knowing, too, that though he'd made a commitment, he was free at last of the specter that had haunted him for years. He was not like this man . . . and he never had been. The two of them would never be friends . . . but they would find a peace of sorts.

JESSICA SAT in the glass booth of the bar at the disco that separated the underage from the overage drinking patrons, letting the frenzy of the New Year's Eve celebration swirl around her like confetti. Streamers wishing a Happy New Year dangled from the bar mirror. Her eyes lifted to its glittering surface . . . and met those of a man at the end of the bar who'd been ogling her for the last hour. He looked young. He must be that, and shy, too, or he would have approached her by now. Maybe he was working up his courage.

While Anita and Todd gyrated on the dance floor, she nursed her second glass of wine, determined to drink it as quickly as she had the first.

Somewhere above her, an airplane was leaving the ground, taking Rourke away.

Her wine tasted bitter. She pushed it away, slid off the stool and threaded through the crowd, heading toward that blond man who'd been watching her.

"Were you going to ask me to dance?"

He blushed and endeared himself to her forever. "I've been thinking about it."

"Would it help if I asked you?"

As if he had gone speechless in the face of her boldness, he nodded.

She tugged him onto the floor, and then realized her mistake. The music glided into a South American rhythm, one he was obviously as unfamiliar with as she.

"Did you see *Romancing the Stone*?"

He shook his head, still not talking.

''Never mind,'' she consoled him. ''Just hang on and follow me.''

Rourke saw them the minute he walked into the room, Jessica, her hair falling forward on her cheeks, laughing, dancing with another man.

It hadn't taken her long to forget him.

All the pain and anguish he'd felt seven years ago when he'd watched Jessica sit on a blanket with another boy and raise her mouth for his kiss came washing back over him. He knew now as he hadn't then exactly what the emotion was. The possessiveness a man feels for the woman he loves.

He had the same choice now he'd had then. He could walk away...and stay safe...or he could take the risk...and go to her.

A lifetime of deep-seated beliefs urged him to walk away. He was used to loneliness, he'd lived with it for years. Yes, that was what he would do. He would walk away and stay safe...carrying the image of love instead of the reality.

He gave the order to his feet to carry him away...and Jessica's laughter rang out in the room, warm, inviting. Memory washed over him, the sound of her voice, bright with laughter, dark with pain, husky with love. This time, when he walked away, he'd carry with him the joy of kissing Jessica, holding her, loving her. This time, there would be memories to haunt him in the night, to make his body ache with need and regret.

Years of living without her stretched ahead of him in bleak, intolerable emptiness.

Feeling as if he were teetering on a high wire with no net under him, he turned toward Jessica.

Warmed by the wine, Jessica whirled away from her partner...and saw Rourke. He was standing there watching her, his face dark, expressionless.

He didn't move. There was no invitation in his face or body as there had been that first night they'd met on a dance floor. Chilled by his impassivity, she felt her partner's arm circle her waist, drawing her away. Her mind numb, Jessica went, turning her back to the cold, stark face of the man she loved.

Rourke felt as if she'd slapped him. No longer capable of clear, rational thought, he thought only of possession. He stepped in behind the man, extracted Jessica from the stranger's hold and turned her into his arms with a neat precision that startled them all.

For a moment, she held herself tense, unyielding in his arms. Then, as he pulled her closer and began to sway with her in a reasonable facsimile of dancing, he felt her body warm and melt against his. She lifted her head to him, her hair falling enticingly down her back. "What are you doing here?"

He slid his hand up through the silken fall, tangling it in his fingers. "Giving the lady a chance to change her mind about my marriage proposal."

"You don't love me."

The words were sultry, feminine, asking for denial.

He didn't disappoint her. "Like hell. Are you going to leave with me peaceably or shall I use brute force?"

"I should insist on brute force...just because it took you so long to get here."

"I was talking to my father. He wants me to take a position on the board of directors. Brute force requires some cooperation. Put your arms around my neck, Jessica."

"You've reconciled with your father?" Jessica swung her arms around his neck, uncaring that eyes were turning in their direction, happier than she thought it possible to be.

He swung her up into his arms, his mouth moving in a smile at seeing the exultant lift of hers. "Reconciled is too strong a word. Armed truce describes it better. Are you ready to be kidnapped?"

Jessica smiled up into his face. "Since when does brute force require permission?"

"Since now," he said, his eyes devouring her as she lay in his arms. "Since you."

Her own eyes were hungry in their passage over his face. "I should say goodbye to Anita," she told him, "just in case you carry me away so far I'll never see her again."

"I don't think it's possible to separate you two that long, but it's certainly an idea. Where is she?"

"Here," Anita said from behind his shoulder. She studied Rourke's face, then Jessica as she settled into Rourke's arms. "Can I trust him to take good care of you?"

"Yes," Rourke answered, his dark eyes alive with intensity. There was purpose there, and a determination that seemed to echo the excitement within Jessica. She glanced back at Anita, then nodded to Todd. "Can I trust him to take care of you?"

As if on cue, Todd stepped forward and took the glass from Anita's hand. "Yes." His tone echoed Rourke's and the two men exchanged knowing male looks.

Anita smiled. "Todd says he'd like to do it for the rest of our lives." Anita leaned over and brushed her lips on Jessica's cheek. "I think I was wrong about your errant knight. It looks as if things are going to turn out right for both of us. Call me in the morning, will you?'' She stepped back and waved a hand dismissively at Rourke. ''Go on now, take her out of here. You're making a scene.'' He needed no further urging.

When they reached Jessica's apartment, Rourke pulled her firmly up the stairs and into the private darkness. ''Would you like to talk now...or afterward?''

To prove to herself she wasn't dreaming, she threaded a hand up through his dark hair. ''Do I have a choice?''

''No,'' he said, burying his mouth in the smooth softness of her neck.

''Then why,'' she chided softly, ''are you wasting time pretending that I do?''

In the bedroom, Rourke showed her with his lips and his hands that he meant to waste no time at all. She gloried in his haste...and, her passion matching his, she showed him how much she enjoyed—and shared—his fervent hunger.

Lying beside him in the soft light, she watched as he raised up on one elbow and looked down at her. His bare chest was golden, dark with crisp hair above the white sheet, his profile strong, classic. Even after loving him, she discovered looking at him still delivered a physical impact. He was solid, lean, male...and hers.

As if he knew what she was thinking, he let his eyes wander over her bare shoulders, the curves of her body sheltered under the sheet, staking his visual claim on her as she had on him.

''If you're thirsty, I'll open some wine.''

''Sounds good.'' She stretched her arms lazily over her head.

He raised his hand to her hair. The gesture was so gentle it unnerved her. ''I don't deserve you.''

"Don't you?" Her heart pounded at a slow, steady beat in her chest, but she felt light-headed, giddy. The love in his eyes and the tenderness in his hands was the stuff of a thousand dreams.

"I'll have to be very careful not to hurt you again."

"That's true," she murmured, wishing he would stop touching her with such bone-melting gentleness, knowing she would feel like dying if he did.

"I'll make a lousy husband."

"Not true," she said, taking his hand and bringing it to her mouth.

At the soft touch of her lips on his palm, he stiffened slightly. Quickly, before she could prevent him, he did exactly what she had done, brushing his mouth over her palm in a kiss so humble it enslaved her. Shivers swam over her arm.

"A man told me once...when I did that to him...that I should only do that with my lover."

He leaned away, looking sleek and satisfied with himself. "Warning you off, was he?"

"He was doing what he thought best...for both of us."

His eyes caught hers and held them with a look of love that nearly took her breath away. "You've always believed in me, haven't you?" He reached for her and brought her head against his chest in an oddly controlled, yet intimate gesture. "It was your belief in me that frightened me more than anything. I tried to walk away from you, Jessica. I really tried. But I couldn't do it."

"Why did you have to try?"

Rourke felt her stillness under his hands. "You know why. I was afraid. Afraid I was like my father. Afraid I couldn't be what I knew I would have to be...for you. Afraid I couldn't make love last a lifetime."

"And are you still...afraid?"

His eyes sought hers. "No. I know now a lifetime won't be long enough to show you how much I love you."

The waiting was over. Secure in her womanliness as she had never been before, her lips reached to his. He lowered his head to receive his reward, the sweetness of her mouth and the silky moistness of her tongue.

She drew away for a breath. "I've always loved you, Rourke. Always. I want to marry you, to have your children." She waited, breathless, watching his face. His own childhood had been so unhappy. Would he want children of his own?

He only said easily, "I want yours, too. Dozens of little girls with topaz eyes—"

"Not dozens!" She drew back in mock horror, joy exploding deep within her. This is what her life would be like from this moment on, teasing and smiles and loving. Years of sharing their love with their children. Her parents would be happy to have grandchildren to spoil at last. And Gavin would come around when he saw how much Rourke loved her.

"Well, maybe one," Rourke conceded. "And a boy, just to keep me from being outnumbered."

She wrapped her arms around him, holding him close, knowing that it was the depth of his love for her that gave him the courage to consider having a son.

"We'll love them so much, Rourke. We'll spend years and years loving them—"

"And each other," he breathed, leaning over her, fitting his mouth and his body perfectly, to hers.

Harlequin
Superromance

COMING NEXT MONTH

#234 THE FOREVER PROMISE • Meg Hudson
Fourteen years ago Claire Parmeter left King Faraday at
the altar when she discovered that another woman was
carrying his child. Now King and Claire meet again.
Mutual desire draws them together, but the ghosts of
their past threaten to separate them once more....

#235 SWEET TOMORROWS • Francine Christopher
Valerie Wentworth thinks she's put Wall Street behind
her forever. But that is before an irate financial planner
waltzes into her antique-doll shop. Not only is Cutter
the most gorgeous man she's ever seen, but he has the
formidable wits to match her own, and their bodies,
well...they fit together perfectly.

#236 HALFWAY TO HEAVEN • Pamela Bauer
Designer Rachel Kincaid can't afford to fall in love with
sexy department store magnate Cole Braxton III. She is
still holding out hope that her missing fiancé will return
home. But Cole isn't about to wait around forever.
Faced with a barrage of difficult choices, Rachel finally
realizes the answers lie within her heart....

#237 CHILD'S PLAY • Peggy Nicholson
Snatching a small boy from under his bodyguard's nose
is no mean trick, even for Tey Kenyon. She can't let
Mac McAllister interfere with her plans, but interfering
with her heart is another matter!

ATTRACTIVE, SPACE SAVING BOOK RACK

Display your most prized novels on this handsome and sturdy book rack. The hand-rubbed walnut finish will blend into your library decor with quiet elegance, providing a practical organizer for your favorite hard-or soft-covered books.

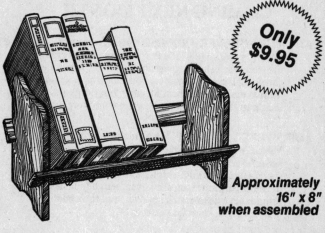

Only $9.95

Approximately 16" x 8" when assembled

Assembles in seconds!

To order, rush your name, address and zip code, along with a check or money order for $10.70 ($9.95 plus 75¢ postage and handling) (New York residents add appropriate sales tax), payable to *Harlequin Reader Service* to:

In the U.S.

Harlequin Reader Service
Book Rack Offer
901 Fuhrmann Blvd.
P.O. Box 1325
Buffalo, NY 14269-1325

Offer not available in Canada.

BKR-1